D1572131

# LORA LEIGH

# SHATTERED LEGACY

ELLORA'S CAVE
ROMANTICA PUBLISHING

An Ellora's Cave Romantica Publication

www.ellorascave.com

Shattered Legacy

ISBN #1419954512
ALL RIGHTS RESERVED.
Shattered Legacy Copyright © 2005 Lora Leigh
Edited by Sue-Ellen Gower
Cover art by Syneca.

Electronic book Publication September 2005
Trade paperback Publication July 2006

# Warning:

The following material contains graphic sexual content meant for mature readers. This story has been rated E–rotic by a minimum of three independent reviewers.

Ellora's Cave Publishing offers three levels of Romantica™ reading entertainment: S (S-ensuous), E (E-rotic), and X (X-treme).

S-*ensuous* love scenes are explicit and leave nothing to the imagination.

E-*rotic* love scenes are explicit, leave nothing to the imagination, and are high in volume per the overall word count. In addition, some E-rated titles might contain fantasy material that some readers find objectionable, such as bondage, submission, same sex encounters, forced seductions, and so forth. E-rated titles are the most graphic titles we carry; it is common, for instance, for an author to use words such as "fucking", "cock", "pussy", and such within their work of literature.

X-*treme* titles differ from E-rated titles only in plot premise and storyline execution. Unlike E-rated titles, stories designated with the letter X tend to contain controversial subject matter not for the faint of heart.

# Also by Lora Leigh

ঙ

# About the Author

∞

Lora Leigh is a wife and mother living in Kentucky. She dreams in bright, vivid images of the characters intent on taking over her writing life, and fights a constant battle to put them on the hard drive of her computer before they can disappear as fast as they appeared.

Lora's family, and her writing life co-exist, if not in harmony, in relative peace with each other. An understanding husband is the key to late nights with difficult scenes and stubborn characters. His insights into human nature and the workings of the male psyche provide her hours of laughter, and innumerable romantic ideas that she works tirelessly to put into effect.

Lora welcomes comments from readers. You can find her website and email address on her author bio page at www.ellorascave.com

# Acknowledgments

## ଚ

*To Lady Lynn*

*for all her encouragement from the very beginning, and her father Gabriel, for being part of raising such a wonderful daughter, and for his enjoyment in my books as well.*

*Thanks just for being you, Lynn, and for all you have given me in encouragement and support.*

*And to Keith Johnson,*

*thanks for the use of the copying machine so long ago. That help was the first brick in the road to a long, exciting journey, and always remembered and appreciated.*

*And for my Muse, Joshau.*

*Thanks for being stubborn.*

# Shattered Legacy

ഇ

# *Author's Note*

## ∞

*Shattered Legacy* is not a "Happily Ever After" that many of you have come to expect from me. This is a prequel, a history and a beginning to the contemporary Legacies series. Here, you will meet the four couples who will begin their individual journeys soon.

*Shattered Legacy* was written to give an in-depth, detailed view of the events that occurred and that enabled the strong, powerful women who return at a future time, the determination and the ability to reach out and take what they know is theirs.

As with all great stories, all manmade legends, there is a tragedy, a brief time of fear and pain that gives payment to Fate and Destiny for a future that will dawn with the shining glory of justice and success. *Shattered Legacy* is the dark past, the bitter payment for a future that will wield the sword of honor and justice. It is the story of four men, four women, and the deceit and betrayals that stole memories, desires, and lives.

This is the Legend of the Shadow Warriors.

# Chapter One
*England*
*Spring, 1040 AD*

The battle had been harder than most. The field, littered with the dead and dying of both sides, was enough to bring turmoil to even the strongest stomach. The warriors who walked through it now had stronger constitutions than most, and still the bile rose heavily within them. So many broken bodies. Warriors and knights, earls and lords, the scourge of death marked them all. For what cause, Devlin wondered. For greed, for power, to usurp and plunder, rape and pillage a land already suffering from the tyranny of one who should protect rather than destroy.

Here was the proof of man's cruelty and disregard, one to another. This was the sum total of a king's vow to protect and cherish life. To lead, guide and rule his throne in justice and compassion. It was a vow the king had made to the warriors and this was the proof of his deception.

Devlin stared around at the broken, wounded, dead and dying, and felt his soul ache. Many were young, too young and too ill-prepared for the death that stalked the land, the evil that washed over it in these dark times. Like a dark malevolent cloud of suffering and violence, it stalked and struck with the viciousness of a rabid dog.

There were no longer days of peace. There was no longer a sense of security or growth. War, disease and hunger were like maggots growing with steady strength on the dark forces sweeping over the countryside. Devlin knew the cause of the evil and the war. He knew the forces pushing the destruction sweeping through town and parish alike but he had been unable to stop the steady force of violence. There were days he wondered if the evil would ever be halted. Or if he would forever be faced with the sight of this, a once beautiful field wrapped in mist, filled with carnage, the moans and broken whimpers of its victims drifting forever through his head. This was his curse, though he had been told it was his blessing.

The Shadow, he was called. His unique abilities enabled him to hide himself with the barest protection of even a small amount of darkness. With the power of his mind alone he could fade into a corner, into a shadow, become one with the night and all that it contained. Yet, he could not hide from this, the merciless games of an unnatural demon intent on possessing the world.

The Guardians, those gods who watched and waited from the stars, had bestowed this power on him decades ago. They had sought to create a warrior who could battle in this land, who could kill the evil they could not. An evil of their own kind, a Seeker of power, a demonic being whose sole aim was the enslavement of a world. So far, the Seeker, Jonar, was winning.

"We were betrayed." Devlin spoke to those following in the mist behind him, his voice seeming to echo about the field. "Why else would we have been called away? This battle was decided long before it was ever fought."

Devlin and his men had heard of the forces moving steadily toward the contingent of warriors he led himself, barely a day after leaving camp. It seemed all had known of the battle to come except those who lay dying about the field this night. Deceit, even within his own ranks, he thought. For the enemy would not have known the time to strike without a spy within awaiting the order from the king.

"Sir Devlin. Sir Devlin, help me," a young voice called out weakly as Devlin approached, his hazy expression beseeching, a dirty, blood-streaked arm stretched out through the mist.

He was just a child, Devlin knew. One of the skinny, gangly young boys the knights brought along as squires. This one had always been the most cheerful, despite his uncertain lot. The one who had seemed perpetually filled with laughter.

"David." The boy's name was a sigh of regret.

Devlin moved toward the small figure with quick steps, aware of the men who followed him. They spread out around him, attempting to see through the steadily building fog that crept over the countryside. They searched, as always, for the assassins that lurked, ready to sever the head of the dark force's greatest enemy.

He reached the boy in seconds, moving to kneel beside him and ease his light weight into his arms. He was so small, Devlin thought. Too small and too young to be lying on a killing field.

"Sir Devlin, we were defeated." The young voice held a measure of bemusement. The boy fought to breathe, his lungs wheezing wearily, his breath gurgling within his throat as Devlin pulled him close.

There was no aiding him. The wound to his stomach was a long, painful death sentence. One such a young boy should never have to endure. Devlin clenched his teeth, fighting the rage and bitterness that filled him.

"Aye, David, in this battle we were defeated," Devlin said roughly, propping the boy up in his arms and wishing there was more he could do other than provide comfort and warmth. All he could do was smooth back the tangled fall of dirty blond hair and stare into the dazed, pain-ridden brown eyes staring up at him in misery.

"I have wanted to speak to you," David's voice rasped in his throat. "I was sent here for you, Sir Devlin."

"Rest, David," Devlin urged him, hearing the sound of lungs filling with blood, the rattle of death in the boy's young chest.

"No, Sir Devlin, hear me." David stared up at him, his eyes glassy from the pain, yet showing his determination to give Devlin his message. "I tried to tell you, and yet I could find no place where other ears would not hear. There are those who would aid you. Those who know the truth of the evil that has come upon us. You must go to them. Seek their aid."

Devlin frowned as he watched the boy's desperate expression. David's eyes were glazing with his fading strength, his body trembling as the cold and shock settled over him.

"What do you know of such evil, David?" he asked him gently. "'Tis the evil of men with nothing better to do than war. You should know this by now."

David shook his head weakly, his gaze steady and knowing on Devlin's.

"'Tis an evil not of our land. An evil that only few can destroy," David whispered regretfully. "Find the wizard, Galen, and his daughter, Chantel. Find them, Lord Devlin. They hold a key, a secret that can save us all."

The young voice was imploring, hoarse with need. His dirty face was twisted into lines of pain and need, his gaze boring into Devlin's with the strength of a man, rather than a child.

"The wizard Galen is dead, David," Devlin reminded him. "Even our king admits to this. If he lived, he would surely have come to aid the family he swore his fealty to long ago."

David's gaze became frightened, his grip on Devlin's arm desperate. He seemed terrified that the warrior he revered would not heed his words.

"No, Lord Devlin. Galen lives. Our king has been influenced by this evil, and Galen refuses to lend hand in his battles. I swear this is true, for I was sent to bear you this message. You must listen to me. You must heed my words."

Tears fell slowly through the dust and grime that coated the boy's face. His dark eyes were wide, beseeching. His fingers bit into Devlin's arm fiercely.

"I, too, have heard such rumors." From the tendrils of mist, Devlin's warrior, Joshua, neared them. "Perhaps the boy speaks the truth, Devlin."

Joshua's voice was low, controlled and dark. He was like an angel of death himself, his amber eyes bright and probing, his harsh expression savage in its intensity.

"Where is this wizard then, David?" Devlin asked him gently as he pushed the boy's sweat-dampened hair back from his forehead. "Tell me what I must know then, and I shall seek him for no other reason than it is your wish." At that moment he knew he would have given this child whatever he asked. So young. Too young to die within blood and pain.

David coughed roughly, blood mixing with the spittle that dotted his chin. The boy was in pain, weak and so near death. Yet still he sought to finish the mission he had taken for himself.

"He resides now within the Norman lands, deep in an enchanted forest, close to the seas. You will know when the way is right, you will feel desolate when the way is wrong. He bid me come to you, to send you on this journey. He awaits you, Lord Devlin. Go now. Tell no one who you seek or where you go, for the way is dangerous and Galen's enemies grow daily."

The boy's breath was growing shallower, as though in the giving of this message his battle had finally ended. Devlin grimaced, holding the child tighter, hoping to ease the passing. He pulled the boy deep within his arms and held him as his eyelids fluttered, his grip slowly slacked, and the life left his body in a long, gentle sigh.

Devlin felt his own heart break as the child sighed his last breath and his body shuddered. The boy had tried often to bring him this message, Devlin now knew. Yet it seemed that other matters had continually drawn Devlin's attention from the imploring look the child often sent him.

"He was just a boy." Devlin laid the body to the ground, staring down at the young face regretfully. "I should have forced Garrison to relieve him of his duties and send him home, as I often considered."

The knight, Lord Dewitt Garrison had been a vain, ego-serving man. He had been cruel to the boy, leaving him alone outside his tent in the cold and damp air. Devlin had often sent him blankets and food, and wood for his fires when he saw the boy's needs. But he had never gone to him, and now he regretted that bitterly.

"Would it have done any good?" Joshua questioned him softly. "The boy knew his fate, I fear. He came anyway, in service to this wizard."

Devlin was silent as he stared down at the lifeless boy. He was barely fourteen years, and his laughter had spread through the camp with his arrival. He teased knights who had not known such revelry in years. He aided the camp whores, helping to carry their water, tend their aches, when his duties allowed such. And through it all, he watched Devlin, always eager, it seemed, for his company. Now Devlin knew the reason for that eagerness.

"What have we heard of this wizard, other than his disassociation with the king?" Devlin demanded softly as he laid the boy's arms across his chest and prepared to pick him up.

"Do we have time for what you are preparing to do, Devlin?" Joshua asked him softly, his tone indicating they did not.

Devlin paused, but only for less than a second. It would not matter if all of Jonar's forces were riding upon them now, he would take the time to finish this task.

"We have time, Joshua, for whatever I deem necessary." Devlin flashed him a hard look.

Joshua stood back as Devlin came to his feet, the small body of the boy lying in his arms, the sandy-brown head lying limply on the chest of the large warrior. Against that broad chest, the boy seemed much younger than he was, his fragile body resting now where before it had not.

"Derek," Devlin called one of the warriors to his side. "Find a shovel to prepare this child's grave. I want him away from this battlefield and the scavengers that will soon descend upon it."

The other warrior made no comment and didn't have far to search for a short-handled shovel that would do the job. Devlin knew his manner was cold, hard. His voice brooked no argument, and yet he could not relent. This child had deserved so much more.

"Joshua, round the horses up. I refuse to leave them for the enemy to gather into their stables. The knights' mounts are most important. Such well-trained animals are worth their weight in gold to Jonar."

The name spread a vile taste in Devlin's mouth as he spoke it. Jonar, the dark lord. The evil cloud of malevolent hatred spreading across the land was a direct result of his malicious designs. Jonar sought power and recognition, to be treated as a god and recognized for nothing save his ultimate decisions of who would live and who would die. He was a master of pain, a dark lord of agony. He was Devlin's greatest enemy.

Others would say the battles, the wars, the great dread and poverty sweeping over the land were the result of mere men seeking more power than they had earned. The power struggles and treachery, the blood running like a river over the valleys and dales were the result of mad kings, desperate lords and greedy peasants alike. But Devlin knew well the workings of Jonar and saw it in the desperation sweeping the land, the hand of that unnatural being.

"Will we seek out the wizard?" A large blond Viking, Shanar, moved to his side, his rough face holding a gentle expression as he stared down at Devlin's burden. "Could he truly be the one we seek to aid us in this fight?"

Despite Devlin's own height, several inches above the mark of six feet, this man stood a near four inches taller. Devlin glanced up at him as they walked farther into the forest, feeling the wash of a gentle breeze, the fresh scent of the night rather than the blood and filth of the battlefield they left behind.

The Guardians, those whom they served, the masters to the great powers the warriors wielded, had told them of one who knew the powers of the earth. That when those powers joined with their own would cause devastation and destruction to Jonar. Devlin glanced up toward the sky, but saw nothing except the mists that covered the land.

"Aye, we will leave this night." Devlin nodded. "When we have seen to the matter of this child's burial, we will then begin our journey."

"There are no messengers to send to the king, informing him of what we are about," Shanar reminded him.

"If what this boy has said is true, then our king has been infected with the evil Jonar spreads as well, just as I suspected. It would perhaps be better for now if he believes our deaths occurred upon this field until I learn the truth of this matter myself."

"He has not seemed a sane king," the larger man remarked. "But it was Harold's wish that we serve him."

"Whichever is the case, until I learn who is the betrayed and who the betrayer, I will resume my own battles. I grow tired of searching for Jonar's forces and finding them deep within the king's instead. This fighting among the royalty of this land wears on my nerves. It is the perfect breeding ground for Jonar's forces and his dark evil."

It was becoming apparent that the king they followed was beginning to rule through tyranny and blood. And Devlin knew that soon William of Normandy would take up the cause and invade this land. It seemed no matter which way they turned, Jonar's hand was in the wars and tragedies overtaking England. The search for power, riches and stable footing in a world gone mad was destroying royalty and peasants alike. Devlin was uncertain how much longer he could hold the line between those of Jonar's forces and the unknowing, unsuspecting lands bowing down to him and his cohorts. Perhaps it was time to go to the Norman lands anyway and search out William. He was sounding by far the better choice for England.

Devlin stopped in a small clearing, far enough away from the field of battle that the moans of the dying and the stench of the dead could no longer be heard or smelled. There he lay the form of the squire to the ground, accepted the small shovel from Derek and began to dig.

The task was not an easy one, for Devlin had fought for weeks on end with little sleep. The barons rising against the king were becoming more numerous, the battles more brutal with each growing year. Weariness was riding him hard. The need to rest was becoming paramount. But each day the situation grew more dire and Jonar's forces stronger, while Devlin and his men seemed to grow weaker in the face of the dark powers the unnatural invader wielded.

"The boy deserved better than his death here," Devlin said with a sigh, though his thoughts were on other matters. "I should have heeded the plea I often caught in his eyes. But I did not wish to tempt the knight's anger toward him, so I let it go."

"Death is all around us, Devlin, more children than just this one is succumbing," Shanar said wearily. "He knew his fate and faced it bravely to complete his task. We could ask no more of him than that."

"We could ask that such a fate should not have been his," Devlin bit out. "What was in the wizard's mind to send such a child to this task? Why could he not have made this journey himself?"

Wizard. Devlin's contempt of such a title often rang with his dark voice filled with derision. There were no wizards, no witches, nor warlocks. There were only the dark powers of good or evil, and those who willingly followed them. More often than not, he had learned that evil shadowed even those professing God's blessings, and those burned at the stake had more faith in their God than those burning them could ever hope to attain.

Devlin did not believe in magic, for he knew the basis of such deception. He just wondered from where the mighty Galen drew his power. Was it God's blessing through the power of the earth itself, or was it the darker unnatural power bequeathed to those who fought for the stars? Power such as Devlin and his men possessed. Power such as Jonar misused, enforcing his dark desires, playing his cruel and merciless games.

He would learn soon, Devlin thought as he lowered the broken child into the cold and damp grave. And when he did, he best never learn that whether graced by God or cursed by Jonar, Galen had known this quest would result in the bloody death of this child.

* * * * *

The dream came to Devlin again when he lay down to attempt to sleep hours later. The darkness of death surrounded him at first. Blood and cries and shattered lives. Then through the pain, the scent of spring enveloped him. Warmth sifted through the haze of cold death, pushing it away, soothing his soul. Sultry, warm and becoming, the woman walked to him as he lay upon his hard pallet, staring up at the vision, his cock rising hard and hot as he viewed the beauty that stood before him.

Her glistening white-blonde hair fell to her hips, thick and lustrous. Her breasts were full and tipped with hard pink nipples. Her cunt was covered with hair so light, so soft, he swore he could glimpse the pink flesh beneath it. And it glistened. He could see her woman's dew lying thick and wet along the soft slit.

He remembered her taste, the feel of her. She came to him when the weariness was at its peak, when he saw no hope in the endless future laid out before him. Only more and more death, then she entered, a breath of spring and hot, sweet desire.

"You came," he whispered, grateful she had, but he had not expected it. In the midst of blood and war, he would not have called her to him.

"I will be here, beloved knight, for as long as I may." She moved to him as he pushed the blanket from his naked body.

He was hard and hurting, needing her touch, the pleasure of her. She knelt beside him, so close he could feel the heat of her body. Her hands went to his chest, smoothing to his abdomen as she bent forward for his kiss.

How could she be so warm when she was but a dream? The heat of her body wrapped around him, stoking his desire and his need for her. Her lips stroked his with a shy, sweet promise. She had been coming to him for a year now, and still he sensed her maidenly hesitation in reaching for her needs.

He pulled her to him, moving her to his pallet, bringing her to her back, partially beneath his body. She was fiery heat, a warmth he needed beyond anything he had known in his life. He could not resist her, would not deny her. God help him, demon or angel, he needed her as he needed the very air around him to live.

"I need you," he groaned against her lips. "Will you surrender to me?"

She tipped her face back, those emerald green eyes shining up at him with love. Such love. How could a vision, no more than a dream, fill him with the wonderment of her devotion?

"There is no surrender," she whispered. "I am yours. Do with me as you will."

"Take me into your mouth." He was more than willing to beg if need be. His cock was certainly in a begging frame of mind. "Let me feel your desire for me. Your hunger for me."

And she did hunger for him. He could feel it in the heated tremors of her body. Ripples of reaction that had little to do with the cold of the night and everything to do with the fires that raged between them.

A small, mysterious smile shaped her lips. Devlin felt his scrotum tighten in anticipation as his cock jerked in longing. His thighs tightened as her nipples hardened before his very eyes.

He could look no longer though. She was moving along his body as he turned to his back. Her hand encircled the pulsing shaft that pleaded shamelessly between his thighs, her grip firm and warm. She moved slowly between his legs, her slender body glowing in the moonlight as her head lowered, her hair covering the sight of her mouth enveloping him.

In desperation he reached down, pulling the silk to one side so he could watch her lips cover him. And what a sight it was. Satin and silk, soft, pink and moist, her lips covered the bulging head of his cock. She sucked at it slowly, seeming to enjoy his taste, the very texture of the satin-lined heat and steely hardness. Devlin ground his head against the pallet as the pleasure tightened his body in fiery waves. Her hands were not still, either. One stroked in long, slow movements down the thick stalk as the other played restlessly with the heavy sac between his thighs.

He was suspended on a rack of pleasure. His hands clenched in her hair, his eyes able to only open to mere slits as he drank in the sight of her loving him in such a way. She savored him. Her tongue licked beneath the bulbous head, her soft moans of arousal and pleasure humming on the sensitive flesh. He clenched his teeth. He didn't want to disgrace himself and her by spilling his seed, but he was close. So very close.

Devlin cried out in denial when he felt the first, warning pulse of his release. Soft liquid spilled in her mouth as he jerked upright, pulling her quickly from the rapidly approaching eruption.

"No," she cried out. "I would know the taste of you."

"Mercy, my love." His voice was strained, his breathing harsh. "I would spill my seed inside you, feeling you milk me with the soft clasp of your cunt, rather than the sweet tenderness of your lips that I so long to taste."

He took her lips. They were silk and satin, her tongue a shy, tempting treasure as he forged into her mouth. Her taste was honey, nectar, ambrosia. She was a lover fit only for the gods, yet she lay here next to his battle-scarred body, bringing him warmth and hope.

His hands moved to her breasts. Firm, warm mounds tipped with the sweetest nipples. He wanted to suckle her into his mouth, hear her cry of lust as she rose up to meet him. His lips moved over her neck as she arched against him, anticipating, knowing his pleasures. Her hands, small and delicate, caressed his chest with a touch that fired his desire for her. Unable to bear such sweet torment, he rose above her, his chest heaving, passion rising hard and hot in his body. Then he was lowering himself again, dragging the smooth muscles of his chest over the hot, sensitive tips of her breasts. She cried, arching to him, her slender fingers digging into his biceps as he held himself carefully above her.

She moved against him temptingly. Her thighs parted for his and, as always, he was amazed that he was naked for her, having not remembered removing the rest of his clothing. But her hot slit was there to tease his cock, wet and slick, a tempting feast.

His mouth moved over her breasts, his lips suckling at her nipples as she gasped in heated need. Pleasure overwhelmed him, drove him higher, hardened his cock until it throbbed and ached unlike anything he had known in his life.

"Your taste would drive even the saints insane with hunger," he groaned as he nipped at her nipple, his hands going to her thighs, stroking through the soft creamy slit and reveling in her broken moan of pleasure.

"I wish only to drive you mad for me," she sighed brokenly, twisting against him, trying to drive the fingers he used to tease her with into her body.

He knew her inner flesh would be gripping, tight and hot. Her juices would coat his fingers when he sank them into the snug depth of her. He would then be lost to his own needs. He wasn't ready for that. Not yet.

He kissed her breasts lingeringly one last time, his tongue stroking over her nipples, loving the hardness of them, the proof of her need for him. His mouth drew a moist line down her stomach, over her abdomen. She cried out, as she had the last time he loved her in such a way. He ignored her hands as she attempted to pull him back up to her, ignored her shy entreaties.

It was the weeping flesh below that he needed. The soft rain of her female juices to fill his senses and his desires.

When his tongue circled the little bud of her clitoris, she flinched with pleasure. How soft and sweet her voice was when she pleaded with him for her climax. For a long second he took the little bud into his mouth. Toyed with it, played with it, made it swell and throb at his touch until the slick excess of her juices began to build around it. He attempted to lick it clean, drowning in the sheer beauty of her cries and the replacement of sweet passion's syrup as he ate at her.

His head moved lower, following the path of sweet cream. It frothed beneath his tongue like warm honey, heated sugar. He licked at it. Drew it over his tongue, savored the taste and went back for more. As he drew lower, he raided the inner secrets of her cunt, stabbing his tongue into her time and again as he groaned out his hunger into her flesh. His hand moved to the needy clit above, his thumb exerting minimal pressure. It was enough. She cried out his name, her thighs tightening on his head, her vagina convulsing, sending the warm flow of her release into his mouth.

Devlin could wait no longer. He moved along her body, spreading her legs wide, bringing them to his hips as he lodged the thick head of his cock against her tender opening.

"Now," she begged him, her head tossing, her hair laying about her like the softest rays of the moon. "Do it now."

He slid in by slow, painful degrees. She was tight. So very tight he had to grit his teeth and fight back his own release. She gripped the head of his cock like a soft oven, pulsing around him, her dew easing his way through the fist-tight channel. She was as tight as a virgin, as hot as fire.

"I need to take you hard," he cried out, unable to sustain his control any longer and hating himself for it. Hating the need that poured over him until he couldn't think, couldn't find the control to ease her way.

"Hard," she agreed with a ragged whisper. "Hard, Devlin. Fill me now —"

Their cries shattered the night. Devlin plunged his cock to the very depths of her gripping pussy, hearing her scream beneath him, arch to him. He cried out himself as she gripped him so tight and hot he knew he would never be free of her.

There was no hope of control then. He held her hips with hard hands, plunging into her over and again, the slap of his scrotum on her ass drawing images he never believed possible to his brain as he wondered how much tighter, how much hotter her vulnerable nether-hole would be.

He groaned, feeling her nails biting into his shoulders as he came to his knees, seeing her face twisting in such beauty, such pleasure it was enough to drive a man insane. He fucked her as he always did, as he could not keep from doing. He drove into her fast and hard, feeling the pulse of her dew-slick flesh, the tightening, the shudders of her slender body.

His cock was on fire. He heaved against her, fighting for breath, burying himself inside her until he swore he could go no deeper. The thick shaft was burning, throbbing, he felt her tighten further and heard her scream of release. It echoed around him, in him, lighting his soul and sweeping away that darkness that had once lingered there.

He came with a harsh, soul-torn cry. His cock erupted, spilling his seed inside her flesh, feeling her grip him, the tremors of her inner body urging more and more of the thick liquid from his straining cock.

Devlin collapsed over her, his breathing hard, rough. Her hands stroked his hair, her lips whispered over his face and he slept once more. His soul eased and as her voice whispered of love and eternities and destinies born, he gave up his battles for but a few more hours.

# Chapter Two
## *France*
## *Spring, 1040 AD*

෨

Chantel stood silently before the open window of her bedroom. A fresh spring breeze drifted through, filling her senses with the soft, delicate scents of the forests surrounding her father's castle.

It wasn't spring that had her staring into the forest below though. It was the gentle green aura pulsating from the crystal at her breast. Warm, beckoning, it heralded the arrival of the men who were, even now, hidden beneath the canopy of trees below.

Four days and nights it had taken them to travel through the forest to her father's castle. Four nights that she and her sisters had been haunted, by ever increasing degrees, by the dreams and visions of the life that would come.

Behind her, her sisters, Ariel, Caitlin and Arriane, sat quietly, disturbed by the foreboding shadows that twisted and curled through their own, once clear, crystals.

The sisters, all the Mistresses of the powers of the earth. Wind, Water and Fire joined the heart of the Mother Stone, the Earth Stone, which Chantel wore herself. As Mistress of the Earth Crystal, her power would always draw them together and give them greater strength. She was the key to their powers. Only with her own strength and knowledge would they find their way among the secrets the crystals contained.

"If this is the answer to the danger surrounding us, why then have the shadows not lifted, Chantel?" Ariel spoke from behind her.

Ariel had questioned her at every turn these last months. She was the least trusting and, for the moment, the most bitter of the four women.

Ariel was a warrior in her own right, made harder and tougher than the others due to the violence of her childhood. She feared the shadows, just as she feared the power.

Chantel turned and met her violet gaze, smiling comfortingly at the chestnut-haired warrior woman.

Ariel wore a gown of pale yellow silk with a deep violet, velvet tunic over it. It had been a chore getting her out of the leather breeches and plain linen shirt she usually wore.

"The crystals shall clear when our destinies are secured," Chantel promised her. "As Mistress of the Wind you will control much more than you know. You must learn the basics of knowledge before you begin your true journey."

"Ye make as much sense as ever, Chantel." Caitlin was a proud Irish lass from the top of her fiery red hair to the pale green of her eyes.

The Water Mistress was forever questioning and curious. She did not agree with the destiny Mother Earth had allotted her, nor was she pleased with the idea that her husband would be someone other than who she chose herself. Getting her agreement to this had been a monumental task, despite the dreams of the coming lover. Chantel knew, with a touch of sadness, that come morning Caitlin would forget all her objections. The warrior she had been promised to would control much more than her heart.

"Understanding will come in time." It was Arriane, Mistress of Fire, whose patient tone ended the questions.

Her eyes were a sapphire blue, bold and bright in her pale face. Her long black hair flowed around her gown of smoke and over-tunic of midnight, giving her an ethereal appearance.

"You sound like Father," Ariel accused her as she adjusted the thin gold belt at her hips.

"Arriane is right though." As Mistress of the Earth, Chantel knew better than all of them how accurate Arriane's words were. "Now is not the time to question the shadows of our future. Are you all ready for the coming night?"

She spoke to them all, but her gaze lingered on Arriane the longest. Of all her sisters, Chantel knew that she, her youngest and most fragile sibling, would have the hardest way. The fact that she was younger by only a matter of months mattered not. Their sisterhood was through Galen, each of their mothers were different. Chantel easily admitted her father had once been a much-heralded part of the King's court, both for his magic, as well as his attraction to the women. That attraction had resulted in four daughters in the course of a single year.

"I will be fine, Chantel," she promised, one promise among many that her worried sister had received.

"He will learn your secrets," Chantel warned her. A warning she had given many times. She wished the time was right to increase Arriane's power, but Chantel knew she would need it herself for a while longer.

"They are not truly bad secrets, though, are they?" Arriane questioned her, a shade of fear in her voice. "He should not hate me for long. Should he?"

"He's a whoremonger and a bastard," Ariel accused Arriane's intended groom as she moved restlessly behind Chantel. "Father was insane to contract that alliance."

Sadly, Chantel admitted the truth of her sister's words, but in all fairness to her father, she knew it was an alliance Arriane was destined for before she had even taken her first breath.

The Mystic warrior she had been given to was the most bitter and the least inclined to know the gentleness of the love he would one day feel for this fragile woman. He would bring her much pain before he realized it.

"I promise I shall be fine," Arriane told them all softly, the confidence of her tone at odds with the shadows of fear in her eyes. "I know it will be difficult at first, but all will be well later.

Yes?" Imploring eyes were turned to the sister who held the knowledge, foresight and control they were all trying to learn. It was to Chantel they turned for guidance and reassurance.

"I promise you all," Chantel whispered softly. "The day shall come when this spring shall be but a dreamlike memory. Jonar shall be defeated and taken from our lands forever, and we shall live in golden laughter with our warriors." Her hand touched Arriane's cheek briefly. "There is much pain ahead for you, dear sister, but your life shines brightest when our battles end."

Unfortunately, Chantel knew that her pain would also be the bleakest.

"Then I shall be fine," Arriane promised her with a sad smile.

Chantel feared that Arriane held more knowledge than she revealed. In those deep blue eyes, Chantel glimpsed the fear and the bitter resignation of what was to come. There was nothing she could do now, at this time. The bargain had been struck, now the terms must be met. And payment would begin this night.

Chantel gave her sisters one last gentle smile then took a deep, fortifying breath. The time was at hand to bring their destinies into the castle and to face the battle to come. She alone knew the full ramifications of what she was doing, and she prayed to both God and to Mother Earth that it would all be well in the end, as she had been promised.

"I will leave now and go to meet them. Await your husbands in the great hall. This night, I pray, shall bring us more comfort than our dreams have."

The dreams had always left them shaky, reaching for a touch, a sigh that always seemed just out of reach. Dreams that haunted them in the darkness of sleep, men who reached for them, shattered cries of helpless desire echoing around them as the dreams receded.

As last night's dream had done. Chantel's body still pulsed with the warm glow of her warrior's release, his shattered moans.

"Yes, by all means, let's get it over with," Ariel said derisively as she followed her sisters. "I'd enjoy sleeping in peace for a change."

Chantel fought the tears that came from the edge of bitterness in her sister's voice. Ariel was nearly shaking with her fears and the bitter memories of her past. But of them all, Chantel knew that this sister would know the greatest love, the utmost gentleness from her warrior for all time.

As they left her room and made their way to the great hall, Chantel fought to keep her own fears at bay. She could not allow her sisters to glimpse her indecision, her fears that she had made the wrong choice. If they saw her own hesitation, they would all become frightened of what was to come. She could not allow that. Chantel knew that future now depended on her and her alone. She could not allow mistakes to slow the way.

As Chantel entered the great hall, her father, Galen the sorcerer, met her at the bottom of the stairs.

He watched her silently, a frown marring his handsome face as his eyes flickered to the soft glow of the crystal she wore at her breast. The pure crystal had been magically inset with a perfect circle-shaped emerald in its center, from which an eerie glow pulsed steadily. Around it was positioned the sapphire half moon of Caitlin's water power, a violet starburst for Ariel's wind power, and a red ruby lightning bolt to represent Arriane's power over fire.

As the Earth Mistress, Chantel could call up all the forces of the earth, but only her sisters could control them. She was the binding in the power, the strength of the others. She knew this, and often that burden was a terrible weight to bear.

"They are waiting," Galen said softly. "Are you certain you wish to follow through with this, daughter? I do not know what you and Mother Earth have planned, but I will tell you I have a vague uneasiness concerning it."

Chantel stopped and laid her hand gently on his arm. This was her father, the man who had raised her, cared for her. His blood and his power were a part of her and the three sisters who followed, and she could sense his fears as easily as she could sense those of her sisters.

"You feel you are losing the daughters who worship you, Father." She smiled gently at his display of love. "You are gaining sons, you must remember this."

Galen's eyes narrowed on her.

"I have a feeling, daughter, you know much more than you have told me. It does not sit well with me." His gaze was centered directly on hers and Chantel could feel his own great powers reaching to break through the shield the crystal afforded her.

Its strength held, though, with no hardship to herself. The crystal wrapped her in a force of power, holding her steady when she could feel her insides shaking with nerves.

"I love you, Father." She reached up and kissed his smooth cheek as his arms went around her in a brief, fierce hug. "Be at ease. I promised you, did I not, that all would be well in the end?"

"It is what comes before that end that is beginning to worry me," he told her as she stood back from him. "Be warned, Chantel, you cannot hide the truth from me forever."

Yes, he would know soon, and when he did, she knew that his anger would be fierce, but his love would ensure his forgiveness. Chantel fought to remind herself that what she did, she did for all of them. What she did, she did to ensure the happiness and the peace they had been promised in the future.

"All will be well, Father, I promise you," she swore. "Now, come, walk to the courtyard with me and I shall go collect our reluctant grooms."

Chantel watched the smile that edged her father's lips and knew that her soft laughter had eased his heart.

"Not so reluctant, once they glimpse the beauty of my children," he assured her. "Each of you shall wrap those men so tightly around your dainty little fingers that they shall be unaware they had ever lived differently," he accused her.

"Is this not the point?" She smiled back at him, though she knew he was aware of the dreams, the bond they had created within the souls of these men.

"Definitely, Daughter, at least according to a woman." He grinned as they left the hall and walked into the bright sunlight of the courtyard.

There, the pure white filly he had chosen for Chantel the summer before last, awaited her. The horse's color was nearly the same as the white-blonde of her hair. This match had so pleased her when her father had gifted her with the animal. That he had taken the time and care to find such a rare color showed his love of her.

Raising the long length of her gown past her ankles, Chantel stepped up to the mounting stone and took her place on the soft lady's saddle that had been placed on the horse. She took a deep breath, gathering her courage as she hooked her knee around the pommel and accepted the reins from the guard who stood beside the gentle animal.

"Is everything ready to receive them?" she asked her father as she built her courage for the night ahead.

"Everything has been readied. Baths are being prepared now, food trays will be prepared after they enter the castle."

"Then I will collect them," she sighed. "I don't know why they could not make this easier on me."

Chantel turned the horse and headed through the acre-long courtyard that led to the castle's outer walls and the drawbridge that spanned a fog-enshrouded moat.

As she left the castle grounds, she carefully pulled her power around her, hiding her wayward thoughts or any secrets that could be glimpsed by the Guardians. She trusted in the crystal's shield, but she knew that outside the enchanted grounds of the castle, it could be weakened, its power breeched due to the immaturity of her sisters' stones.

The others had not yet been shown their own unique gifts, nor the control needed. That would come in time. Until then, Chantel knew that she must be careful and that she must always keep the shields carefully in place when leaving her father's home.

There were many enemies and those who would see the great Galen weakened, or use his love for her against him. She must always be certain this did not happen. Destiny must be concluded. Fate must be satisfied. And the price of that power and that victory would be high, she knew.

# Chapter Three

ɛ◌

The castle sat regally, comfortably above the valley it ruled over. Three stories of stone and rough wooden shingles surrounded by a wall three times a man's height.

The forest grew undisturbed around it. The wizard Galen had not cleared the trees and brush from the land around his castle as other castle owners did to prevent attacks from within the forest. The wizard depended on the magic he possessed to keep his castle safe and all invaders from his land.

Devlin sat atop his horse, just inside the boundary of that forest, watching the castle and those who came and went within it.

Behind him, the three others sat astride their own steeds, as silent as the forest had become several miles back. They were being watched, but not by human spies or human eyes, they were watched by the denizens of the forest.

Devlin was unconcerned with the stalking maneuvers of the wolf pack that had trailed them closely. He had been most curious, though, when those wolves had ignored the stag that had slipped quietly past them and headed in the direction of the castle.

"What man needs an army, when he has the creatures of the forest watching out for him?" Devlin remarked softly as he detected yet another forest creature watching them from the underbrush.

"Galen will already know of our arrival, Shadow," Joshua told him, his dark voice edged with amusement. "That stag was on a mission, else it would not have passed hungry wolves so easily."

"Those wolves are better fed than are we." Shanar made little effort to lower his voice. The big Viking stretched in his saddle and as Devlin glanced back he caught the anticipation in the warrior's eyes.

"The drawbridge is down, there is no sign of knights or an army awaiting us, so perhaps our arrival will be a welcome one." Derek's lilting Irish brogue was thick with weariness.

They had ridden hard to reach this castle, hidden deep within the forests and fabled to be impossible to find. They had ridden through the past several nights, stopping only to eat and rest their mounts before riding on.

Devlin could feel his weariness as he never had before. It pulled at the muscles of his back and made his eyes heavy. It also worried him, this tiredness. Not since the Guardians had gifted him with his unusual powers had he felt such weariness.

As he gazed out at the sheltered perfection of the castle the wizard had built in the middle of the forest, he felt a longing he had never truly been aware of.

His gut clenched tight with the need to feel the peace that seemed to surround the fortress. He could hear the distant echo of laughter, the raised, playful voices of the children behind the stone wall that enclosed the castle. It was as though happiness lived in charmed perfection there and he ached to be a part of it.

It was an ache he knew would never be relieved. Never had the warriors been welcomed into any man's home with laughter and warmth. They were the champions of the gods it was said, rather than God himself, rarely welcomed at all, but tolerated for their fighting gifts. Would it surprise them, he wondered, to know he prayed to the Almighty the same as they?

As he sat there, debating the safety of their arrival, a form rode onto the drawbridge. Devlin sat up straighter in his saddle, his eyes narrowing at the vision that began to cross it.

A young woman of perhaps eighteen years, her hair unbound, the white-blonde mass falling from her head down her back to caress the muscular back of her white steed. Devlin tensed, his memories of his midnight lover rising so clear that it caused his cock to rise as well. That fickle flesh became engorged with heat, demanding the slick, perfect portal it would find between this woman's thighs. This woman who tempted his dreams and had him spurting his seed in lonely splendor.

She rode leisurely, but her head was raised, her eyes looking expectantly into the forest where Devlin sat with his men. It was she. It could be no other.

"Galen's daughter perhaps?" Joshua spoke. "She's leaving without guards. The wizard Galen does not protect his treasures as well as I would have thought."

A growl from the underbrush denied that charge. Without taking his eyes from the young woman, Devlin was aware that the wolves had moved closer to them and now watched them with heightened senses.

"Perhaps her guards are already in place," he drawled in amusement as he continued to watch the woman riding toward them with renewed interest.

What trick of the demon Guardians was this that the very image that haunted his most erotic dreams was also the daughter of the sorcerer he sought? What magic had she practiced on him to bewitch his sleep?

It didn't take her long to reach them, though Devlin no longer cared if this mission was accomplished in haste. He was entranced with the form and the face of the girl meeting them.

Her white-blonde hair framed a face striking in its strength and beauty. High cheekbones and wide, slanted, emerald green eyes were a perfect contrast to the pert nose and full pink lips. Lips that his cock well knew, lips that his own had taken as their orgasms shattered them.

She wore a long white chemise and over it a brilliant green tunic that made her eyes darker, mysterious. There was a suggestion of warmth that reached out to Devlin, one that confused and bewildered him.

As she neared, the wolves once hidden now moved from the shadowed underbrush of the forest to surround her as they watched the men suspiciously. It was apparent that they felt none of the assurance that this woman seemed to carry about her like an invisible shield of strength.

"Sir Devlin." She stopped her mount several feet from them, a smile tilting her lips and sparkling in her eyes. Her voice was a soft caress across his frayed nerves, bringing a sense of peace, of homecoming. "My father, Galen, welcomes you to our castle and wonders at your delay within the forest. We have a hot meal, cool drinks and fresh beds prepared for you and your men. Would you like to come in now?"

She teased them, surely. Devlin had never been so welcomed to any man's domain. The Shadow Warriors were feared and distrusted, even though their services were in high demand. They were the Warriors of the Guardians, undefeated and having powers that even the most wise among men could not explain.

And what man would send his daughter, one so enchanting, to meet such a group of men?

Chantel's head tilted, her eyes watching him curiously as a small smile played at the corners of her lips.

"And why, dear lady, would the wizard Galen welcome us so eagerly?" Devlin leaned forward, bracing his arm on the pommel of the saddle as he regarded her. The frown that crossed his face seemed to have little effect on her though.

The smile that had merely flirted with her tender pink lips now bloomed in amusement and warmth. She seemed to tease him with that look, chiding him for his distrust.

"Sir Devlin, I am Lady Chantel, daughter to Galen. The Guardians have already apprised my father of your quest and the reasons you are here. He is ready to speak with you of it." She paused, a slender white-blonde brow arching questioningly. "That is, if you are willing to enter his castle, instead of lounging within the forest?"

The Guardians had already apprised the wizard of his quest? He should have known better than to believe they would have left this matter alone. Should have known that somehow, somewhere, it had been they who brought him the lover of his dreams.

"Very well, we humbly accept your offer, Lady Chantel." He bowed his head graciously, all the while unable to take his eyes from the beauty of her face. Unable to trust in her, unable to believe she truly stood before him in the flesh.

"Come along then." She graced them once again with her smile as slender fingers turned the reins guiding her steed.

She moved ahead of them, her hair blowing in the breeze, her slender hips shifting gently as she sat regally in the lady's saddle.

"Quite a welcoming, wouldn't you say?" Joshua moved in close as he voiced Devlin's own suspicions.

"The Guardians' interference was something I had hoped to avoid," Devlin sighed as he spoke of the misty gods who led the warriors into their battles. "I had hoped they would allow us to handle this on our own."

Joshua snorted derisively. Devlin didn't blame him for the sentiment—the Guardians were becoming burdensome with their demands and their interference. Devlin was certain there were even times they were working against them.

"Perhaps the wizard will hold the answers we seek," Derek spoke up softly. "If he knows the Guardians very well at all, then he will be aware of their ways. Perhaps that will aid us."

"Perhaps." Devlin wasn't counting on anything. He had learned the hard way how often greed and the chance to please the gods affected other men. He was afraid this quest was just another he had made in vain.

As Chantel rode ahead of the men, she fought to keep her heartbeat steady, her mind clear of confusion. Her father had warned her that once she stepped past the walls of the castle then the Guardians would know of her thoughts. She couldn't risk that, not yet.

So she thought instead of the warrior whose eyes she could feel trained upon her back. She blushed at where those thoughts were willing to lead her.

In her mind's eye, Chantel could still see his fierce frown, the suspicion in his hell's-black gaze. He was dusty and obviously worn from his journey through the mountains and into the forest where her father had made their home. Yet, he still hesitated in accepting the offer of welcome. As though such offers made would always hold the threat of betrayal.

Chantel ached for the life she knew this man had lived. Devoid of love, separated from his home, and destined to fight against an evil such as Jonar. He appeared to be a warrior well able to fight the dark lord though.

The Shadow was obviously tall and well-muscled. His black eyes were filled with danger and mystery, his sun-darkened face strong and masculine. Wide, arching brows as black as midnight, his lips full, but straightened into a controlled line. His cheekbones were well-defined, a hard slash below the bottomless depths of his eyes.

His reputation, of course, had preceded even the Guardians' warning of his arrival. The Shadow was spoken of only in hushed, fearful tones, a warrior who had achieved the approval of the gods and in turn had been gifted with abilities to far surpass any other men.

It was rumored he would disappear into the shadows in a way that even the animals of the forest would be unaware of his passing. He could see into the souls of men with his eyes or carry his own steed with his bare hands.

To Chantel, he appeared every bit that strong, but she had glimpsed more in his eyes. She had glimpsed a man lost, one searching for home. It was there in the slight droop of his shoulders, the way he had watched the castle with an air of envy. This was a man who wanted more than the battles he sought out each day. And she knew from his whispered words, thought only to be a dream by him, how he longed for more than the battles he fought.

Thankfully, the ride back to the castle wasn't a long one. Within minutes, Chantel was passing through the high stone gates once again and was able to drop the shield she had been forced to place about her thoughts.

Peace descended and she relaxed, allowing herself to turn and glance once again at the men following her.

Chantel wondered if they hadn't sensed the change when they passed the drawbridge themselves. They surveyed the interior of the castle walls eagerly, as though they had found something here that they had sought for a long while. Chantel could tell them what it was they sought, but she knew they would still not understand its meaning.

As their horses drew to a halt, the people of the castle gathered within the courtyard to witness the arrival. Visitors were few and far between within the stone walls Galen called his own. This was an event they all wished to see.

"Ah, you have finally arrived." Galen moved through the crowd of gathering servants with a smile on his face.

Her father was still a trim, handsome man. His dark brown hair was barely graying, his misty blue eyes were still sharp and filled with purpose. And as always, he was eager to thwart the Guardians in any manner possible.

Chantel worried that the day would come when the gods would realize how her father dallied with their requests.

"You are the wizard Galen?" Devlin paused beside Chantel as he began to aid her in dismounting as well.

Chantel's breath stopped as his hands spanned her waist, lingering there as he turned to glance at the wizard who now stood before him. The touch of his hands warmed her skin, caused her thighs to ache. And between them, her sex throbbed urgently. She could feel the soft slide of her slick juices there, the moisture gathering, seeping from the sheltering lips that protected her sensitive female entrance.

She ached there as well as in her breasts. She could feel her face flaming as those full mounds became swollen, sensitive, the tips needing the caress she had known only in her dreams from this man. His hot mouth covering them, suckling at her, his teeth nipping. She drew in a deep, slow breath, praying for control.

Slowly, his big hands amazingly gentle, Devlin lifted her from her steed and set her on her feet. If his fingers seemed to caress the silk of her gown at her hips as he released her, Chantel wasn't about to protest. The warmth of them, the magic of their strength, seemed to seep into her very bones.

"I am Galen." Chantel watched as her father noticed the lingering touch, and fought to ignore the blush staining her cheeks. "Come. Come into the castle. I have had water prepared for your baths and food kept warm for your arrival."

Her father turned and led the way through the massive courtyard to the open doors of the castle. Chantel watched as the men exchanged confused looks among themselves.

It was obvious that Galen was not what the men had expected in the wizard they sought. Galen dressed in rough, though clean, gray breeches and a white tunic belted at the waist with a simple rope of leather. His boots weren't fashionable, but worn for function instead. Her father was still known to enter the fields and work side by side with the peasants he protected.

"You will find my father shares many of your suspicions toward the Guardians," Chantel informed Devlin softly. "Come into the castle so you may bathe and eat. He will discuss your request with you at the evening meal or tomorrow's breakfast, whichever better suits your needs."

Chantel led the way, aware they were following slowly, watching the people and the courtyard in bemusement. Sadly, she was aware that these men were rarely welcomed into any man's home. Their fighting abilities were in great demand, but they were still feared among those they protected.

"Your father is too trusting," Devlin told her darkly as they stepped into the open doorway. "He should be more careful."

"Are you here to cause us harm, Sir Devlin?" Chantel glanced back at him, her heart heavy as she glimpsed the hunger in his eyes as he entered the brightly lit great hall.

"No, Lady," he replied huskily, pausing as though to soak in the homey atmosphere of the room spread out before him. "I would never cause you harm."

In his voice, Chantel heard the longing. How he must ache inside, she thought, surely as desperately as she ached these many years as she waited for him.

Chantel battled her tears as Devlin gazed around the warm and well-lit area of the huge main room. His eyes watched with equal parts suspicion and need battling within them.

"Then my father is justified in his trust of you." Motioning to the waiting servants, she turned to face the men fully. "Your rooms have been prepared with a hot bath, as well as wine and a light snack before your meal. If you will follow us."

Three women flanked Chantel, each indicating to the warrior they had been assigned to serve to follow them. Chantel turned to Devlin, indicating that he should follow her.

Chantel could feel the confusion emanating from him as they climbed the stairs set off to the side, to the second floor of the castle.

Devlin moved cautiously behind her, searching the shadows for betrayal as she led him to his room. How many times, she wondered, had he been given a false welcome only to combat his enemies when his back should have been secure?

Galen had told Chantel all the stories he had gathered of the warriors over the years. The many betrayals they had experienced, the pain they had suffered in the years they had been fighting for the gods.

They fought an enemy that Mother Earth assured her the warriors could never defeat in this time. Jonar carried too much magic, too many tools of the gods for man to defeat. Yet, she had promised her that the day would come when Devlin and his men would be victorious and that she herself would be the key to his victory.

Chantel led the warrior to his room, opening the door and walking in slowly. Her heart was beating fiercely, her knees almost shaking as she entered the room first. As Devlin passed by her, Chantel closed the door, aware of the tension gripping his big body.

There was a heavy silence in the room as he turned to look at her. His black gaze was hooded, his face lined with weariness, yet his body alert and ready for action.

In his eyes, she read his suspicions, his bitterness as past lessons rose to taunt him.

"So are you here to perform, Lady?" His eyes narrowed as he watched her darkly. "I was unaware that Galen's daughter played whore for the Guardians."

The pain of his accusation sliced through her heart like the sharpest dagger. It took all her control to hold back her cry as she felt the dark seeds of suspicion that grew within his mind.

Yet, she also knew his need to understand, to explain this sudden welcoming where there had never been such a thing in another place.

Chantel took a deep breath. Her father had warned her that Devlin would be filled with suspicion and less trusting than any person she had ever known. His accusation still hit her with the force of a blow though. She hated the distrust she saw in his eyes, but even more she hated the edge of disillusionment she could feel coming from him.

"I am no whore, Sir Devlin," she told him, standing firmly before him. "I am a virgin and no man's pawn. I am here because it is my wish. What you do with that is between you and your own honor."

Chantel could feel his struggle, see the demons leaping within his eyes as he fought to understand what she was offering him.

Poor knight, she thought to herself, how quickly he had been thrown into unfamiliar waters. He could sense within these castle walls all the dreams he had ever held, but still he was unwilling to accept even the idea of it.

Chantel had known for years that she was destined to be this man's woman. There was fear, but only the fear of innocence when faced with the time of knowledge.

"No man would gladly sacrifice his daughter to the dark warriors of the gods. No virtuous woman would gladly accept such a fate. So what sorceress' spell are you practicing here?" Devlin turned and stared at the bed, turned back invitingly, the wooden tub still steaming with water in the corner, the table laden with breads and cheese and a jug of wine.

"I practice no magic on you, Sir Knight," she told him softly as she moved to the small table and poured him a healthy measure of wine. Turning back to him, she sipped slowly from the goblet herself before extending it to him. "I am here to practice the gentle art of cleansing your body, and perhaps your heart, if you would allow it. I've shared your dreams, warrior. Surely now you will be willing to share the reality of it with me."

Chantel fought the trembling of her own body. She hoped he would ease her into the coming night and not grasp what she offered as a starving man would a banquet spread before him.

He was needy, this she could tell by the tenseness of his body, the bulge beneath his breeches, but she also sensed his control and she prayed it would serve her for just a while longer.

Devlin's eyes narrowed further as she spoke of those shared dreams, and then he raised the goblet to his lips and drank long from the spot her lips had touched. Yet not once did he take his gaze from her, as though he expected her to plunge a knife into his heart should he not watch her closely.

*Dear Knight*, she thought to herself, *we have not the time to overcome your distrust in a way more seemly*. How she would have enjoyed a gentle courtship herself. Lazy days beneath the teasing warmth of the sun, gentle smiles, perhaps a few dances as they flirted softly. There was no time for this now, though, and she knew there never would be.

Chantel watched the color that mounted his cheeks slowly, the hot glitter that began to rage in his dark eyes. This lonely warrior, she felt, sensed this as well. Destiny and fate had spoken, and Mother Earth had whispered to her the secrets of the future. The present was all they would have for a very long time to come.

Devlin didn't move to touch her though. He didn't have to. Instead, he glanced quickly at the tub and then smacked the empty goblet down on the table before he began to undress.

Chantel fought to steady herself, to still the trembling that began in the deepest recess of her body as the clothes were slowly shed.

He was a work of art. Hard, lean muscle, dark skin and the brief glimpse she allowed herself of his manhood sent her heart thudding so fiercely she nearly felt faint. His cock rose thick and hard, the wide head flared and raging. Had she not been assured by Mother Earth that he would cause her no harm, she would have surely run from the room in fear.

"A virgin, huh?" Chantel nearly missed his remark as he lowered himself into the steamy water.

"God, this feels good." He moaned as though the feel of clean warm water had been unknown to him.

"Yes," she whispered as she moved beside him with the bar of soap and a washcloth. "A virgin."

Heavy lidded, his black eyes assessed her as she took a small pitcher of warm water from the floor and held it behind his head.

Chantel knew he distrusted the teasing grin she could feel shaping her lips, but there was such distrust in his eyes, that it was tease him or cry.

"May I wash your hair for you, Sir Devlin?" she whispered, wondering at the husky pitch that had suddenly entered her voice.

Devlin blinked slowly, his breath harsh in the sudden stillness of the bedroom. Finally, after long moments, he merely nodded shortly and moved to sit up in the water.

"Nay, lie back as you were, there is a small basin behind to catch the water from your hair," she instructed him as she moved the large bowl into place. "It is your time to rest, to relax. Simply enjoy the warmth of the water."

The warmth of the water, and someone to care for you for a change, Chantel thought silently to herself. He reminded her of a wounded hound she had once cared for. Eager for her touch and the gentleness she would give him, but well aware that often betrayal was just around the corner.

In time the hound had learned she meant him no harm and Chantel was certain that the day would come when Devlin too would realize that fact as well.

Chantel moved to wet his thick black hair, amazed at the softness of the strands that fell to his shoulders. She moved the thick mass carefully until it flowed over the back of the tub and used the water in the pitcher to dampen the midnight strands.

Next, she took a carefully chosen jar of soap mixed with sandalwood, to lather into his hair. She was desperate to touch him, to feel his skin beneath her fingertips, and yet so was she hesitant. The coming night would be her first, and though the dreams of this man had tempted her, she was still hesitant to tempt his passion.

Devlin watched her carefully as she washed his hair as gently as any mother ever would. Her fingers moved slowly along his scalp, massaging away the dust and sweat of his journey with the rich lather of the soap.

Chantel was aware of the narrowed look that never left his face as she did this. The warrior was fighting to understand the logic of her actions and why her father was allowing it.

He would not easily accept the truth, Chantel thought. Devlin was a warrior, unused to any gentleness, any amount of trust. He would have to learn that it was easily within reach.

Chantel's fingers combed slowly through the tangled mass of black hair, gently working the snags free, then firmly rubbed his scalp clear of any lingering dirt and sweat. All the while, her fingertips gloried in the touch, her heart thudding painfully against her breast as she cared for him.

"You have a gentle touch, Lady Chantel," he whispered as she rinsed the lather out of his hair slowly, careful to keep the suds from his eyes as he watched her.

"Thank you, Sir Devlin." Her voice was just as soft and much less controlled as she fought the heaviness in her chest that forced her breath to feel labored.

Next, she dipped the square of linen into the water and lathered it with the soap.

"Close your eyes," she told him softly. "Else the lather will burn them."

Distrust flared in his gaze once again. Then slowly, his body tensing in preparation of betrayal, he closed his eyes.

Chantel worked the cloth over his face several times, washing the grime from his skin. His eyes were deep set, his brows arching over them strongly. His nose was straight and aristocratic, his cheekbones high and flushed. Chantel worked the soft cloth over each feature, rinsing then repeating, careful to remove the grime of his travels from each pore of his skin.

She found great pleasure in touching him, in feeling his strength and warmth. Her fingers replaced the cloth with the last washing, flowing over his sun-darkened skin and relishing the feel of flesh before she began to carefully rinse the soap, paying close attention to the long-lashed eyelids. Had she ever seen such lashes on a man? She could have sworn she never had.

Finally, she rinsed his face one last time and then dried it quickly so he could open his eyes once again.

"You're washing me as you would a child," he scoffed, his black gaze pinning her in accusation. Yet, the gentle chiding held a vein of pleasure within it. It confused him, Chantel thought, the pleasure he was receiving from her touch.

"Then enjoy it," she chided him with a soft smile. "When was the last time you were taken such gentle care of?"

He frowned at her fiercely, but she merely ignored the look and quickly lathered the cloth once again and began to wash the strong contours of his neck and shoulders.

The muscles there were bunched and corded with tension. Chantel moved closer, working the lather of the soap between her bare hands before she began to work the muscles of those shoulders.

She wasn't certain, but she thought she caught the strangled edge of a whimper of pleasure. She hid her smile as she continued to massage his shoulders, her hands sliding, pressing and relishing the feel of his skin.

"It's not proper that you are doing this," he informed her. "A serving wench would be better."

"Would you prefer a servant's touch to mine?" She smiled as she touched his shoulder with her bare fingers and felt the muscles jerk in response.

He was silent for long moments as he watched her, his gaze shielded, narrowed as he probed the air around her for any hint of deception.

Chantel allowed him in, just enough for him to glimpse the feelings raging inside her heart, the needs raging inside her body.

He seemed to flinch as he retreated quickly from the heated glimpse he was given. His breathing became harsher, his expression nearly savage in its intensity.

"Lady, you do not want to continue this game," he informed her darkly. "I am a man long due a woman's warmth, not a callow youth so eager to please I will forget my own pleasure in the face of your untried state."

Chantel felt her mouth dry at that warning and then water at the thought of this man's touch. After all the years of dreaming, of searching for him, he was finally here. This warning would not stray her from her course.

"Are you saying you will hurt me intentionally?" Chantel looked into his eyes as she voiced her question.

"I will not need to." He swallowed tightly as he met her gaze, his expression now tormented, awash with needs that she could tell he struggled to control. "I will be unable to do anything else. I ask you now to leave and to tease me no more with your silken hands."

"And what of your needs?" she asked him, her eyes flickering to the broad head of the shaft lying just below the water's surface.

Chantel felt her face heat, her body melt at the sight that met her eyes. Her gaze flickered away quickly. What would it be like to touch him there? To hold him in her hands and see pleasure in his face at her touch? In her dreams, she had taken him into her mouth countless times as he pleaded for her to suckle that burgeoning flesh.

She well remembered the feel of hot satin, hard steel. His strangled groans would wrap around her, his hoarse declarations of the pleasure she brought to him would cause her body to flame with her own needs.

Tormented by those memories, Chantel moved the washcloth to his chest, her motions growing slower as her gaze went once again to the sight of his hardness. She longed to taste that flesh again, to feel the power and the heat that filled it.

"My needs may well be more than you can meet, Lady," he warned her, moving until he was sitting up more fully in the water. "Wash my back, then give me the damned cloth so I may finish washing before your gentle touch results in my own embarrassment."

Devlin's husky order had her frowning as she watched him, regretting the move that no longer allowed her to see the proof of his need for her.

"Embarrassment?" Chantel wasn't certain what he meant as she began to wash his back firmly. "How could I be the cause of your embarrassment?"

She felt the harsh breath that exploded from him at her question. Thankfully she had just finished his back when he reclined forcefully, his hand moving to capture her hand as it went once again to his chest.

"Hear me well, woman." His voice was guttural, his black eyes staring at her heatedly. "Keep this up and you will find yourself getting an education you were not counting on. Do you understand me?"

Chantel smiled once again, aware that she was goading him, but unable to help herself.

"I told you, Sir Knight, I am a virgin," she whispered. "How would I know what to count on and what not to?"

His face flushed darkly, the hand gripping her wrist contracting as he fought some internal war. Chantel had no idea if he lost or won the battle within himself, for his next action cleared her mind of all thoughts but him.

Devlin jerked her hand beneath the water and, before she could think, he had wrapped it as far as it would go around the hardened flesh thrusting boldly from between his thighs.

A groan was ripped from his throat as her fingers touched him. His head fell back along the rim of the tub, his eyes glittering from beneath partially closed lids as the hand that held hers trapped moved her fingers against him.

Chantel whimpered, her breath stopping in her throat at the heat and hardness she held in her grasp. Her fingers would not meet around his hard cock, but that did not seem to hamper his enjoyment of her touch.

"God, your touch is like silk." The words seemed to be ripped from his throat as he moved her hand once again. He drew it slowly to the base of his shaft, then in a slow sweep once again to the broad head.

Chantel felt fevered, as though some dreaded illness had taken hold of her, suspending her breath, her thoughts, everything but the feel and the sight of this big man's pleasure.

Her fingers flexed beneath his grip, massaging the muscle it gripped, and she watched as perspiration dotted his forehead, his face tightening with an expression akin to pain.

His hips lifted toward her, causing the flesh trapped beneath their grip to rise marginally above the surface of the water.

"Enough." The words were torn from his chest as he removed her hand and pushed her none too gently away from the tub.

"No," Chantel cried out in protest as she fell back, fighting for breath, her hand still extended toward him before sanity returned and she clutched it quickly within the folds of her now dampened gown.

"Undress." The order was given in a voice so dark, so filled with heat she flinched. "Do it now, woman, or I won't bother when I've finished washing this damned grime from the rest of my body."

Chantel shook her head, watching as the cloth quickly lathered long legs, strong thighs and the near-to-bursting length of his erection before it was thrown aside. He rinsed quickly and then rose from the water, unmindful of the wet floor as he stepped from the tub.

"I warned you." He advanced on her, his face dark, his eyes glittering with a suppressed fury as he reached for her.

Chantel cried out as he pulled her to him, his head lowering, his lips taking hers in a kiss that gave little concession to her untried state.

"I warned you," he repeated against her lips a second before his tongue pierced her mouth and his hand ripped the gown and tunic from her body.

His body was hot and so hard. He pulled her against him, lifting her into his embrace as his lips plundered hers and his shaft nestled itself against her woman's mound.

Chantel gripped his shoulders, her fingers digging into his skin as she felt the heat and longing that ripped spasmodically through her body. She was untried, but not unaware or unknowing. The dreams she had shared with this knight had paved the way for what was to come.

Her lips moved beneath his, opening, her tongue touching his hesitantly as he plundered the depths of her mouth.

"What have you done to me?" he growled as his head lifted and his lips buried themselves at her throat. "You have cast a sorceress' spell that I shall never recover from."

He moved quickly then to the bed, falling upon it as his hands braced his big body above her.

Chantel breathed in roughly, feeling her breasts, sensitive and swollen as they brushed against the hard wall of his chest. Her nipples were hard, aching and hot. She needed this touch, the warmth of his mouth surrounding them as he had done in her dreams.

"First you torment me when I would sleep," he growled, staring down at her, fire and need reflected in his eyes. "Now, you would torment me when my only want is to protect you from the hunger that rises inside me. You, my Lady, are a danger unto yourself."

Chantel fought her grin as she heard the helpless fascination in his voice. She lifted her hand to his face, her fingers tracing his full lips. She watched as his eyelids lowered at her caress, the way his strong teeth caught at a finger and nipped it warningly.

"I have shared my passion and my heart with you in those dreams," she whispered. "I have known your needs and your touch and the paradise that awaits me when you truly possess me for the first time. I give to you all that I am, Devlin. I ask only the same in return."

He shook his head, his damp hair brushing his shoulders, her fingers.

"I want to devour you," he groaned roughly. "My passions were not meant for a virgin."

"I am your virgin." She smiled gently. "All your passions were meant for me."

His eyes narrowed further, the black pinpoints of hunger nearly hidden by his thick lashes. For a moment she wondered if he wavered in accepting her passion, or if he considered refusing it. How could she live if he refused her?

She felt his hand then, calloused and faintly rough against the soft skin of her thigh. Her breath caught in her throat, her neck arching at the pleasure.

"I will not be an easy lover, my lady," he warned her. "My desires are not for one who would wish to be cherished rather than well-loved."

"I prefer well-loved," she gasped, twisting against him as the tips of his fingers glanced over the dampness of her most private area.

She knew the flesh there was slick and hot, prepared for his touch. She felt his fingers slide through the narrow slit, testing her, circling the small bud of intense feeling that was farther above the entrance to her channel.

"You're ready for me," he growled roughly, his head lowering as his cheek caressed one heaving breast. "Why are you so ready for me?"

Tormented need and confusion filled his voice, tore at her heart. She would have answered, tried to answer, but the feel of his finger, broad and hot, penetrating her core was more than she could fight against. Her hips lifted into the caress, a broken cry issuing from her lips.

She could only tremble within his grasp as his lips moved from one breast to the other, covering each nipple in turn, suckling at her with strong, erotic pulls of his mouth as his tongue rasped over each swollen peak.

Chantel shuddered, the pleasure more intense, hotter, deeper than any dream they had shared. His lips moved over her breasts, then down, his hands holding her still now as she writhed beneath his caresses. They were fire and lightning, searing her with a passion she was hard-pressed to survive. How could such pleasure be possible? How could she burn so bright and hot and still survive?

"Devlin," she cried out hoarsely as his lips worked over her stomach, her abdomen, moving she knew, to taste the essence of her need from between her thighs.

Her hands caught in his hair. What they had done in the privacy of dreams, was much more frightening in reality.

"No." He reached up, moving her hands so they lay on the blankets beneath her. "You offered yourself to me, Lady. Now I will have my fill." He stared at her, stretched between her legs, too close to the thick female juices that she knew now coated her flesh. "Your taste within my dreams has tormented me. I will now know if it is indeed nectar fit only for gods. A taste that only I will know."

His voice was hard, his hands determined as he pushed her thighs farther apart. His gaze stayed locked with hers, daring her to look away as he slid farther down the bed until his head was poised over the flesh he would have.

"Watch me," he whispered. "Just as you did within our dreams, Chantel, watch me devour you."

# Chapter Four

೫

Watch him. Chantel could barely breathe. She feared she would lose consciousness entirely if she watched the darkly erotic sight of his head bending to her. But she did just that. She watched as his tongue emerged from his mouth, distended, and swiped through the soaked slit of her female folds. Her juices clung to his tongue as he licked his lips, tasting her, then returned for more. She couldn't halt her cry, the shocking shudder that raced over her body. She shook, her knees bending, her legs lifting to open her body further to him. She needed him. Needed more.

His tongue returned to her, circled the small pearl of exquisite sensation that swelled and pulsed to his touch. Then his mouth covered it, suckling her, his gaze never leaving her face as she cried out and fought to breathe.

"I cannot bear it." Her voice trembled, the passions raging through her body were destroying her. She needed him. Needed his cock filling her as it had in her dreams.

"I'm hungry, Chantel," he whispered as he licked her again. "Starved from lonely nights of dreams alone. Desperate to know in truth, the touch and taste that I have known only in dreams. You offered and now I will take, as I have longed to take all these months that you have tempted me."

His head lowered. Chantel could not halt her scream as sensations too extreme to be borne tore through her body. His tongue pushed into her entrance, filled her as her muscles clamped on him, her hips lifting closer. She could not keep her eyes open. Could not continue the hold his look had on her. She was weak, her mind dazed, her body consumed with a fire so intense, she felt as though her very blood were molten.

His tongue licked and stroked her to levels of sensation that had her crying, begging for the release she knew was just out of reach, tempting her, taunting her with its intensity. He thrust that wicked member into her sheath, swirled it against the sensitive flesh there and set off a firestorm of tremors that had her gasping out his name in exquisite torment.

"Are you ready to come apart for me, Chantel?" he whispered, kissing her thigh as his fingers moved to the entrance of her soaked quim.

Her body tensed, her muscles tightened.

"Yes," she begged. "Please, Devlin. Please, I beg of you."

His finger entered her slowly, then a second, stretching her, burning her sheath with the intoxication of the slow penetration.

He filled her, stretched her, then his mouth returned to the swollen pearl above it and began to suckle it deeply, his heated mouth, the rasp of his tongue stroking her to paradise. Chantel could not contain her scream as the sensations tore through her, violent in their intensity. Her body arched, her thighs clenched about his head as she felt her insides dissolve. Her womb spasmed and lightning raced through her bloodstream as pleasure tore through her.

"Mine." His growl shocked her as he rose above her body. She looked into his eyes, saw desire raging through his gaze and had but a second to draw in a breath before his cock, thick and hard, pushed into the velvet reaches of her cunt.

She whimpered in fear and in pleasure. Her thighs gripped his muscular hips, her hands clenched on the arms braced above her.

"Devlin." She cried out his name as she felt his muscles gather, bunch, then he was surging swift and hard inside her, tearing past the fragile barrier of her innocence and filling her to overflowing.

She moaned against the stretching burn, the lightning flare of pain and heat that turned to a pleasure so intense she felt on the edge of death. She could do no more than fight for air, her head tossing on the pillows, her body shuddering as he began the deep, slow thrusting motions of his hips that threw her past sanity.

He stroked her cunt repeatedly, gasping with each inward thrust as her muscles closed on his invading cock, clenching on it, her pussy weeping its thick juices and easing his way further. She was crying repeatedly now, begging him with a desperation she had not known, even in their shared dreams, for the peak of pleasure she knew would surely kill her.

It was close, so close, pouring over her, through her as his cock began to pound inside her. The hard length of muscle stroked her furiously, driving her higher until she felt the sensations rush over her in an inferno of such heat that she screamed out beneath him. Her body, each tiny portion of her flesh, exploded around him. He groaned out above her, his male cry urging her higher, the flood of his seed, hot and erotic, pushing her into a realm of sensation that hurled her past consciousness.

\* \* \* \* \*

She was asleep. Devlin glanced at the face of the young woman cuddled against him and sighed wearily. What had happened? He had not lost control of himself in such a manner since he was an untried youth. To do so with this woman was unforgivable.

A bloody virgin, Devlin shook his head. This journey to the wizard's castle had gotten out of control so quickly, he wondered if he would ever regain it. To be certain, he doubted he would. The hardness between his thighs assured him that this night, he would concentrate on nothing but the woman whose body was twining slowly against him, her hand caressing the planes of his stomach and moving lower, even in her sleep.

She murmured his name, a smile shaping her lips as her fingers found his erection. Her lips pursed as a kiss was placed against his neck, then in amazement Devlin watched as she moved lower in the bed.

Just as she had done countless times in his dreams, she moved languidly, her lips pressing warm and satiny smooth against his flesh.

Devlin knew he had died and gone to heaven, and heaven was this woman's mouth as it closed delicately over the head of his cock.

He fought for control as her sweet lips moved over him, then died a thousand deaths as her tongue moved in a silky hot trail around the turgid head.

He clenched the sheets in his fists to keep from jerking her closer, to keep from burying his length as deeply into her mouth as he could. It was a torture he wanted to never end, a torture he knew he couldn't bear much longer.

He was helpless as she held him in the soft grip of her lips, her silken hands gripping his shaft as she licked him like a particular sweet and moved her fingers as he had taught her in the bath.

Her pace became hotter, her mouth ravenous as she caressed him, her fingers a gentle vise as they stroked him.

"No…" The harsh exclamation was torn from his lips as he felt his climax rushing through his body.

The temptress between his thighs paid little heed to his raspy command. The tightening of his shaft and quick harsh thrust of his hips against her should have warned her, but she ignored it.

Her lips closed around him, the gentle suckling motion of her mouth, the flicker of her tongue was too much. A harsh cry escaped his throat as he felt himself coming, his climax rushing through his body, erupting from the head of his shaft and pouring furiously into her eager, willing mouth.

Devlin had lost his sanity. He knew he had the moment he threw her to her back and mounted her. He thrust his still hardened shaft into her, stroking, thrusting as her legs encircled his hips and her cries joined with his own.

When his release ripped through his body, he knew he was lost. There would be no more lonely nights staring into the depths of a midnight sky in anger and in need. This woman would fill his nights as surely and as fully as he filled her body now.

Finding their breath, their sanity, was not an easy thing to do in the aftermath of such pleasure. When Devlin managed to do so, he would have pulled her into his arms, whispered his thoughts, but she jerked from him, a startled cry on her lips.

For the first time, Devlin noticed the crystal that lay at her breast, suspended from a silver chain. He frowned as that crystal seemed to warm, to glow against her breast.

"The bastard!" The curse ripped from Chantel's lips as she staggered from the bed and jerked a robe from the wooden closet beside it.

She was breathing harshly, fear laying heavily around her as she fought her way into the robe. Devlin moved just as quickly, but had only managed to jerk his pants and boots on before she was rushing from the room.

He jumped to his feet, snagging his shirt from the floor and pulling it quickly over his head as he rushed to follow her. He wasn't nearly as quick as he would have liked. His legs seemed to want to tremble instead of move as he directed them.

Two of the women who had taken his men to their rooms met Chantel at the bottom of the stairs that led to the next level. From there Devlin could hear the source of the commotion.

Joshua. Pushing the women out of his way, Devlin raced up the steps as he heard a woman's frightened cries and Joshua's rage echo through the halls.

The women were but a step behind him when he burst through the door. Devlin stopped in amazement, blinking, unable to believe what he was seeing.

The young woman hung in his grasp, pleading with him, Joshua's fist was cocked, his eyes watching her in an insane fury.

Devlin's reaction was instant. His eyes centered on that fist, ready to swing, to crush the life from the woman hanging helplessly before him.

"Joshua." His voice was but a whisper, but Devlin knew that despite the cries he could hear, his words would reach the warrior.

Slowly, with only the power of his mind, Devlin forced the warrior's fist to lower, his hand to release the naked young woman. She fell to his feet with a cry, while Chantel and the other two rushed to her side and fought to drag her robe quickly over her nude body.

"You bastard!" Chantel rose to her feet, her hand cracking furiously against the bronzed face of the savage still standing over them.

"Get that devil's whore from my room." Joshua stared into Devlin's eyes, the amber depths lit with fury as he shook with the force of it. "Before I kill her."

"Chantel." Galen ran into the room, taking the scene in quickly and pushing past Devlin.

The wizard went to his knees beside the girl, his hands lifting her tenderly as she cried uncontrollably against his chest.

"It's okay, child." Galen stroked her back, her long black hair, his eyes closing in what Devlin assumed was grief as he tucked her to his chest as he would a daughter.

A daughter. Devlin looked to the other women. They all wore a necklace similar to Chantel's, and though they were vastly different in looks, they all shared a bearing, a presence that proclaimed them.

"Derek." Devlin turned to the man at his side. "Get Joshua out of here until I figure out what the hell is going on."

"We should all leave this place." Joshua turned to Devlin, staring in contempt at the woman still cradled in the wizard's arms. "We were wise to suspect them. They not only deal with the Guardians, but Jonar himself. The little bitch is his granddaughter, Arriane."

The condemning words had little impact on anyone but the warriors. Devlin's gaze went slowly to Chantel, who had stood to her feet at Joshua's accusation.

"Is this true?" he asked her softly, feeling the bitter edge of betrayal rush over his body.

"It is not what you think," Chantel cried as she turned to face her lover. "Her blood matters not, for she is part of Galen as well. He has no excuse for his treatment of her."

"Chantel, take your sisters to your room. I will call for you when it is time." Galen overrode Devlin's demand as he stood up, helping his daughter to her feet as well.

"Father, I should stay." Chantel took Arriane into her arms, but led her instead to the two other women standing with her.

"No." Galen shook his head. "It would be best if you do as I have asked. I will call for you soon."

A long look passed between the two before Chantel nodded shortly and began to lead her sisters from the room. As she began to pass Devlin, he gripped her arm with his hand, staring down at her.

"Have you betrayed me, Chantel?" he asked her slowly. He wanted her to deny it, to ease the suspicions forming in his mind.

"Father will explain." She shook her head quickly, her gaze meeting his firmly. "But we haven't betrayed you, Devlin."

"Go, Chantel." This time Galen's voice had the ring of a command in it. "I will send for you when it is time."

Devlin watched as Chantel flashed her father an angry look. Evidently she did not agree with his hasty order to have her leave. Yet she did so, leading the other women quickly from the anger that thickened the air of the room.

Devlin faced Galen now, aware of the door closing softly behind them as Shanar locked it into place.

Devlin sighed deeply.

"I came here to request your help, but perhaps I came in error," he suggested. "I was informed your hatred for Jonar was as deep as ours. It would appear I was wrong."

"We will address your concerns momentarily." Galen's voice surprised Devlin. It resonated with fury and with wrath as he turned on Joshua. Before Devlin could blink, Joshua was flying through the room, crashing heavily into the wall where he seemed to be pinned helplessly, his feet barely touching the floor.

Devlin turned on Galen, fighting to break the magic that suddenly wrapped about the room. His own powers were ineffectual against the invisible bonds that held him. He could not move and could do nothing to aid the warrior who now faced the sorcerer's wrath.

"The powers those bastards gifted you with are strong, my young warriors," Galen sneered as he advanced on Joshua. "But they can never compete with the power Mother Earth has given her champion. You—" He stood before Joshua, violence barely leashed as he speared the warrior with a look that promised retribution. "My daughter came to you willingly, with no betrayal in her heart, and you would dare to strike her?" Lightning flashed outside the room, thunder resounded in great clashing waves.

"Your daughter is the spawn of Satan!" Joshua screamed out at him, his amber eyes glowing as he fought the hold the wizard had on him.

"And you aren't?" Galen asked him cruelly, seemingly unaffected by the powers the four warriors were combining against him. "Save your strength, pups," he sneered at them all. "You cannot defeat me with your powers, no matter your strength, and this you would do well to learn now."

"She is Jonar's spawn…" Joshua raged.

"She is my daughter. Raised by me since her sixth summer and with none of Jonar's cruelty in her tender heart. Ask yourself, you little whoremonger, why you didn't feel evil in her when you first saw her? Why wait until she was lying weak within your arms to probe her gentle mind and find that for which you thought you searched?"

"Only a whore would know such moves," Joshua sneered.

"Or a woman who has dreamed of your touch since she was but a child, unknowing of what a man would even ask of her," Galen charged. "Only a woman whose heart is too tender to see a bastard for what he truly is."

"No." Joshua spat out the word as his gaze locked with Devlin's. "I will not breed with that bitch. I will see her naught but dead."

Silence descended the room now and Devlin could feel the weight of the sorrow that seemed to fill it.

"No, I will not allow her to breed with you. No child shall ever come of this union until you free your heart from the black hatred enslaving it. It is to my great sorrow that I can do nothing about the love she has for you," Galen told him contemptuously.

Galen turned to Devlin now and Joshua slid slowly to the floor, the magic released. The wizard's face was lined, his eyes filled with sadness.

"You came to me to ask a favor and to collect that which belongs to you, to all of you. I will discuss this with you alone, or you can all ride out now. Alone."

Alone, without the women they had unknowingly searched their lives for. Devlin stared at Joshua as Galen left the room.

"Shanar, you and Derek stay here with him. I want him sane before I return," Devlin ordered him.

"Good luck." Shanar crossed his arms over his chest as he looked at the enraged warrior, still naked, still filled with fury. "Maybe we should just ride out."

"Then get ready to ride, but the women stay here." Devlin arched a brow, much as he had seen Chantel arch hers, as he looked at the other two men.

"The hell you say!" Joshua's voice surprised them all. "I'll go nowhere until I kill that bitch."

Devlin shook his head. The situation was out of control and he had no idea why.

He turned back to Joshua, watching as the other man jerked his clothing on. His savage features seemed even harsher in the waning light of evening, his eyes glowing eerily, and his overly long black hair released from its tie and hanging around his shoulders.

He was like a man possessed, Devlin thought worriedly.

"What the hell is wrong with you?" Devlin questioned him furiously. "Never have I known you to strike a woman and you strike the daughter of a wizard?"

"I didn't hit the little whore, I just wanted to." Joshua breathed roughly as he sneered. "I would have choked the life out of her had I been given the chance though."

"Are you insane?" Devlin asked him softly. "What has possessed you, Joshua?"

The other man was silent as his gaze clashed with Devlin's. His eyes glowed with gathering fury and Devlin knew he was but a step from trying to force his way past them to the women below.

"You leave this room and you will ride with us no longer, Joshua," Devlin informed him softly. "You so much as open that door and you will no longer be part of us, do you understand me?"

Surprise registered with all the men. Never had Devlin threatened them in this manner and Devlin never threatened — he promised.

"She's just a whore," Joshua raged.

"And you have lost your mind. I refuse to ride with a madman." Devlin fought to understand, to come to grips with the fact that what had begun as a quest for help was destroying them instead.

Joshua took a deep breath, speared his fingers through his hair and then muttered something.

"What?" Devlin wasn't certain he had heard correctly.

"I said I wouldn't really kill the little whore unless I fucked her to death!" Joshua yelled at him, fury still pumping through his body. "I was enraged, but I wouldn't really kill her."

"Prove it." Devlin crossed his arms over his chest. "I don't trust you, Joshua, and a lack of trust could get us all killed."

"I'll stay put," Joshua ground out. "I'm horny as hell and ready to explode, and if I don't bury it in the little bitch before long I'll die. So get the fuck out of here and settle with the old man so I can do it."

Devlin stared hard at Joshua, his eyes narrowing.

"Stop probing my fucking mind," Joshua bit out furiously. "You got yours, I didn't. So get the hell out of here so I can get her back."

Devlin turned to Derek and Shanar.

"He's lost it, Devlin." Shanar shook his head. "I've not seen Joshua like this since…"

Since the first dream, when the other warrior had awakened like a madman, tearing apart the small village they had been staying in as he searched for the temptress who had invaded his dreams.

Devlin sighed roughly.

"Stay with him. Make sure he doesn't go after her. I'd hate like hell to have to disown him."

Devlin stalked from the room, tearing down the stairs as he made his way back to the great hall. He was tired, hungry and he was sore. Dammit, he didn't need this right now, but there was nothing to do but take care of it.

His first stop was his room. He threw open the door to find Chantel there, cleaning up the last of the water from the floor with a large dry cloth.

She stood quickly to her feet as he entered the room, alarm crossing her face.

"You shouldn't be here." She gripped the front of her robe tightly as he began to strip the clothes from his body.

"I don't like wearing dirty clothes over a clean body, my Lady," he bit out as he jerked open the small leather bag that contained a change of clothes.

All he wanted to do was find the wizard, negotiate a deal for his aid, and ride out to the next battle against Jonar, Devlin thought. He hadn't anticipated finding everything he had ever needed here, every hidden dream that had filled his soul. He hadn't known he was truly lonely until he gazed into the emerald eyes of the woman standing so solemnly behind him.

He turned to her, finding her gaze fighting to keep from straying to his throbbing erection. Damn woman, he couldn't even be furious with her for the way his body craved her.

"Don't worry, I wasn't about to use it," he growled as he jerked his pants on and laced them quickly.

"Of course." Her voice sounded small in the room, and her expression regretful.

Devlin sighed deeply as he pulled the tunic over his head and adjusted it.

"Come here." His voice was gentle as he pulled her to him, lifted her into his arms and kissed her lips quickly. "Stop worrying. I'll figure something out."

He wasn't certain yet what he would figure out, but he knew he had better come up with something soon.

"Arriane is terrified of him now." Chantel nestled in his arms, her voice sounding incredibly young and uncertain.

"Just as terrified as Joshua is of her." Devlin sighed. "Stop worrying. We'll get it sorted out." He stepped back from her and kissed her lightly once again. "Have someone send some food and wine to Joshua's room. I'll have something worked out before morning, I promise you."

She nodded, watching him uncertainly as he sat down, pulled his boots back on and walked to the door.

"Devlin." Her soft voice stopped him at the door.

"Yes, Chantel?" He turned back to her, suddenly hesitant himself.

"Do you remember the dreams?" she asked him fearfully, as though she were scared they had been a figment of her own imagination.

Devlin closed his eyes and then opened them quickly as fragments were suddenly displayed within his mind.

"I remember the dreams, Chantel." He tried to swallow past the lump in his throat. "I remember them all."

He didn't wait for her to answer, but left the room quickly and closed the door securely behind him. In the hall, he took a deep breath and then stomped back down the stairs to the great hall.

All he had wanted was a bath and a meal, Devlin thought. He got the bath and he was more tired and more satisfied than he had been in his life, but with it came more trouble than he knew how to deal with.

He entered the great hall, his gaze roaming over the room until he caught sight of Galen. The other man sat silently in a large chair positioned before the empty fireplace, a mug of ale in his hand as he watched Devlin.

"Are you riding out now?" Galen asked him as Devlin strode to him. "I'll have your horses readied."

Devlin could see that one happening. He wondered if the wizard truly thought he wasn't aware of how well he was being played within this drama Galen had set up.

"Then have us stopped at the gates?" Devlin asked him as he sat in the chair that had been positioned diagonally to Galen's. "This isn't over yet, old man. Let's finish it."

Galen frowned.

"I didn't think I was so old yet," he reflected. "I'm young enough to sire children and still sit my own horse. Young enough to look forward to my grandchildren and perhaps marry again. Age has not yet dulled me."

"Hasn't it?" Devlin asked him. "Surely you erred when giving Jonar's granddaughter to Joshua. You would have served her better to have hidden her until we left."

Galen thought about this for long moments, his dark brows lowered, his blue eyes distant as he considered the options he must have had.

"He would have known she was here." Galen finally shrugged in defeat. "Why else did the four of you refuse to sleep after entering the forest? You rode four days without rest to get here—he would have begun his search the moment he laid down to rest. The closer he came to her, the more she haunted him, just as he had haunted her."

Which was the truth. The last night they had slept, dreams of the women had tormented them until they were awake well before dawn and ready to ride.

At the time, Devlin hadn't questioned the strength of the dreams. They had been at battle for months against Jonar's forces, had fought hard and ridden harder to reach this infernal forest when the battle had been over.

"You knew Joshua would use his power against her." Devlin accepted the mug of ale a servant brought to him. "You should have known his fury."

Had the wizard known anything about Joshua, he would have known the temperament that plagued the warrior. Joshua was hotheaded and often brutally sarcastic.

"I should have, but I didn't," Galen sighed. "He should know well she was not deceiving him, had he used his powers properly. There was no reason to hurt the child."

"He didn't strike her." Devlin went straight to the point.

He wanted the negotiations finished and the deal set. Chantel was awaiting him, hopefully with hot food and his bed turned down and ready. He was worn to the bone, horny as hell, and ready to finish this night.

"He wanted to." Galen argued his side, obviously in no hurry to finish the event.

"You knew what would happen, and you used it to display your own power and up your hand." Devlin accused him mildly. "Tell me what you want so I can eat and go to sleep. I'm tired, old man."

There was silence. Devlin glanced at him and saw the crafty light in the misty blue eyes. He set his mug down, leaned forward in his chair and offered the wizard what he knew he was after. Devlin saw no need to waste time. He had a feeling he knew what the wizard wanted, just as Galen would know that Devlin had set his course already and would not be convinced to turn back.

"We will wed the women in the morning, but Joshua must have access to Arriane tonight. There may be a lot of screaming and a lot of broken furniture the next morning, but not a hair on her head will be harmed.

"The women will stay here while we fight, but we will have the castle as a home for ourselves. In return, you will provide us with the power we need to defeat Jonar. I know not your reasons for gifting us with your daughters and the power they possess, but I swear to you, I will do all I can to ensure that neither the women nor the power is abused."

There was no need in arguing points, Devlin thought. They both knew what they wanted and the price to be charged. Marriage to Chantel, in Devlin's eyes, was a pleasure not a price, but he wouldn't tell the old man that.

"There is much you don't know." Sorrow still seemed to surround the wizard. "Much I don't know as well. But I will gladly give my sons all I can to aid their fight. What you don't understand is that the power shall come from your wives."

Devlin looked up in surprise.

"I don't possess the Mother Stone any longer, my fine warrior, and it is that which you would ask of me. My daughters carry it, broken into four, its power shared among them, around their pretty necks. The power is theirs and will be given to their mates gladly."

"The necklaces," Devlin whispered in surprise.

"Mother Earth was exacting in her commands. Only her daughters could wear the stone and control the power. No man shall ever hold what is hers to bequeath. Their mates can share in the power and can make it stronger, but they can never possess it."

Devlin shook his head.

"I accept your terms, I accept your demands. But I make one of my own," Galen continued.

"And that demand would be?" Devlin asked him softly.

"You will promise me you will never allow Chantel to leave sight of the castle. Should she ever do so, then Jonar shall take her and she will be gone from us forever."

Surprise lit Devlin's face.

"Is she Jonar's granddaughter as well?" Devlin asked.

Galen shook his head, sadness lining his face.

"She is no blood of his, but he would kill her if he ever manages to take her. Promise me, you will never take her out of sight of the forests, nor send for her in any manner."

"I promise you." Devlin nodded. It was not something he would ever do anyway. Should he need his woman by his side, he would not send for her, but come for her himself.

"The vows will be said at noon tomorrow." Galen nodded then rose to his feet with a sigh. "I shall go to Arriane and take her to Joshua myself."

Relief rushed through Devlin, leaving him weak in its wake. Then Galen turned to him once again.

"There was a young squire sent for you. He did not return," Galen said softly. "I would know his fate."

Devlin grimaced, remembering young David and the pain he had endured.

"He died soon after delivering your message," Devlin told him regretfully. "He was a brave lad."

"Aye." Galen nodded sadly. "He was a very brave lad." Then he sighed deeply. "Go back to your room. Your meal and your bride await you. The rest will come as Mother Earth decides it."

Devlin wondered why he felt no comfort in the sorcerer's words. Rather, he felt a strange foreboding that he feared learning the meaning of.

He sat for long moments, his head tilted back against the chair, his eyes closed. He would move in a minute, he promised himself, as soon as he managed to get the energy.

God, he was tired. The month had been a hellish one, the last battle against Jonar's forces nearly more than he and the warriors had been able to defend against.

It seemed that with each new battle the bastard managed to pull out a new surprise, a new weapon to use against them. Add to the bargain that he was forever surrounding himself with the innocent victims he preyed upon, and it made for an untenable mix.

"Everything okay, lover?" The husky voice roused him from his dozing state and Devlin opened his eyes slowly.

He would have smiled, but he knew something was wrong. Chantel stood before him, her hair in glorious disarray, a sensuous smile on her lips. It looked like her, except for the hardness in her cold green eyes, the half sneer that passed for a smile.

Devlin frowned, watching her closely as she moved nearer. She stopped beside his chair, gazing down at him with all the warmth of a frozen winter night.

Her hand lifted to touch his cheek as her head lowered to place her lips against his. Devlin gripped her wrist, pushing her back gently as he came to his feet.

"What magic is this?" His narrowed gaze took in the subtle differences of the lover of hours past and the woman who now stood before him.

Even her skin felt different. Where Chantel's skin had been soft, silky and warm to the touch, the skin that now covered her arm felt cool, not cold, yet rougher and nowhere near as fine as it had been.

"Antea." Devlin turned in shock to the voice at the stairs.

Devlin shook his head, blinked, his gaze going from the woman whose wrist he held to her duplicate at the foot of the stairs.

"I only wanted to have a little fun, sister." The wrist Devlin held was jerked back quickly, the woman moving several feet from him. "Don't worry, he knew it wasn't his lover."

Devlin watched as Chantel moved further into the room, her pace slow and her green eyes glittering with anger.

"You do not play games with the men of this castle, sister," she warned her look-alike softly. "You were warned of this before their arrival."

"Warned of it and ordered to my room like a child." Churlishness darkened the voice as the woman faced her sister. "What fairness was this, that you and the others should have protectors while I am left alone?"

"You have your destiny, as we have ours," Chantel told her softly. "You will await yours, just as we have awaited."

"Chantel?" Devlin touched the skin of her cheek, relieved to feel the warmth and the soft subtle fire he knew.

"Meet my half-sister, Antea of Oxboro." Chantel indicated the pouting young woman. "Forgive her for her attempt at deceiving you. She has a...difficult sense of humor at times."

Devlin turned back to the other woman, assessing the differences in the two women who could have been twins. As he did so, he noticed one profound difference.

"She's of Guardian birth," he announced softly, finally realizing why she neither held the warmth, nor the vibrancy of a normal woman. Those of Guardian birth were colder and often more mercenary than one who was not.

Chantel sighed. "Aye, and this is why she is here. She is the daughter of Konar. The one Jonar has sworn to destroy before her age of inheritance. She has been given shelter here until her twenty-first year."

"Shelter?" Devlin turned to the woman who would soon be his bride, wondering if she had lost her senses. "Do you have any idea the danger this places you in, Chantel? Jonar would take you as easily, thinking he has the woman he seeks."

"Jonar is aware of her likeness to me. That is why she is safer here," Chantel turned from him as she spoke, watching her sister closely. "It is her only defense at the moment. Jonar cannot breach the castle effectively to learn which is Antea and which is Galen's daughter. With any luck, we can continue the charade until she comes of age."

"Until then, I'm stuck here." A malicious edge to her voice had Devlin frowning.

How could two women look so much alike and yet be so different? It couldn't be the Guardian bloodlines, for Devlin knew several who were born of Guardians who were gracious and kindhearted despite their more mercenary approach to life.

This woman was a brittle, cold copy of Chantel and Devlin feared she would cause his lover more trouble than she may be worth.

"You are not forced to stay, Antea," Chantel reminded her quietly. "Should you wish to leave the safety of the castle, that is your choice. We merely offer you sanctuary, nothing more."

"Nothing more is right." Antea turned back, her eyes assessing the way Devlin had moved protectively to Chantel's side. "Your father should have been kind enough to procure a protector for me as well."

"Perhaps he didn't wish to offend the knight you have chosen just for that purpose," Chantel suggested kindly. "Come now, I don't wish to argue with you. It's growing late and Sir Devlin's meal awaits him upstairs. I'll see you in the morning."

"Of course, sister," the other woman seemed to coo, but Devlin detected the anger in her tone.

"Have a pleasant night."

The woman turned and sauntered slowly from the room.

There was silence between Chantel and Devlin as she left the great hall, moving slowly to a doorway on the opposite side of the room. As she passed out of the room, Devlin turned to frown down at Chantel.

Warningly, Chantel shook her head, indicating silence.

"Come to our room. I have your meal prepared and you can rest. It's been a long day for both of us."

"Chantel…" The hardened edge of his voice caused her to flinch, but he knew no other way to make his feelings clear.

"Not yet. In our room." She shook her head as her voice lowered. "No ears can overhear us there."

Devlin followed quietly, but as he did his worries grew. One who had not touched Chantel in passion, or knew her well, would never be able to tell the difference between the two young women. Jonar would take no time to learn the difference before he would kill one or both of them.

Chantel had no idea the dangerous game she was playing in giving this woman sanctuary. Jonar would play her game until time began to run out, then he would just kill both women to be certain he had the right one.

It was well known the vendetta Jonar harbored against Konar, the leader of the Guardian gods. He blamed Konar for the death of his daughter, Shalene, who was rumored to have been ready to sacrifice her only child to a demon cult she had taken into Jonar's fortress.

The Guardians had struck her down, taken the young child, and in the process assured themselves that Jonar's wrath would fall on any child of Guardian birth. Most especially the child Konar had sired.

As the bedroom door closed behind Chantel, Devlin turned to her, aware that he was growing angrier by the second at the thought of the danger she was now in.

"Chantel, your sister must be moved," he informed her as she led him to the table where his meal had been set.

"Eat. We can talk afterwards." She poured his wine, set it beside his place then moved to the window that looked out over the valley below.

"Not until we've settled this." Devlin moved behind her, his hands cupping her fragile shoulders as he rested his head atop hers. "This is dangerous. The closer she comes to the age of inheritance, the more desperate Jonar will become. He will kill you both."

"Jonar will be handled." Devlin decided the edge to her voice terrified him.

He turned her around quickly, barely missing the edge of sorrow in her eyes.

"What do you mean, he will be handled?" Devlin wanted to shake her, he was becoming so frustrated with her refusal to see the sense in sending the woman away. "That woman would cause trouble even were she not Konar's blood. The fact that she is leaves you in grave danger. We will be wed tomorrow. Do you think I enjoy the thought of my wife in such danger?"

"Do you think your wife would enjoy being in such danger?" she whispered. "But neither can I turn her away. I must do what I can to protect her until she is of age. I can do nothing else."

"Let me send her someplace else," Devlin suggested. "I have friends who would guard her and who would relish the prospect of thwarting Jonar."

"None can protect her as well as she is protected here." Chantel shook her head at the suggestion. "Jonar has not taken her because he does not wish to bring Father into this fight the Guardians and the Warriors wage against him. He knows Father's rage could be the deciding factor in any battle. For that reason, he will be certain he does not harm me."

"You can't predict that," Devlin raged.

"Actually, I can." Chantel's smile was soft, but the edge of sadness in it worried him. "I can sense changes, I can sense those things that can come. I don't have visions, I don't predict the future, but I can sense danger or events that will unfold. And I tell you now, Jonar will take every precaution to be certain I am not taken if he makes a move to kidnap Antea."

"Chantel, you can't be certain of this," Devlin whispered as he felt an irrational fear flood his entire being. "You can't predict one such as Jonar."

"I can only give you what Mother Earth gives me, my love," she whispered, facing him with a soft smile, the warmth of her dark eyes reaching into his soul. "All will be well, you shall see. Now, come eat, and we will rest through what is left of this night."

Devlin allowed himself to be led to the table and ate as she requested. He stayed silent on the subject of Jonar, but he would not let it rest. On the morrow, he would make plans with his men, set a system of keeping them safe. If there was any way to keep Jonar from taking the woman he had searched his life for, then Devlin would find it. Even if it meant turning Antea over to the dark lord himself.

# Chapter Five

∞

Arriane stepped back into the bedroom where childish dreams had disintegrated beneath the fury and merciless hatred of the man she would marry come morning. She steeled herself against the pain she knew was coming. Now that he knew her heritage, she would find no softness from her savage husband-to-be.

At her breast, her crystal pulsed gently, warming her, soothing her. It was her talisman, her last hope in a world that she knew would change too quickly for her to ever hope to save herself.

She was stronger than Chantel knew. The secrets of the crystal were growing closer daily, yet still, she was weak, unable to draw on what she instinctively knew could save her. She was failing bitterly.

"All will be well, child," her father promised her softly as they faced Joshua across the length of the room. "I swear this to you. Have I ever broken a vow to you?"

She knew he could feel the trembling of her body, the pain and anger that coursed through her with no outlet to ease it. She laid her hand upon his arm and looked up at him with what she hoped was an expression of confidence.

"I will be fine now, Father," she promised him, keeping her voice low as she fought the quiver that would have revealed the emotions fighting to be free inside her.

His face was lined with sadness, with regret. He had fought for so long to ease her way and her terrors, and now they were both realizing that the time had come that he could no longer do so.

"Should you need me…" The offer was made in a voice hoarse with his emotions.

"Should I need you, then I shall not delay in calling out to you," she assured him. "Go now. I will be fine."

She felt his hand behind her head, a familiar touch of caring as he caressed her hair, kissed her brow warmly. Galen was a strong, caring father. He had never spanked them as children, had never raised his voice to them in anger. They were unnaturally spoiled, she knew, in a world where women were given only the barest regard.

She stood still and silent as he cast Joshua a hard, furious look then turned and stalked from the room. She knew he would never forgive the younger man for the abuse he had witnessed. Joshua had earned her father's eternal hatred. A burden she would have never wished upon him.

As the door closed behind Galen, the expressionless mask Joshua had assumed slipped. He turned his strange amber eyes on her then and they glowed with fury. Like an animal caught in a killing frenzy. He turned that look on her slowly and his unnatural power began to fill the air and swirl about her like a heavy, invisible fog.

She could feel it beating at her head, her body, searching for a weakness, a way to slip into her very soul. She lowered her head, hiding her tears, and forcibly relaxed the barrier that would have kept him from knowing her innermost secrets.

Her legs weakened and she barely contained her gasp of physical pain. Violence washed through her, around her. The blood seemed to thicken in her veins, clog her heart as she fought for breath beneath his furious assault.

He was taking all that she was and yet casting aside any hint of tender emotions or wishful dreams. She felt him going to the heart of her knowledge of her heritage. The black stain of dishonor that her grandfather had left her. The legacy of insanity that her mother had carried. He bypassed the nightmares of her childhood without a glimpse and sneered at the hopes that filled her. And she stood beneath it willingly, accepting that, for now, fighting against her husband would cost her a measure of strength that she knew would be much needed to survive the shadowed events to come.

"What shadowed events?" His eyes narrowed on her, the hawkish features of his face intent with his merciless expression.

She felt him delving into those shadows, searching for the answers he sought. She was thankful that she herself did not know what lay there.

"You are the Mystic," she finally said softly. "Perhaps you can make sense of those things that even I do not know."

He seemed to snarl. His upper lip lifting in anger as he watched her with a rage she could not decipher. Arriane pulled her robe tighter around her body and fought the sudden chill that overtook her. She was weary, even to her very soul. Fear and need swamped her, conflicting emotions that had her senses rioting.

"I will not harm you," he bit out, though he was careful to keep the length of the room between them.

Arriane cast him a cynical glance. As though being held from her feet by the power of his mind, his hand at her throat, was not harmful to her. She would have laughed at him if she had the strength to feel amusement at the situation.

She, who had waited years for his touch, for his warmth and passion, now found only a cold bed to cushion her and an even colder man who would soon be wed to her. The castle priest had once told her that she would be held accountable for the sins of her mother, and it seemed it was true. As though the nightmares and the pain of her childhood had not been enough, now her future dimmed before her as well.

"I am tired," she finally told him, her weariness beating at her brain, weakening her body.

She watched the frown that crossed his face, the way his amber eyes seemed to glow for but a moment before they were once again merely that strange, yellow brown.

"Sleep then." He waved his hand toward the curtained bed. "If you can."

If she could. She crawled onto the mattress, hugging the side of it as she fought the ache that resonated from the very depths of her spirit. She pulled the blankets around her neck and fought to ignore the tears that finally fell from the corners of her eyes. God help her, but on the morrow, she would wed what could well become her greatest nightmare.

She listened to him move about the room, then flinched in shock long moments later as his weight settled into the bed behind her.

"Remove your robe." His voice was guttural, echoing with a rough, rasping heat that had her shivering in mingled desire and despair.

"Joshua, please," she whispered painfully. "I understand your hatred of me, but I cannot endure your rejection once again."

"I will not repeat the order, Arriane," he growled darkly. "I will rip it from your body instead."

Her breath caught in her throat. Fear or desire? Hesitantly, she rose from the bed, careful to keep her back to him, and shed the only barrier she had been afforded from the heat of his body.

"No," he bit out when she would have sat on the mattress and slid back beneath the blankets. "Turn to me, allow me to see you."

Her breath hitched in her throat, her fists clenching in anger at her sides, but she did as he bid. She could not afford to anger him further, already he risked disavowal by his leader and her father's fury. She would not be the reason that Chantel failed in whatever goal she had set for them. Chantel had promised that no matter her pain, her future shone bright. She had to trust in that. Trust in the man whose fury now terrified her.

She turned to him, staring him in the eye, refusing to lower her eyes. She may have to lower her pride in some measure, but she would be damned if she would let him think she enjoyed it.

Dark color flushed his face as he stared at her, his eyes going over her full, high breasts, her softly rounded abdomen and then her thighs. His gaze paused there, narrowing on the bare flesh of her cunt.

"Truly a child of the Guardians," he grunted.

She arched a brow mockingly, her gaze flickering to his unashamed arousal and the bare flesh surrounding it.

"I could say the same of you," she reminded him bitterly.

"Aye," he snarled in disgust. "Birthed by one of their whores and cursed by them for all time. It does not mean I embrace it as easily as do you."

"Nay, husband, you do not embrace naught but your bitterness and rage," she agreed. "Rather than accepting those things you cannot change, you curse them instead. Truly a productive course of life."

Arriane trembled as she stood before him naked, arguing her parentage and the personal areas of her body. Never had she known such anger, such humiliation as she did to realize that her very private flesh heated and moistened alarmingly as his gaze went back to it.

"That is of little consequence," he told her absently. "Come here, lie beside me."

She took a deep, nervous breath.

"I cannot endure it again, Joshua." She hated the pleading note in her voice. "I beg you, do not do this to me again."

His gaze rose slowly to hers. "Do not force me to repeat myself, Arriane. You will not like the consequences."

She bit her lip, blinking back more tears, and moved hesitantly to obey him. Her body shook until she could barely keep her teeth from trembling. Despite his earlier rage, his insults and near violence, still, her body ached for him in ways that she found most shameful.

She lay beside him then, stiff, frightened of herself and what he would do now. He had sworn he would not complete a taking of her. Had reviled her as a witch and dismissed her pleas that he not hold her parentage against her. And now, he wished her to lay with him naked? His erection brushed her thigh, thick and hard. It looked like a blunt-tipped weapon now, rather than the thick object of pleasure that she had seen it as before.

"Such a tempting body," he said with soft regret as his hand spanned the width of her stomach. He had such large hands, long-fingered and a bit calloused. Her body ached with the pleasure she knew those hands could bring.

"Joshua," she whispered his name breathlessly, staring up at him, needing him in ways she could never name.

"I will not take you," he told her, his voice hard, firm.

Pain washed over her, through her, slicing at her heart.

"Why then must I lay naked before you? Allow me at least my rest." She fought her tears, hating the thought of crying before him.

"Not yet," he whispered. "You brought me to pleasure earlier with your sweet mouth. Now, I will see to yours as well."

Her eyes widened in alarm. "No, Joshua." She fought to jerk from his touch, to reach the blankets now tangled at her feet. Such cold arousal was more than she could bear.

"Not so fast, witch," he growled, an arm and thigh bracing over her body, holding her still to the mattress as he stared down at her with hooded eyes. "You will know the same torment, the same pleasure that you brought to me."

"I wanted only to please you," she cried out. "You want only to hurt me in return."

"Hurt you?" he asked her with heated arousal now. "Nay, Arriane, no pain will come from this touch."

His fingers smoothed over the bare flesh of her cunt then, pressing between her thighs to cup the moist mound whose inner secrets throbbed in hunger. Arriane groaned at the touch, sensation streaking through her very womb and causing her body to clench with a hard, ragged breath.

"Such a soft, pretty temple," he whispered with rising heat as a finger slid through her moist slit and his hand moved back, caressing the soft flesh. "Do you taste as good as you look, my little witch?"

Arriane shuddered in exquisite arousal. Her heart was thundering hard and fast within her chest, her breasts swelling, her nipples aching nearly as desperately as the wet flesh he caressed. When his fingers reached the little knot of nerves at the top of her cunt, her hips arched from the bed, a strangled cry escaping her throat.

"Easy, Arriane," he whispered as he moved down the bed, spreading her thighs slowly as he came between them.

She watched him, fire spreading through her body at the sight of his jutting cock, its blunt head dark and angry-looking as he stroked it with one hand and her with the other.

"I remember your hungry mouth sucking my seed from my cock," he growled. "So hot and tight, wrapped about the head, your tongue licking me like a flame."

Her face flushed, heated at his explicit words, but her mouth watered to taste him once again. Her eyes tracked the movements of his hand as he stroked his own hard flesh. Slow and easy, he caressed the thick stalk until a tiny pearl of semen graced the sensitive tip. She licked her lips in greedy hunger.

"Ah, not yet, my little witch." He stared down at her, his eyes glowing, his long mane of black hair framing his savage features and flowing down his back.

The hand between her thighs pressed more firmly against her as his fingers slid down the juice-coated slit once again. Her hips bucked, her back arching as the tip slid inside her clenching entrance, and a strangled cry left her throat.

The sensations were too much to be borne. Her body rioted with the conflict of her mind. A need for more and yet a need for satisfaction that clawed through her womb, her cunt with raking talons of desire.

"Joshua, I need you," she whimpered, beset by a tidal wave of flaming need. "Please, do not torment me in this way."

His eyes flashed with dark fire, his face flushing as he came over her. The length of his cock wedged between her thighs, pressing on her swelling clit as his big hands cupped her face and his lips possessed her with ravaging greed. His tongue possessed her mouth like a ravenous conqueror, greed and hunger striking fire to her already over-sensitized body.

Between her thighs, his hips rotated, pressed and ground the searing length of his erection against her tormented bud as her legs raised to clasp his hips. The moist, plump lips of her cunt parted easily to the sensual weapon that slid against it, teasing her, taunting her cruelly with what she could not have.

Her hand dug into the hair at his nape, her fingers clenching as she cried out beneath the onslaught of his rapacious kiss. He gave her little chance to breathe and even less to move. His body held her captive, his cock rocking against her sensitive flesh as pinpoints of fire shot through her body.

Arriane fought for breath, for her very sanity, as the deep caress at her clit drove her higher into the dark sensations attacking her body now. She was raging with her needs, her lusts fanned by the near possession, the sensuality of Joshua's restraint, and her own overwhelming pleasure.

He tore his mouth from hers as they both gasped for air. Hips ground together, moist heat pooling between her thighs as her passions fired through her body with the force of an inferno. And still he did not move to complete the act. He only drove her higher, destroying her mind with the growing hunger that sped through her system.

Her clit was an aching, brutally sensitized point of need as his velvet-sheathed cock caressed it with quick, rapid motions of his hips. The juices that seeped from her body coated it, as well as the thick sensual sword he used against it. She moaned, cried out, then her eyes opened, widening as the sensations built.

Her gaze locked with his, dazed, unfocused, his vision wavered as her trembling womb began to spasm in deep, hard contractions. Then there was no breath, no will, no Arriane, no Joshua. There was only a flaming catapult of sexual intensity that exploded through her body with such force that she felt herself, her very soul, fly free of her body as she disintegrated beneath the demands of his rotating hips and pulsing cock.

Arriane heard herself cry out as her body tightened and shock waves of heat bombarded her body. Above her, Joshua moaned in a long, drawn-out sound of agony a second before his erection throbbed, pulsed, then spilled its heated explosion against her abdomen.

Weak now, a strange hollowness filling her, Arriane allowed her legs to lower from his lean hips and turned her head away from him as he stared down at her. Long seconds later he moved from her, then left the bed.

She stared at the wall, her mind a haze of confusion, her body still trembling with hunger as the last waves of her release quivered through her body. She was aware of Joshua returning to her, cleaning his seed from her stomach, then covering her gently before collapsing on his side of the bed.

"I would have loved you deeply," she whispered into the silence of the room as she watched the flickering shadows cast by the thick candles that flickered from his side of the bed.

She felt him sigh.

"There is no love for ones such as us, Arriane. No love and no hope. Best you know that now, before your dreams and your hopes destroy your very soul. I will wed with you, but I will not take you. I will not allow you to breed another such as us, a target for Jonar's merciless fury. Nor will I allow that power to strike against me. Comfort yourself, wife, that as the blood of Jonar, I allow you to even live."

And with those words, he sealed a brutal, dark fate that twisted and churned within the shadows of her mind. She felt such sorrow, such grief raging in the unvoiced screams of her soul, that she wondered how she would survive the aftermath.

# Chapter Six

**ဢ**

The weddings went off smoothly. Four warriors and four fragile young women joined hands, repeated their vows and joined their lives to each other. Joshua looked decidedly put out at the ritual. He believed it to be archaic, a manmade ritual created to make servants of warriors. He didn't seem well-pleased with his new bride, but neither did she seem well-pleased with him.

Derek was, of course, besotted. The Irish Prince had found the woman of his dreams and the fact that her accent proclaimed her of that sunny isle pleased him to no end.

Shanar, the fierce, rough Viking, appeared to have found a mate that suited him just as well. A tall, redheaded temper in waiting who would soon have the giant of a warrior doing parlor tricks to please her.

Of course, Devlin knew he was no better. He was thoroughly enchanted by his bride. Her soft voice, the warmth in her eyes, the stubbornness in the set of her delicate little chin fascinated him to no end.

The Shadow Warriors had fallen this time and they had fallen hard for the daughters of a wizard. Joshua swore it was a wizard's spells, cast upon the other men because of their weak minds. But there were moments when Devlin caught the savage warrior watching the delicate Arriane with a bewildered expression. Devlin knew this would not be a relationship that would flow smoothly.

Joshua's hatred of Jonar ran so deep and so bitter, that despite his passion and his need for Arriane, he would put her through hell until he could learn to deal with it.

Several days later, lying amid the scattered blankets of their bed, Devlin stared down at his wife, still unable to believe what he found here, in this place where he had come to merely seek a wizard's aid.

She lay on her stomach sleeping, her face turned to him, relaxed and innocent, her expression mesmerized him. She tempted him past bearing and satisfied him in ways he would have never believed possible. But there was still more, so much more that he had yet to show his new bride.

Devlin lowered his head, allowing his lips to caress her smooth shoulder as she whispered a moan of rising heat through her slumber. She was ready for him, even within her dreams. His teeth clenched at the thought.

His needs raged within his body, pounded through his cock, and made his hunger for her flame with blistering heat. He couldn't resist the need to kiss his way down her perfect back, then over the rise of her buttocks. As her throaty moans drove him on, his fingers tested her heated quim, drawing from it the slick, thick honey of her juices.

Her back arched, her hips lifting for him as his eager hands pulled her to her knees. His fingers shaped the firm curves of her derriere, smoothing over the creamy skin, clenching and drawing the soft globes apart as he positioned his cock to slide into the tight, hot depths of her cunt.

He groaned roughly as her sultry moisture kissed the throbbing head of his cock. He pressed in, feeling the gripping muscles tighten on him, stretching slowly, wrapping about his burrowing shaft like heated silk.

Devlin couldn't help but watch as her soaked pussy grabbed at the hard muscle pressing into it. It milked him in, clenching on his cock, caressing it with a tight, rhythmic motion that had his abdomen tightening, his loins burning with his need to explode inside her.

He could feel his scrotum tightening as his seed rose, hot and fierce inside him. His hands clenched on her hips as he pulled back, stroking her pussy with slow, deep strokes that finally had her screaming, begging him to ride her as hard and fierce as he longed to. But first he needed to enjoy her.

He watched his cock retreat partially from her cunt, slick, glistening with the juices that clung to it like streams of honey. Gently, he pushed inside her once again, relishing the heat, the tight grip that wrapped around his erection.

His gaze turned to the small jar he had laid beside them on the bed. The creamy lubricant was said to ease another area, to provide the moisture needed to slide into the tender nether-hole he had so dreamed of taking. Keeping his movements slow, his thrusts inside her gentle and shallow, he dipped his fingers into the thick essence and moved them to the little opening awaiting him.

Chantel stilled at the first touch. Devlin heard her breathing escalate, the little whimper of pleasure, of carnal fear that escaped her throat.

"I will not harm you," he promised, his fingers spreading the thick lubricant into the crease, the tips dipping into the sensitive little hole.

The entrance opened easily to his fingertip. Devlin stilled, his cock lodged deep inside the rhythmic pulse of her cunt as he tested the tight heat of her anus.

Her muscles bit at his finger, clenched in rhythm with the muscles of her pussy as she groaned a low, sweet sound of passion and demand. Gently, he pulled back, allowed another finger to join the first and returned to the heated grip that awaited him.

His fingers slid inside her as his hips bucked against her. She tightened and his control shattered. Holding her to him, his fingers lodged hard and tight in the blistering heat of her nether-hole, his cock began to pump hard and fast inside the hot grip of her cunt. He could feel the rippling pulses of her arousal around his erection, hear her need in her heated cries. When her climax tore through her, her pussy contracted with such strength around his pistoning root that he could not hold his own back any longer.

Devlin felt his scrotum tighten further as pleasure tore through his body, arching it, tightening it as his seed exploded from his cock. It blasted into the furnace of her cunt, each pulse of rapture ripping a strangled cry from his throat until he could do nothing but collapse over her, drawing his fingers gently from the clenched muscles of her ass as the last tremors of release shook his body.

He rolled carefully to his side when he could once again breathe, and drew Chantel gently into his arms. She stared up at him with lazy adoration, her soft lips turned up in a smile, the warmth of her dark green eyes warming his soul.

He could not get enough of staring at her. Watching her, touching her. He wanted — nay, he needed — to learn each and every secret of what made this unique woman.

"Why do you stare at me so intently?" He could hear the laughter in her voice as his hands played with the strands of white-blonde hair that fanned out around her head.

"Because of your beauty?" he asked her by way of an answer, aware of the grin curling the corners of his own mouth.

He had smiled more since his marriage than he could remember smiling in his life.

"Ahh, because of my beauty." She giggled drowsily. "'Tis not beauty, my love, but your poor eyesight. I am actually a woman of haggish features, you just refuse to see such."

The laughter in her voice assured him she was jesting with him, but Devlin knew it would not matter. Had a spell been cast upon him, he would gladly linger beneath its power for his lifetime.

"I see only your beauty, wife." He leaned down to kiss her lips one last time, then rose lazily from the bed. "But, I must tear myself away from this bedroom for a while. I'll grow lazy staying abed all day like this."

"Ahh, laziness is it that keeps you in my bed?" She laughed at him, but rose as well and donned the soft emerald green robe they had tossed to the floor the night before. "And here I thought it was my passion that held you captive within this room."

Passion and so much more, Devlin thought as he watched her walk to the door and open it swiftly.

"Alya, I need hot water for bathing, and breakfast brought up for my husband and myself," she told a servant who was moving through the hall. "We shall eat while the tub is being prepared."

"Aye, mistress, Cook has the water warming even now." Devlin heard the soft voice of the servant as she paused. "I will have it carried up while you take your breakfast."

"Thank you, Alya," Chantel said before moving back into the room and closing the door behind her.

"I've bathed more since coming here than I have in my lifetime." Devlin shook his head, though he was secretly pleased at the cleanliness of his wife and the home she had given him.

There was not a hidden corner within the castle that housed so much as a speck of dust. Chantel refused to allow it, often chiding the servants and lecturing them on the hazards and the illnesses that plagued such keeps that allowed it.

"'Tis good for you," she assured him with a smile as she went to her clothes chest and extracted her clothing for the day.

Soon, breakfast was being brought in, water carried to fill the huge tub that sat in the corner of the room and the day began with the laughter of his newly married life.

Devlin felt the contentment that filled him as he bathed with his wife and watched her prepare herself for the day.

"Are you riding out to the village with Father?" she asked him as she ran a brush hurriedly through her tangled hair.

"Perhaps." Devlin never tired of watching her. "I believe he wanted to check on some of the outlying farms this morning first."

Chantel nodded.

"And what shall you do today, lovely wife?" He pulled her close for a kiss as she secured her scarf to her head and turned to him.

"I have many things to do today." She smiled up at him. "But first, I promised Antea we would get the seamstress working on a new gown she wanted. I promised to meet her in the great hall this morning to get started."

At the mention of her half-sister's name, Devlin felt a ragged edge on his contentment. Antea was becoming a thorn in his side as he watched how easily she maneuvered his wife.

"Can Antea not secure her own garments?" Devlin asked her.

"I promised to help her," Chantel told him firmly. "I haven't spent much time with her of late and she's lonely."

Lonely. The woman had more men around her than a bitch in heat, Devlin thought. Antea was not lonely, but merely securing Chantel's time for her own selfish reasons.

"About Antea, Chantel," he began softly, preparing to put forth the idea he had come up with the night before to take the risk of the woman's presence away.

"I will not send her off, Devlin." Chantel faced him now, a determined light in her dark green gaze. "She is my sister and her life is in danger."

"And she places your life in the same danger," he told her just as softly, but with a thread of steel in his voice. "That I cannot tolerate."

"I am safe within the walls of the castle," she promised him yet again.

"Only because Jonar has not pitted his strength against it," Devlin assured her. "When Antea gets closer to her age of inheritance, he will try harder."

Chantel was silent for long moments as she stared down at the food before her. Devlin wished he could see the expression in her eyes. He had noticed that often while she was thinking deeply, he was not given leave to see her expression. Devlin had a feeling he would learn much if he could gaze into her expressive eyes at such times.

"Jonar shall not succeed in killing her." Chantel finally shrugged. "She will be fine. I promise."

"It is not Antea I worry about." Devlin's fears pushed him to continue. "It is you I worry for, Chantel. If you see Antea's life so clearly, what do you see in your own future?"

At this Chantel raised her head. Despite the happiness and the hope he saw on her face, he detected a shadow of sadness as well.

"I see a future where you and I shall be a part of defeating Jonar. A future surrounded by our children and our grandchildren."

"Do you just wish this, Chantel, or do you see this?" he asked her gently, understanding the unique gifts she had to "feel" the future.

"I know this, my love," she promised him as the last bucket of water was carried to the tub and several others sat steaming on the floor.

As the last servant left the room, Chantel stood, removing her robe slowly.

"Would you like me to bathe you?" she asked him, the husky pitch of her voice making his blood beat harshly in his veins.

"Perhaps I would like to bathe you this time," he told her as he led her slowly to the steamy bath. "Let's see how long you can endure such torture."

There was much to do, he knew. But he could not resist bathing her. Touching her body, smoothing the soft, scented soap over her skin as she sat atop his thighs in the large wooden tub. Her head fell back on his shoulder, shudders working over her body as he pinched her nipples lightly between his fingers. Her breasts were swollen, her body hot. He dipped one hand beneath the water, spreading her thighs as he scooted down further in the tub, lifting her as he did so.

His cock slid smoothly into the scorching heat as she cried out. His fingers moved to the small bud of pleasure above the tight entrance to her cunt. He rubbed it gently, feeling her muscles clench on his surging length.

She was so tight. So heated and slick with her woman's honey that he could barely hold on to his control.

"Cry out for me, Chantel," he whispered as her moans strangled in her throat. "I want to hear you as I fuck you. Hear the pleasure I give you with my body."

"Devlin, you will kill me with such pleasure," she whimpered, her body undulating against him, driving him deeper inside her.

Devlin gritted his teeth, his hips surging beneath her as she began to ride him with slow, control-destroying movements. There was nothing that mattered now but her. The taste of her, the feel of her. One hand clenched her hip, the other plucking firmly at her clitoris as she began to moan heatedly.

"Harder," she finally begged, fighting for breath as her sheath began to heat to a fiery temperature, her honey thickening, sliding over his cock. "Please, Devlin. Harder, harder…"

His hips surged forward, driving him deeper yet as the movements on her clit increased. She thrashed, causing him to hold her tighter, to moan at the tightening of her sleek, hot muscles around his cock.

As he forged inside the tight depths of her cunt once again, she cried out rapturously, her inner flesh quivering as he felt her release wash over his engorged flesh.

"Chantel." He had only the breath to whisper her name before he followed her.

He couldn't control his own dark cry or the grip on her hips as he pushed in hard, deep, erupting inside her, spilling his seed, his passion and his heart into the woman who completed him.

* * * * *

In a bedchamber down the hall, Derek stared morosely at the cold fireplace across from the bed, contemplating his life and the bitter choices he had made. At the moment, his latest choice seemed more bitter than all those that had gone before it.

He glanced over at his wife. She slept deeply, though a frown marred her forehead as she traveled whatever dream had come to her. Dark images? he wondered.

His hands clenched as he fought to keep from touching her, fought not to take her. He could not forget the words she had whispered when she had seen him unclothed on their marriage night, when she had glimpsed the brand that marred his thigh. His fingers moved unerringly to the wound that could still burn with mind-destroying agony.

He had been but a child. Barely ten winters. Taken from his parents' castle, branded and sold for a pittance in an effort to be rid of him. How long ago was it? he wondered. So many years ago, nearly a century.

He stared up at the ceiling. His name had been struck from the records of his family by their own hand. His memory had been washed away by indifference and cold determination to see his birth wiped from the face of history. He had been born a prince and reviled as a demon.

Beneath the brand was the mark of the gods. A dark swirling design, like a star encircling itself. The mark of Jonar. The mark of the demon. He had no idea how the mark had come to be on his flesh, but he remembered his nurse's bloodcurdling screams, his mother's horror. Hours later, he had been slipped from the castle, branded and sold to slave traders. Branded as a demon. A brand still clearly remembered, even if the child had been forgotten. A brand that his lovely wife had seen.

Derek blinked back his pain, swallowed his rage. She was the descendent of his brother's wife. The very same brother who had claimed Derek's throne all those decades ago. She had known the moment she had seen the brand who he was, and though his name had been forgotten, she knew he was the black mark, the curse upon the family who had adopted her. A widow, her mother had caught and held the eye of the man who now ruled Derek's lands. She was not a child bound by blood to his family, but rather bound by love and loyalty.

A snarl shaped his lips as satisfaction filled his soul. They still feared him, feared what they believed he was, but even more, feared the curse a ten-year-old child had placed upon their family and upon their lands. And in part, he wondered if he had somehow whispered the right words, the right plea to the forces of the land, for it seemed it was now coming back to haunt him.

*When the land is stripped of fertility, and the gods cry out for mercy. When fairy folk scream out at the destruction, and your daughters lie as whores beneath me, then shall my name be whispered in fear. Then shall you remember…*

The lands of his father now lay bare, infertile and poor. There were whispers of demons stalking the land, and the fairy folk cried out in the darkness of the night. And now. Now his brother's wife's descendent lay beneath him, her horror and her memories wiped away, after she had vowed that to lie with him would make her a demon's whore.

He fought to ignore the moisture in his eyes now. The memory of those dark, torturous days haunted him still. To see the land he had so loved stripped bare of life, and to know that Jonar was the cause, was a burden upon his heart, for he had wished such destruction on them at one time. Now Caitlin had placed a burden upon his soul. For he knew her distaste and her fear of him. And he had taken it. He had wiped it away as though it had never been, but he alone knew it was.

He gazed down at her again, lifting his hand to smooth back the fall of silken flame that was her hair.

*You are a demon!* Her pain-ridden cry echoed around him. *I am not a whore to lie beneath the bastard who cursed our lands and our families. A harlot to lie in the bed with a man who would have been my uncle...*

*Many times removed, and not in blood,* he had snarled in fury. He would not admit to a relationship with her, for he lusted too desperately after her. Besides, there was no blood bond, he assured himself, to ever count the relationship.

"Derek," her whispered sigh washed over him now.

He had shed his tears for her. As he cradled her unconscious body, stolen her memories and her will, his tears had washed her face. And he had remembered. Remembered begging his father as the brand was applied to his thigh, pleading in desperation as he was sold to the slaver, and screaming out in agony as the lash was applied to his back. And through it all, he had cursed them. His father, his brother, and all they could ever love, he had cursed them. And now, he cursed himself.

"Yur still awake?" Her soft, lilting voice was drowsy, edged with sensuality.

His cock spiked beneath the blankets at the sound of it. She had wanted him with fiery intensity before seeing the brand. Her heart was bound to him, her soul a part of him no matter what she had believed later.

She rose up in the bed, her eyes heavy-lidded, the pale green eyes glittering behind the fiery color of her lashes. The color of connemara marble. The color of home. His heart clenched.

"I have only been awake a few moments, precious," he lied. He had not slept well at all since the night he forced his will on her.

She sighed restlessly then, cuddling in his arms as he pulled her tight against his body.

"My dreams were dark," she whispered against his chest. "Shadows and screams and blood lay within them. They terrify me, Derek."

She trembled in his arms then, as though the memory of those dreams still held a part of her.

"They are but dreams," he tried to reassure her. He had such himself, had had them for more years than he cared to remember.

He smoothed his hand down her fall of hair, grimacing at his own inner turmoil. He was terrified now, in ways he never had been before. If he lost her, how would he survive? All his life he had searched for the completion of his soul and now he had found it. Yet, already, it had been taken from him.

The haunting, pain-ridden blow of her words that first night could not be forgotten. He had taken her will and, in doing so, had taken his last chance of happiness. Yet he knew, in the very depths of his heart, that had he not done so, then she would have reviled him and found some way to escape him. Could he have survived it? Aye, he knew he could, but it would have ripped out his heart, made him the fiend that his family's history had already proclaimed him.

"I fear for us, Derek," she whispered against his chest as her hands moved slowly over his muscled back. She touched him with love and with tenderness. So long it had been since he had known such caring.

"Do not fear, love." His arms tightened around her, though tears moistened his eyes. "Do not fear. All will be well."


Caitlin lay against her husband, feeling the beat of his heart beneath his broad chest, the warmth of his flesh against hers. The heat and strength of his body drew her in all ways. If she wasn't touching him, then she was longing to, if he wasn't in her sight, then she worried desperately for him. Yet, there was a feeling of impending doom, a shadow that lay across her mind from which she could not escape.

Her hand smoothed from his chest to his tight, hard abdomen. A grin crossed her lips as she felt the muscles there spasm in response. Turning her head, she kissed the bare skin of his chest, her tongue peeking from her lips to paint a swirling design of passion.

She heard his hard intake of breath and allowed her fingers to scratch against the taut flesh of his abdomen, her nails raking the skin in a way she knew he enjoyed. His faint moan and the jerk of his hard cock that jutted toward her hand was her reward.

His hands weren't still as she touched him though. The hand at her back smoothed lovingly over her skin, toward her buttocks, causing her to moan with the sensual threat explicit in the direction his fingers took. The other gripped the long strands of her hair, pulling her head up to him, intent on a kiss she knew would fire her soul.

She smiled as she tugged her head back away from him, refusing him the kiss they both needed. Not yet. She loved tempting his passion and the dominance he displayed as she fought his touch.

His fingers tightened on her buttock in implicit warning as his eyes narrowed on her. He tugged at her hair again to pull her to him. Caitlin shook her head, tossing it back as she moaned at the erotic little bite of pain along her scalp.

His expression, heavy with sensual promise, made her cunt clench in hunger. His sun-darkened flesh was a heady contrast to her lighter, creamy skin. His deep, brilliant blue eyes darkened to a near midnight as his hungers rose inside him, the long-lashed lids lowering halfway as his lips became a shade fuller, sexier as passion overtook him.

"'Tis a dangerous game you play, wife," he warned her, his voice dark, husky.

She pressed against his chest then, as though to escape him. She tugged at the hold he had on her hair, her eyes closing involuntarily for a second at the pleasure, as his hand tightened in an attempt to pull her back to him.

"Perhaps I enjoy living dangerously," she whispered breathlessly as her cunt clenched at the need to feel his heavy erection stretching her sensitive muscles. But she had other needs as well. Needs that shocked her, that often left her embarrassed to think of them outside their bed.

"Aye, wife, sometimes you do," he agreed roughly, his eyes darkening further as he tugged harder at her hair.

The blend of pleasure and the light sting of pain was a heady aphrodisiac. She gasped with the combination, her nails pricking the skin of his abdomen as he forced her lips to his.

He nipped at the sensitive curves. Her mouth opened to him on a passionate cry as she still struggled against his hold on her hair. His tongue swept in to tangle with hers, to conquer her. She nipped at the invader, a gasp escaping her as he returned the light punishment with a bit more force than her own had been.

Before she could react, Derek moved in a display of muscle and power. He came to his knees, his hand still wrapped in her hair, his eyes watching her with a force of lust so intense, she nearly exploded in release. Her body jerked in arousal as he tipped her head back, his lips slanting over hers, forcing them to open, to accept the sweep of his tongue within her mouth.

His other hand caught her wrists, shackling them both in a grip of heated steel behind her back. He arched her to him, pressing her breasts against his chest, growling as she bucked against him.

"How much do you wish to play, wife?" he bit out as he pulled back to stare down at her intently. "Continue this game and there will be no calling it to a halt if you cannot take the heat of it."

Caitlin felt her heart speed up in excitement, the blood pounding through her veins now and in the hard little nub of her clit. She loved the excitement of this game, the rougher than usual passion, the needs given free rein and the fierceness of the lust that flowed between them.

"I can take whatever you would give me," she challenged him, gazing at him from beneath lowered lashes.

She watched his face flush, felt his cock jerk against her belly in heated excitement.

"I will take you in ways you never dreamed," he warned her, his eyes gleaming with anticipation. "Once started on such a course, beloved, I cannot pull back."

Caitlin tossed her head. "Once started on such a course, you will be lucky to find the stamina to satisfy me, husband."

It was a dare and one she knew would fire his passions. She knew he held back with her, had known this for many nights. The brief forays he had taken in releasing a measure of his needs for her had not been enough to satisfy either of them.

His grin was suddenly sensual, carnal, as his hand tightened in her hair. She bit her lip. It was a sensual threat, a prickling at her scalp that echoed in her very womb.

"Ah, wife, how daring you are becoming." His voice was laced with approval, dark with passion.

Before she could do more than gasp, his lips were slanting over hers, his tongue forging its way past her lips and conquering her mouth with a kiss so heated it stole her breath.

Caitlin strained against him, moaning as his powerful arms lifted her into his hold, giving her little chance to escape. One arm was wrapped tight around her back, the other moving with slow deliberation to the curve of her buttocks.

Caitlin whimpered, clenching her muscles there as pleasure overwhelmed her. He palmed the cheek of her ass, his tongue tangling with hers once again. As his kiss rocked through her system, he delivered a light, stinging smack to the rounded curve.

She jerked in his arms, her nipples rasping against his chest as she moved against him. His lips moved from hers to her neck, then lower. The arm at her back arched her, thrusting her breasts to his hungry mouth. His teeth nibbled at the curve before he enveloped the tip in the hot depths of his mouth. He suckled her hard and deep, his tongue flicking at the nipple, flaying it with a sensual promise.

She could feel the juices of her cunt gathering along the passion-swollen lips now. Her clit throbbed in need, her womb spasming with the intensity of emotion.

When his head raised, his expression was savage with his passion. His blue eyes were glittering with his need, his lips swollen and damp from his feast at her breast.

"My turn," he growled, one hand locking in her hair as he pressed her down his chest. "Take me in your mouth, Cait. Dear God, before I die of need of it."

She nipped his chest, smiling as he began to push her head down to the thick, thrusting erection that so needed her attention. The purpled head was swollen and throbbing, a drop of creamy seed lying on the tip as his anticipation heightened.

She reached out with her tongue, licking the drop free of the bulbous head as he groaned in rising desire.

"Cait," he growled her name warningly, tilting his hips, pressing the thick tip between her lips.

Caitlin swirled her tongue around it, sucking at it as though hesitant of the experience, knowing it would drive him wild. And it did. He groaned, both hands at her head now as he held her still and pressed harder against her.

She laved the head, then groaned in excitement as he forced it further inside her, filling her mouth with several inches of hard, thrusting cock. She was ravenous for him. A hunger unlike any she had known before overcame her. His hands were bunched in her hair, creating a pressure along her scalp, holding her still as he began to fuck her mouth with strong, shallow strokes.

She suckled at the throbbing head of his cock. Licking it as he retreated, suckling with hungry, strong movements as he returned. Her hands gripped his thighs, her nails prickling at his skin as she strained to take more of the heated erection driving into the grip of her lips, the strokes of her tongue.

He tasted like a thunderstorm, male and intense and so addictive she hungered more for him with each taste. She felt the tautness of his body, heard his desperate moans, and felt his cock jerk as he pressed it into her once again. The sweet-salty tang of his seed lingered on her tongue as he fought the release she knew was only moments away.

"Not yet," he growled, pulling back from her, ignoring her cry as she reached for him.

Before Caitlin could do more than whimper in frustration, he had moved, pushing her shoulders to the bed as he came behind her and lifted her hips until her knees rested fully beneath her.

"Stay there," he bit out, delivering a sharp, erotic smack to her raised butt. "I have a surprise for you, Cait. One you will like."

She restrained her whimper as she felt him move from the bed. He walked around the bed where she could watch as he lifted the lid to his trunk, then pulled free a leather satchel from its bottom. He watched her as he opened the drawstring, then pulled the article it contained free.

Caitlin frowned. The object was clear, like crystal, tapered from a thinner rounded top to a thicker base. At the base, a deep, wide groove surrounded it before it flared out thicker in a wider bottom. It wasn't smooth but rippled. She could see the waving effect around the object as Derek then lifted a small tin from the bag as well.

"It is a pleasure that only the gods possess," he told her, his voice dark and seductive. "It was given to me for a particularly dangerous mission I accomplished. I was given my choice of payment and I chose this."

"What will it do?" she asked him, suddenly nervous as he opened the tin and drew out a coating of clear, thick oil.

He spread the oil over the thick object, watching her with a brooding gaze as he stalked back to the bed. He came behind her once again and she jumped in surprise as she felt his hand, slick from whatever oil coated it, slide through the cleft of her buttocks. As he reached her tightly closed anus, he paused.

Caitlin moaned in excitement then anticipation for the moment his finger would thrust into the hot depths there. How many times had he made her nearly insane with his caresses?

She forgot about the object, forgot everything but his touch as he pushed first one, then two fingers expertly into her ass. Her fists clenched in the quilts of the bed, her cunt burning with unashamed need as she pressed harder against his fingers.

They retreated slowly as he murmured to her gently of his desperation for her, his need to take her in ways she could never imagine. Then he was holding her tight and she felt the cool, tapered tip of the object at her tender opening.

"Derek," she cried out, suddenly frightened, wary of what he would do.

"Shhh, I would have you do this for me, Cait," he groaned, pressing the object deeper inside her as a sudden, heated pleasure began to tear through her body.

It was thicker than his fingers, harder. It stretched her, burned, made her aware of needs she had only dreamed of.

"When you can take this easily," Derek was breathing fast, hard as he pressed it deeper, working the thicker length into her anus, "then you will be ready for my cock, Cait. I will fuck you there and drown you in my seed as you tighten around me."

He pushed the object in to the hilt then. A smooth, firm thrust that parted her protesting muscles and sent a streaking pleasure-pain flaring through her vagina.

"Derek," she nearly screamed out his name as her pussy clenched, spilled more of her thick moisture and almost threw her into an orgasm.

"Oh no, baby, not yet," he bit out as he twisted the device.

She bucked in tormented pleasure, feeling then the reason for the small, raised ripples along the device.

"Derek, you are killing me," she pleaded for relief then. Her body was humming in hungry demand as her ass stretched around the alien device. Her cunt was on fire, needing to be filled.

"Not yet," he promised her. "Do you know, Cait, with your ass so filled, your sweet cunt will be tighter, hotter around my cock? When I fill you it will be like pushing into a tightly closed fist."

He held her hips as she sobbed into the blankets. Her body was on fire, the blood rushing so fast and hard through her that she could barely breathe. She could feel the hard thickness inside her anus, heating from the grip of her body, stretching her to the point that her tight channel burned in protest. A heated lash of prickling heat that edged her pleasure higher.

Derek's hands gripped her hips then, raising her, positioning his cock. She whimpered as the broad head paused at the entrance to her vagina. Then her back arched as a strangled cry ripped from her throat.

Her head tossed as she pushed herself up until she could bear her weight on her hands and knees. His cock was burrowing slowly inside her slick pussy, pushing past the tightened muscles and caressing nerve endings she had never known she possessed.

Perspiration dampened her flesh as the scent of lust became nearly overpowering, surrounding her, driving her pleasure higher. He thrust against her with shallow movements, working the thick stalk of his cock deeper and deeper inside her.

Caitlin was panting, whimpering, fighting for breath as he finally surged inside her to the hilt. One hand held her hip, his fingers tightening as she trembled at the thick, dual penetration of her body. Then she bucked against him as she felt the device lodged in her ass being moved.

She screamed out at the wicked pleasure that assailed her as he began to move the device, pulling it nearly free of her anus as his cock thrust hard and heavy inside her cunt. She shuddered with the driving lusts filling her, the dual fucking driving her insane. She was possessed by such overriding pleasure that she could do nothing but give herself to it.

When his thrusts began to gain in speed and depth, her muscles contracted around him. Her body fought for an orgasm that she knew would destroy her and in turn bind her forever to the man taking her with such brutal desire. A desire she longed for, craved, as she did nothing else.

He pushed her higher, harder, until she was unaware of the desperate, agonized moans that echoed through the room. She was aware of nothing but the hard driving thrusts into her body, the alternating, searing pleasure pushing her higher, higher...

Her body tightened as the ripples began in her cunt, spread to her anus, then exploded through her body with such power and force that she straightened against Derek's body, forcing him to wrap his arm around her hips to steady her as her orgasm began to rock her body.

She was only dimly aware of his hoarse shout of release in her ear, but the feel of his semen erupting inside her quaking pussy pushed her past a pinnacle she could have never known existed. It pounded through her, ripped through muscle and tissues in such forceful convulsions that she saw stars erupting before her eyes.

"Cait. Cait. God, Cait, I love you," his words were barely heard through her cries as yet another explosion ripped through her womb.

She felt her juices, his semen, dripping down her thighs as another hard burst of sensation caused her juices to splatter from her vagina. Derek held her tight, close, his lips at her neck. His breathing was hard and labored as he held her through the crisis of overpowering pleasure.

She was weeping, wondering if such carnal pleasure was the sin she knew she felt it should be. She would have spoken, would have expressed not just her pleasure, but her love as well, had she the words.

"You have remade me, Caitlin." He rocked her gently, easing her back as she felt the device being slowly pulled from the sensitive region of her anus.

She shuddered with remembered pleasure, but was too weak to do more than breathe out roughly as he moved back from her, then helped her to lie down gently.

She drifted in a sea of exhaustion and satisfaction, dimly aware of Derek as he cleaned and stored the device back in the trunk. Within moments he climbed back into the bed beside her and drew her carefully into his arms.

"I love you," she whispered, snuggling into his arms, hoping that when sleep came the dreams did not return.

# Chapter Seven

Antea watched as Devlin and Chantel entered the great hall. The warrior walked beside her, his head tilted, a small, almost bemused smile on his face as his wife spoke softly to him.

It was sickening, she thought, to see how they teased each other whenever they were together. The soft smiles, the silent, long glances they shared. The warrior was so besotted he nearly tripped over his own feet whenever his precious Chantel was around.

There was one bright spot in the matches Galen had secured for his daughters, though, she thought as the warrior Joshua came down the stairs behind them. The match of Arriane and Joshua seemed less than content.

Once again Joshua was entering the great hall alone, a scowl on his rough, handsome face. That meant Arriane was likely still in their room crying.

The problems between Arriane and Joshua were making the rest of the household tense as well. Even the servants were talking about it and speculating on how long Chantel would put up with the treatment the warrior was giving her precious sister.

"Are you ready to see the seamstress, Antea?" Chantel's quiet voice disturbed the happy thoughts she was having at the reason for Arriane's tears.

"We're late." Antea shrugged. "She has likely returned to the village by now."

"I doubt it." That patient smile on her sister's face was enough to cause Antea to clench her fists with the need to wipe it away. "Mary knows I am often running late."

"It doesn't matter." What could she say, Antea wondered. To say anything more would bring Galen's wrath down upon her for daring to treat his daughter with any disrespect.

"Come, Antea, I'm certain Mary is still awaiting us."

"No, when you had not shown up, I told her to go on back to the village." Antea was proud of the even tone of her voice. "The dress didn't matter."

But it had. It was her first new dress in months and she had been looking forward to it. But that peasant Mary never seemed to get things right unless Chantel was there to watch over everything.

Chantel frowned at that news, as though she were distressed by it. Of course, Antea knew better. Chantel hadn't wanted to arrange the appointment to begin with, putting it off for this reason or another for weeks.

"I can send for her to return," Chantel suggested softly. "I truly am sorry I was late, Antea."

"It is not important," Antea tried to speak evenly, but fury filled her the longer her sister stood before her with that pitying expression. "I didn't need the dress anyway. It is not like there is anyone here to appreciate it. Please worry yourself no more about it."

Unable to stand her sister's presence any longer, Antea turned from her and left the great hall. She walked quickly to the stairs opposite those Chantel had come down and went back to her room. There was no sense, she thought, in standing around debating the matter any longer. The seamstress had been sent home and there would be no dress. And as she had said, there was no sense in a new dress when there was no way to enjoy the effects of it.

There were no parties at Galen's castle, no trips to other castles past the forest, and there were very few visitors other than messengers.

As she climbed the stairs, Antea entertained the dream that she was Chantel, the golden child. That her word was obeyed and her wishes granted and it was her bed that the knight, Devlin, shared.

As Antea walked from the room, Chantel breathed a frustrated sigh. Her half-sister was becoming more and more discontented within the castle. She was becoming more dissatisfied with the life she was being given and longing more for those things she could not have.

Chantel felt the warmth of the crystal at her breast as she considered this problem and the moves her sister would soon make to change that status quo. It grieved her to know that the events were moving so swiftly and soon would be out of her control.

"Chantel, you should send her away, as Devlin wants." Her father came up behind her as he spoke, his tone filled with worry.

"We cannot send her away, Father." Chantel turned to him, hating the sadness she saw in his eyes. "I thought you were riding with Devlin this afternoon. Something about checking out the outlying farms?"

"I was heading to the stables when I saw you talking with her." Galen sighed wearily. "I cannot concentrate on what needs to be done. There is trouble brewing and I feel that girl is in the thick of it."

"Antea will be fine, Father," Chantel smiled, fighting to reassure him, to take the sadness from his eyes.

"It is not Antea I worry about, Chantel." Galen met her gaze directly. "It is you who I worry for."

"I shall be fine, Father." She smiled up at him as his arm came around her shoulders and he kissed her forehead. "But your sons-in-law may not be if they ride to those farms themselves. I can see our people taking up arms when first confronted with Joshua, should you not be there to intercede."

"Be damned if you are not right there," he bit out, moving quickly away from her. "That damned man would try the patience of a saint."

A saint, as well as a woman's love. Chantel felt weariness gather over her as she glanced to the still deserted stairs. Arriane still had not come from her room and the sensations of her pain seemed to echo in the silence of the castle.

Chantel was seriously debating this habit Joshua had of stripping her sister's feelings and leaving her lost in the emotional abyss he was creating. She could help her, ease that pain, but in doing so, she would curse Joshua to feel the same resounding agony before it could be lifted.

For this alone, she hesitated, hoping the warrior would ease in his anger that Arriane was Jonar's granddaughter. Should he do much more to harm the gentle heart that had been given him, then Chantel knew she would lose her own patience and extract revenge.

*   *   *   *   *

Later that afternoon, Devlin had still not solved the most immediate problem of keeping his new bride safe.

As his men rode through the outlying village, Devlin was still pondering this problem, much to the disgust of his men.

"I say we point her out to the spy, let him take her, and be done with it." Derek looked to the other men as he made his suggestion once again.

"Chantel would know." Devlin shook his head as he reined his horse in outside the small village.

"And we can't do anything to upset Chantel." Joshua's voice held an edge of bitterness that had not been present before his wedding.

"Just because you enjoy upsetting your bride, doesn't mean we want ours in a constant state of tears, Mystic," Shanar spoke up disparagingly. "We need to solve this little problem to the satisfaction of both Devlin and Chantel."

This good marital advice had Devlin stifling his laughter as he glanced at the irate giant. Shanar was becoming fanatically intent at providing his wife with not just the most happiness he could manage, but also an over-abundance of pleasure.

The maid, Alya, had informed Chantel that morning that Shanar and Ariel had yet to unlock their door or to answer the maid's knocks as she was sent to see if they were ready for breakfast.

Chantel had hidden her laughter, frowning at Alya for gossiping, though the look had caused the girl to do little more than giggle.

"Humph, good luck," Joshua snorted. "Those women have the three of you performing jester's tricks now to please them."

Devlin looked over at the bitter warrior, an edge of frustration beginning to bite at him from Joshua's attitude.

"Try pleasing your wife more often, and perhaps she would cry less. I've grown tired of watching your snide attacks cut into her," Devlin informed him.

"She's my wife, not yours," Joshua reminded him. "And I will treat her as I please."

"And I would remind you that these women have the power to aid us, if they are working together," Devlin bit out. "Keep hurting that girl for no reason, and she will turn on you."

"She wouldn't dare." Joshua's voice was dark with anger as he issued the threat. "I would treat her the same as a rabid dog."

"I've seen you treat rabid dogs gentler." Shanar turned on him now, his gray eyes flaring in anger. "The girl has committed no crime, Joshua. She comes to you eagerly and wishes only to please you. Can't you give her so much as a kind word?"

"Can't you attend to your own wife, and leave mine the hell alone?" Joshua shot back, his amber eyes blazing now, filled with a fury Devlin could not name.

Devlin was tempted to look into the warrior's mind for himself and see what set him off so fiercely. It was a power he detested using, though, and most especially on his own men.

112

"This is not solving our most immediate problem," Devlin reminded them shortly, put out with Joshua's attitude. "I will secure my own bride's safety before I tackle the task of teaching a certain warrior the meaning of honor."

The men were silent now, but Devlin knew Joshua was thinking more of ways to torment his little wife than he was in saving Devlin's.

"How old is the lass anyway?" Derek asked him with a frown.

"She's a year older than Chantel, so I would say nearing nineteen." Devlin sighed. "That woman is hard enough to be twice her age though."

"She's a whore." Joshua's voice was flat with disgust. "She met me on the stairs this morn and assured me she could fulfill my needs much better than Arriane."

"That is your fault." Derek rounded on him. "Speaking of it, you have done nothing but give that woman leave to be cruel to your wife. I caught her at it last night, informing Arriane that she would do better to turn her husband over to a real woman."

"If I remember correctly, my little bride took care of herself well."

Devlin wondered if that was an edge of satisfaction that he heard in Joshua's voice.

Arriane had taken great offense at the offer. Before anyone had realized the power she had called up, the hem of Antea's gown had begun to gently smolder.

The sparks had been quickly doused and Antea rushed to her room as her enraged cries echoed through the castle. There had been no doubt though of who had caused the fire.

"We digress once again," Devlin sighed.

"Devlin, there is no other choice but to give the little bitch to Jonar," Joshua reminded him. "I understand your hesitation to do so, but what other answer is there?"

What other answer was there? Devlin settled himself into his saddle and tried to come up with a solution.

"Jonar will kill them both." Devlin could feel the fear that rose inside him.

Chantel had assured him countless times that this would not happen. But the fear that ate at Devlin would not go away.

Devlin leaned forward on the pommel of his saddle, his hand rubbing worriedly at his chin. There had to be a way to preserve Antea's safety *and* Chantel's.

He had tried to catch Galen alone several times to question him on the matter, but the wizard seemed to be mysteriously absent each time Devlin had the chance.

"We better think of something soon," Shanar warned him quietly.

Devlin turned a questioning look on the Savage and then glanced in the direction he nodded to. There, riding furiously to catch up with them, was one of the king's messengers.

The warriors were about to be sent to battle again and there was still no solution to the problem of protecting his bride.

\* \* \* \* \*

Chantel sat silently in the cavern hidden within the bowels of her father's castle. She held the crystal she wore in the palm of her hand, gazing sadly into the mists that had formed inside it.

Before her, a tenuous, lightened form wavered, the figure of the Mother watching her silently.

*You can turn the tide, Chantel,* her voice whispered through the cavern. *You can release Antea to the forces that search for her and live your life in happiness. You can forgo the destruction of Jonar, you can deny the price the Fates and Destiny have demanded for his complete destruction and the gifts you will need to see his end. None could blame you. What they have demanded is more than many could ever bear thinking of, much less do.*

"I can betray a solemn vow and grow old while my husband remains young to fight an evil that shall eventually destroy all I hold dear?" Chantel fought her tears. "This is not much of a choice, Mother."

*You know the alternative,* the figure warned her, her voice caressing as her form wavered closer. *Can you continue this course and see it through to its final end?*

"If you can keep your vow, then too can I." Chantel kept her head lowered, fighting the tears that hovered on her lashes.

*My vow shall be kept, but you must also remember the conditions to that promise. That will not change, my child.* The Mother's voice was saddened, tired. *I tried, but I could not secure that the knowledge of this time would come back to you.*

Chantel nodded shortly, she had not expected that Mother Earth could secure that. There were limits, no matter the sacrifice.

*Are you certain you're ready, child?* the Mother asked her softly. *We can delay this.*

"No, it must be done soon, else I shall lose my nerve all together." Chantel shook her head, losing the battle with the tears that came slowly from her eyes. "Each day I am with him, my heart aches stronger for what I must do."

*Then it will begin, as you desire.* The Mother nodded, then slowly her form receded and Chantel was left alone with the growing darkness of the cavern with the darkness and her fears.

She had made the bargain and now Fate would begin the actions that would secure Destiny's plans for her and her sisters. Death would come. She shuddered violently, the tears falling faster now from her eyes. He would be alone, her precious Devlin. So alone…

Chantel took a deep breath, fighting to still the rapid beat of her heart and the fear that filled her. Mother Earth had been unable to learn the full details of what was to come or how it should end. Just as she had been unable to secure for Chantel the knowledge she now had, for a later time.

The bargain had been made though. Years ago, after first accepting the crystal, the Mother had come to her. She had shown Chantel the visions of her life with Devlin. The few years of happiness, then the pain of her aging as her husband continued in the youth the gods had gifted him.

She could accept that destiny or she could choose another. She could be parted from him for but a brief time, leaving him alone in the dark recesses of his own loneliness and the pain to follow. Then she would be returned to him, when the time was right to defeat Jonar. Only with Jonar's death would the warriors complete the quest the gods had given them and have their mortality returned to them once again.

It had been a choice that had tormented the young Chantel when the dreams of the warrior invaded her sleep, bringing with them strange, heated desires to which she could not put a name.

Now she knew it was the passion and the love that she could feel growing between them each day. Just as she knew that soon, much too soon, he would be torn from her arms, and when fate and destiny obtained their price, only then could Devlin and Chantel be allowed the happiness for which they would be destined.

* * * * *

Chantel was waiting when the warriors rode back into the courtyard with the king's messenger. She watched Devlin, sitting strong and tall on his horse, and fought the weakening thought that she could halt the events beginning at any time.

It would be disastrous to allow herself to delay any longer. Already her soul ached until the pain was like a physical blow each time she saw his smile.

He was her warrior. He was irrevocably her heart and her very soul.

She watched as he spoke to the messenger, a frown crossing his brow at something the man said. His black eyes were narrowed, his arms crossed over his broad chest as he seemed to be deliberating some point.

"They will be leaving?" Arriane moved beside her, her voice husky from yet more tears.

Chantel smiled gently at her sister. Arriane had not smiled since leading Joshua from the great hall the night of the warriors' arrival.

"In a day or two." Chantel nodded, watching the shadows that crossed Arriane's expression.

"Is he unbearable, Arriane?" Chantel whispered painfully, hurting for the tears Joshua had caused her.

"No more than I knew it would be," Arriane told her, her voice trembling. "The child will arrive soon, he says."

Chantel's lips thinned with a growing fury. The child was Joshua's bastard, born of a highborn whore who seemed to follow Joshua about the countryside.

"Joshua wishes for him to be raised in the castle," Arriane continued. "Lady Denning arrives with him." Those words were torn from Arriane's throat as she gave Chantel the news.

"He wouldn't dare!" Chantel's hands trembled with her fury as her eyes centered on the warrior's back.

"He assured me he would." A sarcastic, pain-ridden little laugh erupted from Arriane's chest. "I tell you to prepare you, Chantel. He has had her room prepared on our floor. I would ask that you do nothing to harm her while she is here."

It wasn't that Chantel was a cruel person or would needlessly harm another. But she was protective of her sisters and would harm anyone who would attempt to hurt them.

"Father won't allow it," Chantel bit out.

"He has not asked Father's permission. And I will not have you interfering either. This is the only reason I tell you of it now, to warn you to let me handle this."

Chantel turned on her sister, seeing the shadows of sleeplessness and rage that made her appear tired and worn.

Arriane did not have the ability to hurt anything or anyone. How Mother Earth could have considered her alliance with the Mystic warrior, Joshua, Chantel could not fathom.

"Do not allow him to do this to you, Arriane," Chantel pleaded with her. "He will destroy you."

Arriane smiled softly, regretfully, her blue eyes appearing bruised and filled with sorrow.

"Not in this lifetime, my sister," she whispered, her voice filled with knowledge and despair. "He won't have the chance."

Chantel could feel her face paling as she read the knowledge in her sister's eyes.

"How much have you seen?" she whispered.

"Only enough to know better than to look into the crystal. Joshua probes my secrets nightly, and holding my suspicions from him is becoming harder each night. I want no more knowledge than I have already."

"Block him," Chantel bit out in fury. "Don't let him take the power from you, Arriane, it may be all that will save you later."

"As I said, I have my own suspicions and they tell me there is no need to worry about needing the power later." Arriane smiled sadly. "Besides, could you block Devlin? Even knowing his fury and his hatred, could you refuse him?"

"With little or no effort were he such a bastard," Chantel growled, turning back to see the men heading for the castle now.

Chantel knew her fury was still evident on her face when she saw Devlin frown. She fought to give him a welcoming smile and to ignore the warrior who was causing her sister such pain.

"Telling tales, little wife?" Joshua's voice was a cold blow that caused his wife to flinch. "Did I not warn you against such a thing?"

Chantel pinned the man with a cold look, allowing the force of her power free rein and ignoring the shock that filled the men as an emerald glow shot from her crystal to encompass herself and Arriane.

"Hurt her and you hurt us all." Chantel was aware of her voice echoing around the men.

"Chantel. No!" Arriane's cry was a distant protest as the aura surrounded her, blocking her from the husband who would have snatched her back from it.

"Warn you now, I warn you well. A lock of hair, a tear now shed. No peace shall come, nor child be born, 'til fire falls and water flows, 'til the winds howl and the earth does whisper. Hear me, Mystic, hear me well. 'Til your lips touch fire and your heart bleeds in vengeance. 'Til rebirth is given, 'til legend fulfilled. No more shall she cry, no more shall you know. Tender mercy wiped away. Gentle love shall sleep 'til that day."

Thunder vibrated, the winds howled and the skies rained down tears of sorrow. Then in a flash, lightning split the ground and flames converged, surrounding Arriane, burning bright, burning hot.

Joshua screamed out in rage, reaching for Arriane who disappeared amid the conflagration.

"Mistress of Fire," Chantel's voice sang out above the frightened cries gathering within the courtyard. "Flame high, flame deep, and gather strength, for no more shall you weep. Draw your power, reach for the fire, flame high, flame bright; gather strength, gather life and mourn no more."

As quickly as it began, it had finished. In a blink of an eye the storm and flames were gone, leaving Arriane standing strong and radiantly unharmed.

"Chantel, what have you done?" Arriane cried out in grief as she turned now to her sister who slowly collapsed in her husband's arms. "Take it back. Take it back, Chantel."

"Sleep," Chantel's whisper was weak, ragged, as her eyes closed, her head falling limply against Devlin's chest.

"Take her to her room," Arriane ordered him harshly. "The others shall be there within moments."

119

"What have you done, you little bitch?" Joshua caught her as she made to follow Devlin, his fingers biting into the tender, already bruised flesh of her upper arm.

"Not I." Arriane turned on him, fury overtaking her as the impact of what her sister had sacrificed crashed in on her.

Before she thought, her free arm swung back and flew out. Her fist, tightly clenched, connected with the hard flesh and bone of his jaw.

Joshua staggered back, surprise flashing across his face as Arriane stared back at in him in fury.

"You did this!" she screamed up at him, frightened now at the lack of tears to shed the pain within her heart. "You, with your senselessness and total lack of consideration while in my sister's presence. You have no idea what you have just done. No idea, Joshua."

Ignoring the shock in his expression, the growing fury in his eyes, Arriane turned and rushed to Chantel's room. There had to be a way to reverse the spell, she thought desperately. There had to be a way to save her sister and the lives they had fought so desperately for.

\* \* \* \* \*

As the warriors rushed into the castle, Devlin holding Chantel close as he bore her to their room, Antea stood in the shadows of the great hall and watched with narrowed eyes.

Hatred burned in her heart. Hot and bitter, it flowed through her as she watched the dark warrior, his face filled with concern and anger as he carried his wife up the stairs.

It wasn't fair, she thought. Each of those bitches was doubly protected now. First by the crystals that held such power, then by men who were not just handsome, but gifted by the gods as well. They were gifted, while she was stuck in this miserable hole fighting to keep Jonar from killing her because her father, the god of gods, refused to grant her protection.

Chantel had all the protection she could ever need now and refused to even consider sharing that damned crystal so Antea could leave the castle for just a little while.

For the most part, she was stuck upstairs, hiding in her room, because the spell Galen had cast upon the castle allowed only those trusted few past the stairs. She could not even have the comfort of a lover in her room, but rather had to take her chances with her life to steal outside when the opportunity presented itself.

Chantel had her lover, her husband in her room each night. A virile, lusty man. Antea had stood outside her room, listening in fury to the shattered cries the warrior brought from her sister's lips each night. Such pleasure the warrior brought her. Antea shivered in longing as she thought of the hours that Chantel's cries would drift through the door into the cold hall where Antea stood.

She had done everything she could think of to tempt one of the virile warriors into her own bed. So far, she had failed dismally. Even the strangely golden-eyed warrior they called the Mystic refused her advances. And how could he receive any pleasure from the pale-faced bitch who shared his room? He spent more time screaming at her than he did pleasuring her, yet he refused to take Antea up on the many offers she had made him.

As she stood there, watching the now deserted stairway, she felt the anger and the desperation eating at her. Were she to be caught, Galen would surely destroy her. Should he ever learn that she had found the way to work past his magic spells, then he would never allow her to live, no matter Chantel's pleas. But she had to find a way to secure her sister's power. Through it, all her dreams of immortality could be fulfilled.

With all the power Chantel held in that crystal, it had to be powerful enough to reach the Guardians. If she could reach them, surely her father would come for her and give her the gift of immortality.

"Spying again, love?" Antea jerked around, a startled gasp slipping past her lips as she came face to face with one of Galen's knights.

"I do not spy," she informed him coldly, wondering if Galen was near to hear the accusation. The last thing she needed was to give him another excuse to confine her to her rooms, as he had done the night before Chantel's wedding.

"Then what would you call it?" The knight watched her with a careless grin, as his eyes went over her form slowly.

He was rather good-looking, Antea thought. Broad-shouldered, not very tall, but heavily muscled and she knew from the talk of the women of the castle that he knew several ways to pleasure a woman. She had been a long time without pleasure, she thought.

"Merely curiosity." Antea shrugged, allowing a teasing smile to slip over her lips. "She is my sister, after all."

"Yes, she is." The knight nodded, moving closer in the shadows until his form surely would hide hers should Galen glimpse them. "A sister with a lot of power, it would seem."

Antea shrugged, unwilling to speak, fearful of one of Galen's traps. She feared he had been looking for an excuse to get rid of her since Chantel's guards had brought her to the castle.

The knight was silent now as well and in the dwindling light of the great hall, Antea was unable to see much of his expression.

She could hear his altered breathing, though, and feel his hunger in the quick puffs of air that blew gently across the top of her head.

"I can't enter the upper floors," the knight told her softly.

"I'm growing tired of the stables." Antea moved to push past him. If she was going to lower herself to let this man touch her, she at least wanted a bed. She was sick of having to mask her moans and rush her pleasure.

"There is a room, in the back of the castle," he told her softly, his voice soft, suggestive. "It is little used and has a cot there for the cook when she needs it. I can make certain the cook doesn't need it this night."

Antea paused, staring up into his dark eyes, his handsome face. It beat a stack of hay, she thought.

"Perhaps." She shrugged as she moved past him. "Perhaps I'll be there tonight."

Antea moved away from him slowly, her hips swaying softly, her steps slow and measured. She had not had this particular knight as yet—he had always held himself aloof, merely watching her. It could be a pleasant diversion until she found a way to borrow the crystal Chantel possessed. Then she could contact the Guardians and she would no longer need to settle for a lowly knight. She would have kings at her feet.

* * * * *

Galen watched Antea sway across the room, his brows drawn into a frown. The knight who had stood within the shadows with her was watching her intently, his eyes seeing nothing but a whore's swaying hips.

Galen's fists clenched, his eyes closing tightly for precious, control-gathering seconds. He had witnessed the display of power within the entrance to the great hall. He had felt Chantel's power vibrating throughout the castle, felt the forces of the earth as it rose to do her bidding, and felt grief swell in his heart.

He wanted only to delay what he knew would come and yet he could think of no way to do so. Mother Earth was silent when he pleaded with her, Father Time could give him little consolation.

He was forced to stand silent, forbidden to aid his daughters now when he knew they needed him the most. Forced to give aid and safety to a woman he knew would betray them all.

Galen wasn't a fool. He knew well the type of woman Antea was, just as he knew that her envy would one day injure Chantel.

He couldn't stop whatever was to come, but as he watched the scene that played out before him, Galen swore he would make certain Antea would pay should any of his daughters be harmed by her.

Then his eyes turned to the knight. They narrowed in contemplation as he caught an echo of menace around the man. This knight had never been one to invite friendships, yet he was one Galen had always depended on. He wondered if somehow that had changed.

\* \* \* \* \*

Devlin carried Chantel quickly to their bedroom, aware of the others that rushed behind them. Arriane was calling out orders to a servant as she rushed after them, fear echoing in her voice.

As they neared the bedroom door, Shanar stepped ahead of Devlin and threw it open quickly, then stood back as Devlin pushed past him and strode to the large bed across the room.

"What the hell happened, Arriane?" Devlin laid Chantel on the bed, staring worriedly at the pale cast of her skin and her shallow breathing.

"She will be fine, my lord," Arriane assured him as she squeezed around him to jerk the blankets over Chantel and tuck them close to her neck. "It is merely the effects of releasing her power in such a way."

It didn't sound as though she would be fine. Devlin could hear the tremble of fear in the woman's voice, the guilt and sorrow that flowed through her.

"Do not lie to me, Arriane." Devlin gripped her arm to turn her, but quickly released her as she cried out softly, flinching at the contact.

Rage lashed through Devlin. He turned Chantel's sister to face him and then ripped the sleeve of her gown unceremoniously. What he saw there nearly had him shaking with his own anger.

As bruises went, it was slight. Devlin admitted he had seen much worse on women much more delicate than this one. Never had he known those bruises to be inflicted by a warrior who fought beside him though.

The finger marks were dark, a vivid blue slash across the white skin of her forearm.

"Is this why?" he asked her softly, his gaze moving to hers slowly.

"It was an accident." Arriane shook her head softly. "I shouldn't have fought him."

"Is this why she cursed my warrior? Why she now lies here, looking near death?" Devlin questioned her again.

"She did not curse your warrior, my lord." A single tear slipped down Arriane's cheek as she spoke. "She merely spoke the truth and lent to me a bit of her own, much-needed power. Your lady is not harmed. She will be fine."

"Is this why?" he asked her again, his tone warning her to answer this time.

Once again Arriane shook her head.

"Chantel did not know of the bruise," she told him softly. "This was not why."

"And are there others?" His voice was demon-dark, vibrating with some unnamed force that caused Arriane's knees to tremble with fear.

"No."

"You lie to me, woman," he accused her, staring into her eyes, seeing her fear as she felt the power he could turn on her. "Do I need to strip you here before the others to prove it?"

"Let her go, Devlin." Joshua's voice was soft, warning. "If you want to know about my wife's body, you can ask me."

Devlin turned his gaze to the warrior. In Joshua's eyes he glimpsed an edge of remorse, a sensation of pain as they flickered to the bruise on the delicate arm of his wife.

"Does she carry other bruises, Joshua?" he asked the warrior, suddenly sick inside that one of his men could abuse any woman, especially his wife.

"She carries several other bruises." Joshua stared back at him. "I promise you, though, only the one on her arm was given in anger."

No excuses. Devlin clenched his teeth in anger.

"Do you see what the abuse of your wife is causing, Joshua?" Devlin looked to his own wife, unconscious upon the bed now. "Do you think I will allow this to continue?"

Silence reigned within the room. All the warriors and the sisters of Chantel were aware that Devlin was holding onto his temper with the thinnest of threads.

"My wife is my business." Joshua was tempting that anger with every word out of his mouth.

"Lord Devlin, Chantel's anger was my fault." Arriane's soft statement turned Devlin's attention back to her.

"And how, my good woman, is it your fault?" Devlin frowned, wondering how Arriane could have caused such wrath to be directed to her husband.

Arriane's gaze flickered uncertainly to her husband.

"He is not the one you need to fear, Lady Arriane," he bit out. "Tell me why, and I promise you, you will have no need to fear reprisals from him."

"I fear nothing from him now," she relied sadly. "Chantel was angry when I informed her that Joshua was bringing Lady Denning and their child to the castle and installing them in one of the rooms on our floor. She seemed to believe it an insult to me, as well as to herself." The last was said with a bitter twist to her lips.

Incredulity washed over Devlin until he could do nothing but stare at Joshua in surprise and contempt. Surely he would not have tried to humiliate his wife in such a way, Devlin thought. Then realized that he most likely would have.

Lady Denning's hold on Joshua had concerned Devlin more than once, but now it frankly terrified him.

Joshua stared back at him darkly, making no excuses, saying nothing. There was little doubt to Devlin that the Mystic had lost his mind.

"Leave this room. I will deal with you when the matter of my wife's health has been dealt with," Devlin ordered him.

"Come along, Arriane." Joshua's order was met with silence as he turned and walked to the door.

Arriane, however, did not follow him. She stood beside her sister, watching her husband with a flat, uncompromising expression. Devlin wanted to grit his teeth in fury.

As Joshua reached the door, he realized his order had not been heeded and turned back to her with a frown.

"You did not hear me?" he asked her arrogantly.

"I heard you, my lord, I just refuse to come to your call like the bitch you already have following you." Arriane smiled tightly. "I shall come up later. Right now, Chantel needs me."

"Chantel has her husband," Joshua bit out.

"But her husband does not have fire." Arriane touched the crystal at her breast. "As I said, I shall be there later and you may then rage to your heart's content. Until then, I will stay with my sister."

Devlin watched the anger that washed over Joshua, the promise of retribution in his amber eyes as he watched Arriane.

"Leave us, Joshua," he ordered him once again.

The door to the bedroom didn't slam. It didn't have to. The soft, almost gentle click of it being pulled closed was a threat enough in itself, considering Joshua never once touched it.

"Shanar, you and Derek should take your wives out of here…"

"No." Ariel moved away from her husband, facing Devlin strongly. "It is you who needs to leave now—you and Shanar and Derek. Chantel needs her sisters right now and the power we share."

Devlin rubbed his hand wearily over his face at this announcement.

"Is she ill?" He finally asked the question that he feared the answer to. "Did she harm herself for Arriane's sake?"

"Chantel shall be fine," Ariel promised him as well. "She is weak. The power she released against your warrior was deep and strong, Devlin. She needs us right now to help her to replenish the energy she lost."

Devlin sighed deeply.

"You should go take care of that bastard you call a friend," Ariel's tone was very nearly an order. "Because I promise you, should that whore Denning take up residence in this castle, then there will be nothing left of her, or of him, to carry back out of it."

She didn't wait for him to answer, but moved instead to the windows of the bedroom and began opening the shutters that had been closed there.

The strength of her voice, the order it carried, would have amused him had the situation not felt so desperate.

Devlin glanced at Shanar's and Derek's closed expressions as they watched the women begin to care for Chantel.

"Ye really need to leave, my lords." Caitlin gave Derek a gentle nudge toward the door as she broke her own silence. "What needs to be done cannot be done with you here. We shall come to you when we are finished."

Devlin looked down at his wife one more time. She was still pale, her breathing shallow, but the crystal at her breast seemed to pulse with vibrant life.

He leaned down, his lips caressing her cheek briefly.

"I'll be near," he whispered, hoping she could hear him in some way. "Hurry back to me."

Then he straightened and walked quickly from the room, aware that Shanar and Derek followed behind him.

He was denied his wife and he knew the man responsible for this. Devlin was determined that Joshua would mend his ways once and for all, or there would be more hell to pay than the Mystic could possibly endure.

# Chapter Eight

## ෨

Devlin was silent as he watched Joshua approach him. The warrior was standing stiffly straight, his shoulders thrown back, his hair loosened from the leather that usually held it secured at the nape of his neck.

That hair had caused the warrior much trouble, many times in the past. His hair was straight, as black as a raven's wing, and when loosened flowed around his shoulders and halfway down his back. He was called Pagan. Demon. Oft reviled and greatly feared.

The features of his face were savage. High cheekbones, a slightly crooked nose that bespoke the break it had suffered before the Guardians' gifts, and those piercing amber eyes staring beneath the hard slash of his black brows.

His heritage, his very parentage was only guessed at. All that was truly known was that his mother had been of Guardian birth and one who held powerful gifts. Even Joshua's true age was unknown. He had come to the home the warriors shared as boys, no bigger than a child of five. But his knowledge and his gifts were already apparent.

It had been difficult keeping the child they called Mystic in line. The woman who had raised them, Kanna, had often despaired of ever teaching him the finer arts of consideration. Keeping his power under control had been a trial that was not often remembered fondly.

It wasn't until Devlin received his own first gifts from the gods that they had been able to establish any sort of a hold on him. Kanna had sworn that Devlin had been given his gifts early because of the wild, reckless nature the Mystic often displayed.

"I'm here." Joshua faced him, fury trembling along his body as he came to a halt in front of Devlin. "You had only to send a message. This display was uncalled for."

The display being the psychic command that had forced Joshua to leave his rooms and trek through the castle to the gardens where Devlin awaited him.

"As it was uncalled for when you took Arriane from her dinner the night before in the great hall and forced her to follow you to your rooms?" Devlin asked him, remembered the paltry few bites of food the woman had eaten before Joshua had dragged her off.

"We ate later," Joshua reminded him, his gaze flickering away from Devlin's harsh gaze.

"What did she eat, Joshua?" Devlin crossed his arms over his chest as he confronted the man.

"She ate. That is all that should concern you," Joshua growled.

"She ate so little that my wife felt her hunger," Devlin charged. "The women of this castle are being needlessly upset because of your ungrounded fury on an innocent. But what concerns me even more are the bruises that girl now carries on her body. I want to know to what extent you have been abusing her."

There was no need for Joshua to speak. The answer flashed through his mind quickly, but he still did not have the control it took to keep the knowledge from Devlin.

"Goddamn you, Joshua." Shock filtered through Devlin's system as he reacted to the information his abilities had detected.

Rage was the furthest thing from Devlin's mind, as he was confronted with a side of the warrior he had not known existed.

"It didn't happen." Joshua broke the hold Devlin had allowed to slip. "I did not…"

Devlin shook his head. This was more than he had ever expected. No wonder the warrior's emotions were so ragged.

"Why have you not…" Devlin could not finish the thought. He could only shake his head as he completely released the hold that would reveal to him the secrets Joshua would keep.

"She is so tiny, Devlin." Joshua shook his head, moving away from him as he fought his own inner demons. "I cannot do it."

"She is your wife." Devlin shook his head once again. "But even beyond that, she still deserves a bit of kindness, Joshua. This is not her fault."

"It is her fault," Joshua ground out. "She tempts me at every turn, knowing what she is doing."

"So you bruise her?" Devlin asked him, still furious over the abuse. "Why do you not just walk away?"

"The bruises were an accident." Joshua shook his head, confusion surrounding his emotions as he turned back to Devlin. "What I said to her offended her and she would have slapped me. I grabbed her arm to twist her away from me and we fell. I would not strike my wife, Devlin."

Devlin breathed out roughly. He would not strike her and he refused to make love to her.

"The night we arrived…" he began to ask, confused about the warrior's actions that night.

"I would have, when she returned," Joshua growled, his fists clenched as he fought for his own control. "I was going to. But when I moved to—" he broke off, shaking his head, his body seeming to shudder. "She is too tiny. She is small, so delicate. Dammit, Devlin, I feel like I'm molesting a child."

"She is of age," Devlin argued, still not understanding. "She has been part of your dreams, just as Chantel experienced mine."

Joshua shook his head.

"It does not matter," he bit out. "She knows those dreams, swears they do not frighten her, yet I still cannot for fear of hurting her. I look into her eyes and suddenly there are so many fears, so many secrets swirling around us, that I cannot."

This, Devlin knew was the truth. Joshua had never made any secret of his lusty nature when with a woman. He never chose innocents, but always women who were experienced with the darker side of passion, such as Lady Denning.

"Can you not control your passions?" Devlin asked him, fighting his own confusion. "There is a medium, Joshua, surely?"

"I lose control with her, Devlin," Joshua finally sighed roughly. "This is why she often carries bruises. I touch her in my sleep and her cries awaken me. I will look and can see the strength of my grip on her. I fear breaking her should I actually try to take her."

Devlin was silent for long moments as he gazed around the sheltered area of the gardens. He had no answers for Joshua and yet he knew that one must be found.

"I will have her moved from my bedroom," Joshua finally told him. "That was my plan to begin with. Perhaps in a year, two years, I will be able to overcome this. Until then, Marissa must be allowed in the castle."

Lady Denning. Devlin sighed.

"Chantel cursed you this day, Joshua." Devlin looked into the tortured depths of those amber eyes. "Arriane says she did not, but I heard what she said. You will have no peace until this is resolved."

"I am aware of this already." Joshua grimaced. "That, even, would be preferable to the hell I am in now. Lusting for a woman I cannot take and my fury hurting us both. Bringing Marissa here is for the best, Devlin. I did not do this lightly."

"Neither did Chantel curse you lightly," Devlin informed him. "Knowing her, she is as aware of your problem as she is of Arriane's and yet she hates you all the same. Bringing Marissa here can only make that worse. You will have her stay at the village, not here within this castle. And as long as Arriane carries no more bruises, then I will interfere no more."

Joshua nodded, his gaze going to the mountains that rose in the distance, barely visible over the walls of the castle.

"That means consideration, if nothing else, to your bride, Joshua," Devlin informed him. "The women are too upset right now. With the threat Antea brings here, we must be careful. The power these women hold is immense. It can benefit us, or it can work against us."

Joshua frowned as he nodded slowly.

"This power, Devlin, there is something wrong with it." He turned to face him once again.

"What do you mean?" It was a feeling Devlin had felt himself.

"When I touched Arriane's mind last night, there were shadows there that swirled around thoughts of Chantel. There was a fear, a flash of fire and blood. It worries me."

Devlin felt his heart clench at this news. It confirmed his own fears, his own sense of impending doom.

"We must be certain the women are at peace as much as possible," Devlin ordered him. "If Arriane is distracted from that power by your petty cruelties, then it could work against them. Should Chantel be harmed because of it, then you, my friend, shall ride alone."

The hard edge to Devlin's voice as he said the words imparted the truth of his statement. Devlin would allow no man, whether he be friend or foe, to threaten the life he held above all others now.

"I understand this." Joshua nodded. "I shall have Arriane leave my room this day. I will bother her no more."

Devlin stared once again into the gaze of a man tormented past a point Devlin thought any man could bear. He felt sorry for the warrior, but not sorry enough to lift the threat. He could only nod, then turn and leave the gardens quickly. He would wait in the great hall for news of his wife and pray there would be no lasting damage from the curse and the power she had used.

* * * * *

Chantel watched her sisters in silence, from Arriane's forgiving gaze, to Ariel's stubborn one, and then Caitlin's soft understanding. Her sisters, they were so alike and yet so very different. Mother Earth had chosen wisely in gifting them with the powers of the earth.

It saddened her, the events of the past days. She had no clear answers to give these women who depended on her to guide them. No way to help them to understand the coming tide, so instead she hid the knowledge from them, aware there was no way to ease them, nor was there a way to aid them.

"Chantel, you must reverse the curse," Arriane whispered once again, her gaze imploring. "This is not his fault."

"It is his fault," Chantel told her quietly. "He was man enough to draw you into his dreams, he should be man enough to allow you to share his passion. Only Joshua can break this curse, Arriane."

"And you know he will not," Arriane sighed. She hurt for that, yet Chantel could detect no anger from her. The hatred that had been building was slowly easing now, thanks to the spell Chantel cast with her own power. "And besides, it wasn't worth what you did. You have weakened yourself, Chantel."

"I have not weakened myself," she denied. "I am just tired, I promise you."

"Chantel, yur lyin' to us." Amazement filled Caitlin's voice as she looked to her sister. "Why did ya lie to us?"

Chantel fought to hide her own startled reaction. Damn, she was weaker than she thought she was if they were able to catch her up so easily.

"Not lying, merely trying to reassure you," Chantel sighed. "My power shall be returned, Caitlin. Perhaps not today, but it shall be returned. I do not want you to worry."

They watched her now suspiciously, but the obvious truth of her statement was all they detected. For this, Chantel was grateful.

"We should let her rest." Ariel stood, catching the gazes of the other women. "Devlin will be pacing the great hall, eager to see her for himself. We should go now."

Chantel reached up and touched her sister's hand gently. Ariel smiled down at her, clasping her fingers briefly before releasing them and heading for the door.

Caitlin and Arriane followed her after casting worried glances back at Chantel. She smiled at them reassuringly, watching as they left the room.

As the door closed behind them she leaned her head back with a weary sigh. She was not all that eager to see Devlin. The first thing he would do was use his own gifts to detect any weakness in her. It was hell, dealing with those who had been given the gifts of the gods and of Mother Earth. It often took all her energy to close herself from the varied powers turned against her, seeking answers.

If only she could fathom the mysteries of her crystal, then she could learn to block those probing thoughts and shield her knowledge without such effort. Of course, Chantel herself was well aware that the deceit she was practicing was like a fire lit on a dark moonless night. Easily sighted by those who would search for it, unless her powers were used to carefully mask it. It was tiring, she admitted, moving through each day, watching each thought, shielding each piece of knowledge.

*Shall I give you the power to shield these demons, child?* The voice whispered through her mind and Chantel opened her eyes to gaze once again on the luminous form of the Mother as she stood by her bed.

"I reacted too soon," she whispered. "I should have waited to shield Arriane."

*The outcome shall be the same, in any course*, the Mother whispered, her hazy form bending as she reached out to touch the crystal that lay just below Chantel's gown.

Energy flared, a brilliant green, a vibrant amethyst, a rich sapphire, and a glorious ruby red. For an instant Chantel lost her breath as the power once again filled her.

*Use the power to shield and for that reason alone, Mistress*, the Mother told her softly. *Be careful that the others do not know your true course, for in knowing it, they could harm the future to come and the happiness that awaits you all there.*

Chantel nodded, inhaling slowly as she allowed this new knowledge to flow through her. She had fought the mists of the crystal for months, reaching for this power, and now she knew why she had not attained it.

*This deception does not sit well with you and this I understand. But for now, it is imperative that you succeed, even in this, Mistress, if you are to succeed later.*

And there lay the root of Chantel's problem. The deceptions did not sit well with one who had never lied in her life. Her honesty had always been a much-valued fact of her life. Betraying it had bothered her more than she had known.

*Your warrior returns, intent on answers and explanations that relieve his troubled mind*, the Mother told her softly. *Be prepared for this and for the days that are traveling quickly nearer.*

Chantel could only nod. She knew well the days that were quickly approaching and the need to carry this load to its bitter end.

*I shall be near, at all times, my child*, she was promised. *Be at ease now and reassure the heart that comes so quickly to you. Soon, the days of darkness shall begin, but fear not, for I shall be near and shall ease you when you are in need.*

The figure was abruptly gone as the door to the bedroom was opened and Devlin rushed to their bed, the door crashing closed behind him.

She was enveloped in his arms, her head tucked securely against his chest as he held on to her as though he feared for his very sanity.

"I nearly lost my mind, waiting on those women to allow me to enter my own bedroom," he whispered huskily. "I died a thousand deaths, Chantel, when you collapsed in my arms."

He moved back from her, his black eyes going over her face slowly, his mind whispering through the webs of the shield the Mother had given her.

All was well. That thought was given him as he searched for weakness, for any sign that she had been harmed.

"Rein in your powers, my mighty warrior," she teased him softly as his gaze began to clear. "What an exceptional experience, having your soul so close to my own. Perhaps we should try that again later."

"Do not tease me." He moved back so he could gaze once again into her eyes, frowning down at her fiercely. "You should not have cursed Joshua so, Chantel. He would have worked this out before long."

"And he will yet." Chantel nodded, suddenly tired and unwilling to debate the bastard's merits. "He shall just have a little help now."

"What form of help?" Devlin asked her suspiciously.

"Arriane's." Chantel shrugged. "If he wants so desperately to deny her charms that he would bruise her tender heart so easily, then he shall now have help. I did not curse the fool, I merely gave Arriane the help she needs in standing up to him. She loves him too fiercely and her childhood is still a stumbling block to her own strength."

"Her mother?" Devlin asked, aware of the rumors of Shalene's insanity.

"The child Jonar's daughter would have sacrificed to that cult was Arriane herself," Chantel revealed to him. "Her mother was a sadistic, abusive monster who would have used her daughter for her own ends. Father was unaware during his brief affair with her that she carried his child. She hid the knowledge from him, convinced that a child of such a great wizard would be power to her demon goddess and then to herself. This is the only reason the Guardians stepped in. Mother Earth demanded that the child of Galen be saved and they did that the only way they could."

"By killing the mother." Devlin sighed. "Unfortunately, the result ended in many deaths, Chantel. Jonar still searches for any child of the Guardians. When he finds them, they suffer in their deaths."

Chantel nodded, more aware of this than her husband knew.

"Arriane is safe here, just as Antea is," she told him. "But Arriane does not clearly remember those days or her mother. They are still yet fraught with nightmares and confusing contradictions. Joshua's rages are a clear reminder of her mother's, though. I will allow her to be terrified of him no longer."

"So you did what?" Devlin asked her.

Chantel shrugged. "What I should have made Father do long ago. I took those memories and those fears from her. But until they are regained and dealt with, Joshua will have no wife. And only he can break through the shield I placed on them. Whether she loves him is now up to him."

Devlin could only shake his head.

"He will now learn that his actions can come back on him," Chantel continued. "I am aware of the woman he brings here and so too is Arriane. Joshua will have no peace as long as he goes to that woman, no matter the reason he does."

"He may yet end up hitting her deliberately now, Chantel," Devlin warned her.

Chantel only laughed at this.

"Now, he has my leave to try," she assured him. "Arriane is no longer terrified of her own power, as she has been since she was a child. Joshua may find more than his heart burned when she gets through with him. He had best remember why she is called the Mistress of Fire."

"You are a more calculating woman than I anticipated." Devlin smiled at her, his hand reaching up to caress her cheek gently. "Are you certain you are fine? That your own powers will still protect you?"

"I am certain." She turned her head to kiss his hand gently. "But I am tired. If you would lay beside me, perhaps I could sleep for a while before you must prepare to leave."

He was leaving her, her heart was heavy at the thought, but she knew it must be done. The king had called, Jonar was attacking once again, and only a few men were capable of planning the battles against his forces. Devlin was one of those few.

He stood to his feet, quickly removing all but his breeches, and moved to lie beside her. He drew her gently into his arms, once again tucking her head against his chest, close to where she could hear the steady, strong beat of his heart.

This was where she wished she could spend the rest of her days. Sheltered, held safe from all the worries that lingered outside his arms. She knew that was not to be though. So she closed her eyes and breathed in deeply of his scent and allowed sleep to take her. She would rest here for the brief time she was allowed, then she would once again forge ahead to the destiny laid out for her.

# Chapter Nine

## ✎

Arriane watched Joshua prowl the room, keeping her silence, calculating the growing anger she could feel building inside him as he digested her earlier declaration.

"There will be no other women. If you cannot bed your wife, then I will be damned if I will allow you to bed some whore who follows after you like a bitch in heat." She had stated her case calmly, coolly, watching him carefully, fully expecting him to erupt into violence.

Joshua had maintained a very tight leash on his control where she was concerned and she could feel that leash slowly slipping as he paced the room.

Arriane could also feel the force of his power swirling around her, searching for a weakness in her new armor, a way to sift through the secrets she now held carefully hidden. Joshua wasn't a fool, he knew that in sharing some of her precious strength, that Chantel would have also shared some of the secrets she held. Secrets he had been desperate to learn since first entering the castle.

It was no secret that Joshua did not trust them or Galen. He had been quite vocal on the subject several times, especially to her. But she had known nothing, so he had been unable to learn anything. Now he was aware that beneath the shimmering veil of her newfound energy, there were secrets, if only he could tap into them.

Finally, he turned to face her, his amber eyes watching her broodingly, his black brows lowered as he tried to intimidate her by the fierceness of his look.

She merely watched him silently from her seat beside the bed, awaiting the coming storm.

"You are playing a dangerous game, wife," he warned her darkly. "I think that for once you are aware of it."

"No, my husband, it is you who are playing the games and I who am fed up with them." She crossed her arms over her breasts and regarded him in determination. "I will not be humiliated while you set that whore up within my home and go to her, instead of me. The child I will accept, though I would prefer that it were our own child. But your own stubbornness and bullish attitude has taken that from me for the time being. I will tolerate the child, I will not tolerate the whore."

"She is no whore. I pay her nothing for her services," he sneered. "She is also the mother of my child."

"She is a whore to willingly spread her legs for a man who is wed to another," Arriane stated calmly, though her own anger ate at her insides. "I will not debate the matter with you. I have stated my demands. You can accept them or can stand aside while I throw her from the castle myself."

Incredulity marked his face as he looked down at her.

"You could throw her no place." He had the gall to laugh at her. "She would surely make two of you. You could not toss a child should your life depend on it."

Arriane said nothing, she did nothing. A display of lightning aimed directly at his conceited, ignorant head would get her point across, she thought, but what was the use? He would soon learn well enough that she meant what she said.

He watched her, waiting on an eruption, tears, pleading. All those things she had done before Chantel had shared her power with her. There would be no more, Arriane swore.

She ached just as brutally as she had before this morn. Ached until her soul felt filled with the pain and the loss of the dreams she had held, but there would be no more tears. Just as there would be no children, no laughter or joy until the heart frozen within his chest warmed to forgive her for her birth.

Had she known the words to say that would release his heart, she would have surely shouted them to the world. She did not know the words, nor the actions that would release them though. She had tried all she had known before this day. She had tried to tempt him to her bed, to her heart, but he had refused more than once. She swore she would never again throw herself at this man's feet.

"What makes you think you can control my actions, Arriane?" he asked her softly as he moved slowly to stand before her. "You can have Marissa barred from the castle, but there are many other women here. I could share my lust with any number of them, Antea included, should I wish to."

He could tempt his own death in such a way, Arriane thought. But perhaps it was best not to say that to him at this time. Besides, she had a much better threat to give him instead.

"This is true." She nodded, sighing in resignation. "Very well, my lord, you may spend your desires upon the widow, but be warned. I am just a woman and will assume that when you do so, then I too am given leave to do the same with another man."

Arriane almost believed she could hear his heart beat, so silent was the room now. Amazement filled Joshua's face, his eyes, his every pore as he stared at her in disbelief.

"You wouldn't dare." His voice was harsh, savagely controlled as he stared at her.

Arriane felt a shiver race over her spine, as his eyes seemed to focus intently on her, brightening then darkening in fury.

"I would very much dare, husband," she assured him softly. "I have made every attempt to bring you to my bed. The last offer I gave, you refused so cruelly that you have assured yourself of never receiving it again. But be warned, you go to another woman, then too shall I seek my relief with another man."

His mouth opened as though to scream. His eyes widened in fury, then his mouth closed abruptly as though he were so amazed by her proclamation that he could not speak.

"I am aware I cannot keep you from the Widow Denning." Arriane rose from her chair. "I think it only fair that since I know which woman you will be fucking, that when I choose my own lover, I will, of course, inform you of the fact and of his identity."

The coarseness of her words registered on him immediately, Arriane could tell. The white-hot flare of rage that flamed in his eyes was a sight to behold.

"He will die before he has the chance to take you." Joshua's voice was guttural, his face flushing darkly as she stood before him, staring up at him without a hint of fear.

"Then so will the Widow Denning die at the same time? For every lover of mine you harm, such will be the same fate for a lover of yours. Are we agreed?" Arriane was amazed that her voice was so level, so very calm.

She could have never faced him in such a way before. With his face flushed, his fists clenching until the fingers appeared white, the muscles in his jaw working frantically, he would have filled her with an unreasonable dread. Now she merely watched in fascination as he struggled to hold his temper in check and keep his hands from her throat.

"We are agreed in nothing." The words seemed to echo around the room, they were torn so harshly from his throat. "Should you take a lover, madam, be very certain you do so with the utmost secrecy, for the moment I learn of him, he will be dead."

"Then we are agreed." She smiled in approval. "For should you take a lover, then she will meet the same fate. Perhaps it would be best should you keep your appetites in check, then no blood shall be shed from the venture."

As she moved to pass him, to leave the room and the fury she sensed building inside him, his hand shot out, grasping her arm at the elbow and holding her back.

The grip wasn't tight enough to bruise, but the threat was there. Arriane looked up into his tormented gaze and though she felt her heart ache at his pain, she could no longer find within herself a reason to shed the tears he could not.

"You are too small," he whispered through clenched teeth, his face flushing at the force of his emotions. "Should I dare to take you, Arriane, I would harm you."

He was taller than she, Arriane admitted, broader and more muscular, but she saw no reason for him to worry as he did.

"I am a woman, fully grown," she informed him bleakly. "I have shared with you dreams that left me gasping, aching in need and crying out your name for more years than I care to remember. Your empty excuses mean nothing to me now, Joshua, no more than your anger does. Now release me. As you have asked me to sleep elsewhere, I would like to do so. I grow weary from battling with you."

Arriane felt the slight tremor that shook his body as he moved closer to her.

"You do not understand, Arriane," he growled, his voice dark, husky, filling her with the remembrance of the dreams. "I will hurt you."

"Then release me and let me seek sleep, since you have nothing else to offer me, husband." She smiled up at him mockingly. "And I hope you enjoy the cold bed you are making for yourself."

She jerked her arm from his grip, mildly surprised that he let her go easily, and after collecting one of the slow-burning torches from the wall, walked slowly from the room.

As she opened the door, she turned back, a frown on her face as she heard him whisper her name. But he was not watching her, he had moved to stare into the gathering night outside the window instead.

Arriane left the bedroom and moved tiredly along the hallway. Her old room awaited her. The bed where she had dreamed in heated arousal, touching him when their minds met across the distance that separated them.

She wondered if her dreams would haunt her now or if the cold bed Joshua was making for himself would be forced upon her as well.

* * * * *

Joshua heard the closing of the door and closed his eyes tightly, his teeth clenching with the effort it took to not call her back to him.

Every moment he spent with her taxed his dwindling control and it seemed there would be no relief in sight. He had hoped the arrival of Marissa would bring him some relief, but it appeared his little wife would have none of it.

He had thought, had been so certain, he could use his rage to frighten her enough to keep her by his side and yet unresisting when Marissa was installed in the castle.

Joshua cursed Chantel. Whatever the spell she had released had overshadowed Arriane's demure nature and turned her instead into a woman who refused to back down.

Had it really changed her, he wondered, or had Chantel merely allowed his wife to get past her own fears? He had glimpsed the nightmares of his wife's life, the terrors that haunted her, and though it shamed him, he had used them. Used them against her, but only to save her, he thought.

His hands grew damp as he remembered that first night within the castle. How her hands had washed him in the bath, her gentle voice so filled with laughter, soothing the ache in his soul.

He had known this woman was the one who came to him in his dreams and his desire to possess her had nearly driven him mad. Until the moment he had touched her woman's mound. He had seen how small his wife actually was.

Joshua drew in a deep, fortifying breath. She was too small, he agonized. If he took her, he would hurt her more than she could ever forgive him for. Joshua had seen the consequences of such actions years before when a young girl had been killed by the warrior who had taken her.

The warrior had been in his prime, a man fully grown and each muscle of his body in proportion to his great height. He had been given a young woman by a lord he had aided in battle. The girl had been grown, entering her seventeenth year, but fragile and small-boned.

The screams that had come from their bedroom that night could be heard through half the castle. When the warrior had finished, it was only to find that the girl had died beneath his rutting body, her eyes still staring up at him in agony.

Joshua had been one of the first to see her. The pain had shocked his senses, the horror of what the girl had felt those final moments before her life had slipped away caused him to nearly kill the warrior who had caused it.

Now, as Joshua stared out at the star-studded night, the screams of that woman were suddenly all too clear.

Joshua jerked, his head turning to the door as the screams came again. This was no remembrance returning to haunt him, but rather the screams of his wife.

"Arriane…" Agony ripped through Joshua as he ran for the door, throwing it open and rushing down the hall.

As his feet pounded down the hall, he was aware of others rushing from the lower floors, drawn by the screams.

Fear quaked his muscles as he threw open her bedroom door and stared in horror at the sight that met his eyes.

Arriane stood alone in the center of the room, a room awash in blood. The stuff soaked the bed, the tapestries on the walls, even the floor seemed to ooze the thick, sticky liquid in an uneven pentagram, in the middle of which several snakes twisted and hissed attempting to reach the tender skin of the woman who stood just out of reach. And there she stood, her blue eyes nearly black in shock as she stared at the floor.

"Arriane." Joshua rushed to her, jerking her into his arms and pulling her back from the twisting, deadly forms of the snakes that curled about the oddly drawn pentagram.

She was shaking so hard she could barely stand. Her hands gripped at his shirt, clawing as she fought to push herself deeper into his arms. Terrified, half-formed cries were ripped from her throat, muffled now as he pushed her head against his chest.

As Joshua pulled her back toward the door, he backed into the men and their wives who rushed in behind them.

"Get her the hell out of here," Chantel's frantic voice and pushing hands propelled him out of the room. "Get her out, Joshua. Get her to your room and don't leave there."

"You get her there," Joshua shouted as he tried to push her into Chantel's arms. "We have to get rid of those damned things."

"No!" Chantel shook her head furiously. "This is one that I must handle. You must protect Arriane whether you desire it or not."

Joshua sustained not his first shock of the night, as he gazed into the overly bright green of her gaze.

The crystal about her neck pulsed, flaring in brilliant green sparks as her gaze locked with his.

"Get her to your room. Only you can protect her from this, Joshua, not I. I will be there momentarily."

Ariel and Caitlin moved around him, and Joshua felt confusion gather and spread through his consciousness as he glimpsed the violet and sapphire auras that surrounded the two women.

"Go now." She pushed at him once again. "Get her out of here, let her see no more of this, or she may never be able to return from the horror."

"Chantel, what the hell is going on?" Joshua heard Devlin's furious voice as he pulled Arriane through the hallway, back to the room it seemed he would be sharing with her after all.

Joshua didn't hear Chantel's answer, he was too concerned with the sudden droop of his wife's body and the strangled cries he could hear fighting to burst forth from her chest.

"Easy, love, we're almost there," he whispered, swinging her into his arms and rushing into his bedroom. "It's okay, you're safe now."

Arriane only shook her head, her hands still gripping his shoulders, her head buried against his chest as she fought whatever demon the sight of her room had unleashed.

"Arriane, that's enough." Joshua shook her gently as he pulled her back from his chest, fighting to bring her back to sanity. "I have you now, you are safe."

"They will take me." She shook her head, denying his words as hysteria echoed in her voice. "They will take me to her and she will kill me as she always planned."

"Who would dare to harm you, Arriane?" Joshua fought the huskiness of his voice, the fear that rose inside him as she continued to tremble in his arms.

"Hold me, Joshua." Her plea was more than he could bear.

This was not anger, nor the pain of a broken heart. This was horror stripped down to its most basic form. His wife shuddered in his grip, seeking naught from him but the safety and the solace of his embrace.

"I am holding you, love." He tightened his arms further around her, glancing desperately at the door as he awaited an explanation. "Don't be frightened. I will let nothing harm you."

He soothed her, he rocked her, and when that did little good he unleashed his power against her. He couldn't break through the protective veil that surrounded her to probe her weaknesses, but he could surround her with warmth, with safety, and ease the terror filling her in some small way.

It didn't happen instantly, but slowly her limbs relaxed against him, and she was no longer emitting those heart-rending whimpers, which had come from her throat earlier. She lay still in his arms now, her shudders slowly lessening.

"Arriane, tell me what it meant," he whispered when he felt her body slowly relax against him. He kept his voice quiet, soothing, as he questioned her.

"It means I am doomed." She trembled against him once again, her arms tightening around him as his hands gently stroked her back. "She has returned for me and there will be no escape."

The hollow echo of betrayal in her voice tore at him. He opened his senses, not probing, but merely accepting whatever slipped past the protective veil.

Joshua was shocked at what came to him. A remembrance of the scene played out in her bedroom this night. But this time, it was not a woman who held such startling powers, but a child, hollow-eyed and moving slowly, hypnotically toward the twisting, deadly forms of the snakes.

"Who has come for you, love?" He kissed her brow tenderly, fighting his own fury against whoever had set up such a scene for her. "Who would dare to hurt you here?"

"They would dare." Her cry was ripped from her soul and Joshua fought the hysteria he could feel rising inside her once again.

Joshua closed his eyes and fought to wrap her senses in safety once again, terrified that the horror filling her would take her so far away from him that he would never be able to draw her back.

Some dark premonition slid softly around him as he did so. A relaxing of her guard, a brief glimpse of the shadows, the blood, and a death that would destroy them all, slid around him. It wasn't clear, it came to him like a brief glimpse through a thick, darkening mist, but it was there all the same.

Then it was jerked back just as quickly, the veil sliding between her and his senses as she became aware of the shift in the power.

"Easy, love," he whispered when she would have moved away from him. "There is no need to fear me. I swear to you, I will not slip past your guard when you're so weakened. What good is a sparring match when your partner has been weakened by someone other than yourself?"

The vein of self-mocking amusement in his voice must have reached her, for but a brief moment he felt her breath hitch as though in agreement with that ironic laughter.

As Joshua held her close to his body, he gritted his teeth with the pain her warmth caused him. God, he could smell her arousal, even through her fear as she rested against the rigid length of his manhood.

He shifted, attempting to draw her back, then nearly cried out from ecstasy. Ah God, she would not, not again?

He had worn no shirt as he rushed from the room. Arriane's lips were stroking the smooth expanse of it, her tongue darting out to lick and to caress.

"Let me touch you," she pleaded with him, her hands moving over his body. "Give me at least that, Joshua. Please take this nightmare from my mind."

"Oh God, Arriane, I will not survive it." He swallowed tightly, his head falling back as her tongue raked his abdomen.

"I could give you pleasure again," she whispered. "You allowed me that first night."

"I forced you that first night." His cock was raging as he remembered the agony, the pleasure that was so close to mind-numbing pain that he could not bear it.

"I gave to you," she told him, her fingers plucking restlessly at the laces of his breeches, where the stays were taut and difficult to open for the straining length of his shaft. "You did not force anything, I found joy in you."

The ties parted, her hand, soft as silk and warm as fire, lifted his erection free.

He looked down at her, watching her tongue, soft and moist, touch the straining head.

He would not be able to find his control, he thought as his hips strained closer to her touch. God help him, he would take her and he would destroy her as he did so.

He was but a second from jerking her to the bed and burying his shaft between her thighs, when the hard knock came at his door.

Joshua jumped from the bed, closing his breeches quickly before allowing the intruders to enter. Ariel and Caitlin did just that, rather quickly, their eyes locating Arriane huddled on the bed, then flashing to Joshua with a light of knowledge.

"We will stay with her," Ariel announced, her fierce frown and wary tone of voice warning Joshua that this night had yet to come to an end. "Chantel asks that you join her, Devlin and Father in the room."

Joshua sighed wearily, his hand smoothing over Arriane's hair as she now lay silently upon the bed.

"I'll be back soon," he promised her as Ariel touched her shoulder, sitting on the bed as he eased away from her.

Joshua stared at her worriedly as she curled up in the spot he had vacated earlier, as though searching now for his warmth.

"She will be fine until you return, Mystic," Caitlin whispered as he looked over at her, her sea-green eyes dark and concerned. "You need to join Devlin now. There are things you should know, if you are of a mind to help her through this."

He wanted to snap his refusal to do so, but the words wouldn't come. He shook his head abruptly and headed from the room.

Joshua did not like the way events were so carefully orchestrated within this castle, he admitted. It was as though there was darkness surrounding them, drawing the warriors so close to these women that they would become part of their souls, while something seemed to hover over them as well, a threat, a promise to snatch them back just as quickly.

# Chapter Ten

ର

Joshua returned to the bloody room, his senses open now that the shock had worn off, his eyes staring around the room intently as Devlin and Chantel stood back and watched him.

Each warrior within Devlin's small group had a particular talent. Devlin's, of course, was leadership, combined with a gift of disappearing into the shadows of darkness.

Shanar's was strength — of the four he was the only one who possessed no psychic or extrasensory gifts. Derek's was complete mind control — one Joshua wished he possessed. It would make controlling his wife much easier.

For Joshua, his gift was the ability to probe both people and places. His psychic powers were extensive and could of course do many things with training. So far, the gods had been unwilling to provide the training though.

What he felt now chilled him to the bone. Hatred, fury, a need for revenge and a need for blood had fueled the attempt on his wife's life. And it had been an attempt to kill her. Whoever had done it had fully expected her to walk into the pentagram they had drawn on the floor, right into the deadly little nest of vipers awaiting her.

The question was who? As Joshua searched the area, probing into the lingering emotions he sensed there, he was confused by the fact that it lacked identity. He could put no name to the person who had done this.

"Whoever it was knew well her past," Chantel told him softly. "The scene reenacted was the same that the Guardians saved her from as a child. Arriane had been programmed from birth to walk into the pentagram and give her life to the snakes."

Joshua flinched, understanding now the memories he had sensed within his wife's mind.

Why? Joshua whispered to himself. Who but her mother and the cult she had followed would wish such a death on Arriane?

"Why wait until now to make another attempt?" he asked her quietly, his senses still open, searching for an identity, a clue to explain the attack.

"Because soon she will come into her full power, gifted to her by Mother Earth. When we all reach twenty-one, just as the Guardians will gift a child sired by them, so too does Mother Earth gift the children she has chosen to fight the battle they wage."

This explained the alliance Galen had set up between his daughters and the warriors. Though only Joshua himself was of Guardian birth. The others were born of the earth and they were now the defenders of the earth as well.

"They will try again," Joshua told her as the emotions behind the attack sifted through his mind.

"There is a bigger problem attached to this, Joshua," Chantel said softly as her eyes met his.

"Someone knows who she is." He grimaced, remembering himself that Jonar believed his granddaughter was well beyond his reach. It was common knowledge among the forces that fought Jonar that he believed her to be raised by the gods.

"Yes, someone now knows who she is. The question is how they learned and what now will they do with this knowledge? And who could have been strong enough to pass through the power Galen has placed on these upper floors?"

"If Jonar learns she lives, their chances of harming her will be slimmer should he take her. They won't want Jonar to know this information," Devlin suggested as his eyes searched the room as well.

"There is always a rogue in the mix, Devlin." Joshua watched his commander, feeling the dark cloud that suddenly settled over his senses. "I refuse to leave the castle while Arriane is in this danger."

Joshua well understood the surprise he saw reflected in both Devlin's and Chantel's eyes. He had been all for riding with the king when the message had come earlier. His eagerness to leave his wife's side had been loudly voiced.

"I'll send the messenger to Barak instead." Devlin nodded as he spoke of another Guardian warrior who would take the task.

Joshua looked to Chantel, expecting a comment, a protest, something. She was entirely too silent, too willing to let them take the task of decisions where at any other time Joshua felt she would have had a comment at least to throw into the mix.

She stared back at him steadily, those brilliant green eyes lacking neither approval nor censure in the decisions being made around her.

"The cult Arriane's mother was a part of..." Joshua asked her. "Are any known members within this area?"

Chantel glanced away from him, and in that action Joshua had his answer.

"How many?" The violence in his voice was uncontained as he faced her now.

"Joshua." The warning in Devlin's voice was just as dark.

"She knows something," Joshua bit out. "Something she is keeping to herself. Her father is not here, for he knows the answers we would demand. And she hides the truth from us."

"There are members of the original cult which reside in the village." Chantel moved to the pentagram drawn on the floor. "They are being protected. They no longer practice the rituals of the Damned. My father meets with them now, to warn them of this threat. He does not hide from anyone or anything."

She wasn't certain though. Joshua could feel her uncertainty wrapping around him like a cold, penetrating slice of winter.

155

"Why does Galen protect them?" he asked her. "Is he unaware of the threat they represent to his daughter?"

Chantel shook her head, her eyes still on the markings on the floor, the crystal that lay outside her gown throbbing with a vibrant color.

"They are the same who warned him years ago of the daughter Shalene bore. They are the same who came to him, bearing the news that Arriane would be used as a sacrifice to their god. He swore his protection for their actions."

"Well, someone has reneged," Joshua informed her sarcastically. "And that someone is now threatening her life."

Chantel raised her gaze, her eyes staring deeply into Joshua's. He fought to pierce the veil of her power. These women of the earth held more secrets, more knowledge than he could fathom. But there was one thing he was becoming certain of as he watched her.

"You knew this threat was coming." Joshua fought the fear that suddenly assailed him. The fear that the darkness he could feel overtaking the castle would have such far-reaching effects as to nearly destroy them all.

"I knew the threat could come," she corrected him sadly. "I just hoped you could prevent it."

"And how was I to prevent it, Lady, when I had no knowledge of it?"

"You stole the knowledge when you probed her thoughts that night," she told him. "You took what she would have freely given you, while denying the one thing she had waited to give you. Your denial of her will result in your own downfall, Joshua, are you not extremely careful."

The bleak certainty in her voice struck him like a fist to the gut.

"Chantel, what are you not telling us?" Devlin asked her now, quietly, his voice laden with his own suspicions.

"I would tell you anything I know that would aid him in this, Devlin." She shook her head, her shoulders drooping as though in defeat. "There is nothing I know. I know not who has done this, only that those Galen protects would have no reason to. They are here because they cherished her life, not because they would have seen it ended."

There was more, but no way to call her a liar without gaining Devlin's fury. Instead, Joshua raised his gaze to Devlin's. There, Joshua saw the other man's knowledge that his wife was holding back.

"Watch her well, Joshua," Chantel told him sadly, her gaze moving to the darkness beyond the window. "Her life is now in your hands, whether you wish this or not."

She lowered her head and turned and walked slowly from the room. Resignation lay over her like a thick, suffocating blanket. This worried Joshua far more than tears would have.

He looked to Devlin, wondering now what should be done. His wife's life was in danger and he was certain Chantel knew much more than she was telling.

"I'll find out." Determination laced Devlin's voice. "Go to your wife and sleep while you can tonight. Tomorrow we will plan."

\* \* \* \* \*

The castle was silent, the echo of the last bedroom door closing lingering for brief moments before it was silenced as well.

In their bedroom, Shanar watched the worried countenance of his wife, Ariel, and frowned at the soft amethyst glow he could detect within the moon-shaped heart of the crystal. Ariel sat cross-legged on their bed, her sword braced across her leather-clad legs, her hand moving a sharpening stone carefully, slowly over the gleaming steel she was slowly honing to razor-sharpness.

"What's going on, Ariel?" he asked her, wishing he could ease whatever fears made her caress her sword so gently.

She was his warrior woman from the top of her auburn head to the dainty feet that were shod in smooth leather boots. And now she was fighting back in the only manner she knew. Preparation. Ariel was preparing for the danger she could feel stalking the castle.

Shanar had no psychic gifts, but he knew none were needed to be aware of the cloud that was moving steadily around them.

"Can you not tell me, Ariel?" he asked her softly, sitting carefully on the edge of the bed as she continued to stroke the stone over the gleaming edge.

She was silent, her gaze intent on the sword, the stone, and the edge she was bringing to her sword.

"I love you, Ariel." He whispered the words softly, beseechingly. "There is naught you could tell me that would change that."

The love he felt for her had been carried in his heart long before he touched her outside his dreams.

Her breath hitched. The hint of tears, of sadness was conveyed so deeply in the sound that Shanar's heart clenched.

"Tell me, husband," she finally whispered. "Why did you never speak of the fact that I was not a virgin when I came to you?"

Startled, Shanar's eyes widened as her tear-laden gaze met his.

"It did not matter to me, Ariel." He frowned, trying to figure out why this should hurt her now.

"You were mine. I've known it for years. There was no reason to chastise you for something that came before that night."

Ariel glanced away from her husband, her heart breaking, fear filling her as it never had before. She hated doing this, hated telling him the shame she had carried for so very long, the terror that filled her each time she thought of him leaving her now.

"A man would want to know who his wife's lover had been," she finally whispered, her gaze centering on the sword, the gleaming edge reassuring her that she was protected here if nothing else.

"Some might." She sensed his nod. "I will not say I would not like to kill the bastard for having touched you first, but were it your choice that he did so, then I would not. What is the meaning of this, Ariel? Why should this concern us now?"

"And the scars on my back?" She ignored his demand for answers, but questioned instead. "Did you not wonder about the scars on my back?"

There was silence, thick and heavy and when her eyes finally rose to meet his it was to confront the abject misery of his cloudy gaze.

"You were raped." It wasn't a question, but a certainty as he watched her.

Ariel swallowed tightly, tears fighting for escape as she held his gaze.

"If they know Arriane's secrets, then they may know mine as well," she whispered. "I would not have you harmed by learning them from another."

"It doesn't matter." He shook his head, but Ariel feared that the day would come when it would matter.

"I sold myself, Shanar," she told him bitterly, her rage and her humiliation rising to nearly strangle her. "Does this change your perception of me?"

He shook his head violently.

"You were raped," he repeated, his certainty overriding anything else she would say.

"I did not know who he was at first," she continued. "My mother lay dying, and he swore he could save her. I was terrified of her leaving me. I was a very fearful child, jumping always at shadows, seeing demons where there were none."

Ariel's gaze went to the shadows of the room and she felt the terror of that night as surely as if it had just finished.

"Don't do this to yourself, Ariel," Shanar pleaded with her. "It matters not to me, you are my wife, and I do not love you less."

"It was Jonar." There was no sense in delaying the truth, she thought. "I was twelve when I sold myself to him, and when he did not save my mother, I tried to escape him. When he caught me, he had me beaten until he thought he had taken the life from me. He left me lying in my own blood and waste, laughing at my foolishness for thinking he would save a whore such as my mother or myself."

It was the truth, such as truths went. What excuse could it be that it had been Jonar's hand that had dealt the deadly blow to her mother? That in her terror, her shock, she had believed that for the price of her virginity he would make certain her mother received the help she needed.

"Virginity taken by force comes with no power," she whispered the words he had sneered down at her. "But innocence given freely comes with more than one could ever know. As he took me, he laughed at me and told me my mother would die and that I would die with her. That is how Father found me, hours after Jonar left. Spread naked upon my mother's bed, slowly dying. He healed me and brought me here. But he warned me that the power Jonar took from me could one day be used against me."

When she finished, she refused to look in her husband's face, refused to acknowledge the tears that ran in silent rivulets down her face.

"Chantel, Caitlin, and Arriane bring that power to their husbands. The power of Mother Earth given to us at our birth, secured by our innocence and given to the one who takes it. She never stipulated whether it should be by choice or by force. Jonar stole that power which was yours to possess and mine to give you." She finished, fearing this blow would sever the tender feelings she knew he had for her.

Long moments passed and still he had not spoken. Ariel raised her eyes, her breath catching at what she saw in his face. His eyes swirled with thunderclouds, dark gray emotions that pierced her heart. His large, rawboned face was expressive with his need for her and his unconditional love. Tears shimmered in his eyes, and his expression was drawn into lines of grief and pain.

Bemusement surged through her. He should hate her. Should be raging in fury rather than staring at her as though she held all that he was in the palm of her hand.

"One day, I will have my sword at his throat, and I shall return your power to you with his death." A single tear ran down the hard, strong-boned face she cherished so deeply. "My hatred for him only grows now, just as my love for you deepens, Ariel. You were a child, unaware of your gifts or the evil of the man you were dealing with. The fault does not belong on your fragile shoulders, my love."

Ariel could only watch in shock as he lifted the sword from her hands, laying it gently on the long padded bench at the end of the bed.

"You should hate me," she cried when he returned to enfold her in his arms. "The gifts I held would have given you powers you do not have, a strength tenfold what you possess now."

"How could I ever hate such courage?" He pulled her against his body, his lips touching her hair, her cheeks, and her brow. "You are my life, Ariel. I ache and I hate him for what was done to you. But I do not lay the blame at your delicate feet."

Her delicate feet? Ariel was aware that she had feet larger than any of her sisters or any other woman she knew. She was tall, long-limbed and had feet that carried her body comfortably. How could he see anything delicate in her, anywhere?

"I am not delicate." She felt in all fairness she should point this out.

"I top you easily by a good foot and am much broader, so I say you are indeed delicate in every manner," he assured her softly. "And you are my wife, Ariel. You own my heart and you share my soul. What in your right mind makes you think I could ever blame you for what he did to you?"

"Joshua hates Arriane for her birth," she whispered. "How much more should you hate me?"

This had terrified her. That the husband whose gentleness healed her soul could come to hate her as her sister's husband hated.

"But Joshua has always been a fool," he scoffed, setting her back so he could look deeply into her eyes. "I will kill Jonar one day, for what he did to you alone. But never could I blame you. Do you understand this, wife?"

Joy exploded in her heart as she saw the truth in his eyes.

"I do understand, husband," she whispered as a smile fought through her tears. "And I love you. Until there is no tomorrow, I will love you."

His lips met hers, sealing the vow as his arms wrapped around her, and his big body bore her steadily to the pillows of the bed.

She was in his arms, the pain of her past was wiped away, and she prayed that only joy would follow them through the rest of their days. But she feared, in some distant part of her, that it was not destined to be.

As Shanar rose over her, his gaze holding hers, she relaxed beneath him, no longer fearing the great strength she knew he possessed. From the first moment she had laid eyes on the large Viking, she had felt sheltered, protected by him. She should have feared him for his size alone. Instead, she desired him, as she had no other man.

"Now, I think perhaps we have other matters to discuss." His voice became graveled with his passion as he lowered his head to touch her lips with his own.

"Such as?" Ariel felt her breathing escalate. Suddenly, there wasn't enough air to draw into her body. Her heart raced, the blood thundering through her veins.

"Such as how beautiful and delicate my new bride is," he whispered against her lips as his darkening gaze stared into her. "She appears to believe otherwise."

"Oh." It was more a gasp than a comment of any sort. "She is most stubborn at times. You may have to convince her."

Ariel loved the way her lips moved against his as she spoke. Unable to escape the lure of his sexuality, she allowed her lips to lick at his, loving the warm male taste of him.

"Convince her?" He drew back, ignoring her sudden pout at losing the access to those firmly shaped lips that brought her such pleasure. "I can indeed convince her. I have been known to be quite stubborn myself."

His hands went to the drawstring of her breeches before his gaze came back to hers questioningly. "Do you mind? You must of course be dressed properly for such serious discussion."

"Dressed?" She arched a brow in mock seriousness.

A frown of concentration shaped his brow. "Undressed perhaps?"

Ariel stilled her laughter at his comic games. He filled her soul with such joy that she wondered how she had ever survived without him.

"I can see where this would be necessary." She nodded with solemn thoughtfulness. "Proceed then with your plan."

Ariel fought to keep her breathing measured as he loosened her pants, then pulled them from her legs. She wore nothing beneath, and her breath caught as his gaze went to the juncture of her thighs with heated longing.

"Dear God, you make me weak with longing when I see how wet and hot you get for me." His fingers glanced over the curls between her thighs.

Ariel stilled her rising moan and fought any embarrassment that her husband should see her so slick and wet for his touch. She allowed her thighs to open further and watched as his cheeks flushed, his tawny gold lashes lowering over his eyes as sensuality washed over his expression.

"A feast to please any warrior," he growled, his head lowering to the heat he gazed at with such longing.

Ariel's hands went to his hair, her fingers locking in the long strands as his tongue took a lazy swipe through the slit of her cunt. It was decadent, watching him between her splayed thighs as he licked at her most private flesh. But the pleasure he gained from glancing up and seeing her watch him, transformed his expression and filled her heart with joy. He loved her. He truly, completely loved her.

"Such a precious treasure here," he sighed, his voice rough and vibrating with his passions as his fingers smoothed over her cunt once again. "I could drown in your sweetness and die a happy man."

Her hips bucked as his head lowered again, those sensually firm lips covering her clit as his mouth suckled at her for long moments. His tongue joined in the play, rasping over the swollen bud and making her insane with the heat building in her pussy.

A second before she would have exploded in ecstasy, his head raised, his lips glistening with her juices as his tongue flicked against them sensually. Ariel whimpered, her hips shifting against the bed, rising to him in need.

"Not yet," he whispered.

She watched as he loosened his breeches and shed them quickly. His cock, so thick and hard, weighed heavily between his thighs, the dark head flared wide, perfect for driving her insane as he pushed inside her body.

He came back to her then, lifting her until she sat up. His hands were gentle, his expression savage as he pulled the rough shirt from her body. He held her still when she would have lain back, pushed back her arms when she would have embraced him.

"Like this." He helped her to lean back, showing her how he wanted her hands, to force her body to arch forward. "Nice," he whispered, his slumberous gaze locking on her breasts.

Ariel had never been overly proud of her breasts. They weren't as ripe and firm as her sisters were. She was a warrior. They had been bound for most of her life in an attempt to be certain they did not hinder her fighting abilities. But Shanar seemed not at all displeased.

A growling sound of hunger issued from his throat as he leaned forward, his tongue curling around a hard, elongated nipple. Ariel shuddered as she fought to keep her eyes open, to watch as he licked and nibbled at her nipple, his large hand cupping the under-curve of her breast, lifting the swollen mound more fully to his lips.

"You are beautiful and delicate here as well," he murmured against her, his lips caressing her flesh with sensual fire. "Beautiful and giving, and as delicate as the finest silk."

"Shanar." She didn't know how much longer she could hold onto her own control. He was shredding it bit by bit with each caress.

"You are fragile in my hands. See how pretty and how delicate you are." He glanced down and Ariel followed his gaze. She fought for breath as she saw his fingers, so long and broad, cupping the weight of her breast. His thumb smoothed over the hard, reddened peak, plumping it further.

"Shanar, you are killing me." She fought for breath as he watched her, his head moving in again so his tongue could lash the tip with such moist heat that she nearly exploded with the pleasure.

"I love your body, Ariel." Desire and adoration filled his voice. "Every part of you, all that makes you, I love."

And she could believe no less. His eyes were stormy with the emotion, his expression so filled with it that she could do no more than stare at him in awe. She would have spoken, would have vowed her love to him again, had his hand not moved between her thighs, had his fingers not rasped over her straining clit.

"Oh God." Her hips rose to meet his hand as her arms collapsed and her body fell back to the bed. "Shanar, I need you now."

"Then take what you need, little warrior." A long, broad finger slid into the drenched channel of her gripping cunt. "Ride me, Ariel. Show me your need."

He moved back from her then, lying down as she rose quickly above him. She lifted her leg over his thighs, watching as his hand gripped the base of his cock, holding it steady as she lowered herself to it.

She bit her lip at the first slight penetration of her pussy. A strangled groan escaped her throat as the head pressed tightly inside her. His hands rose to her breasts, his fingers plucking at her nipples as he watched her with such naked arousal and emotion that her pussy spasmed. The hard, almost brutal contraction nearly took her breath.

Shanar bared his teeth, grimacing as she tightened further around him. Then his hands gripped her hips, his thighs bunching as he held her steady and pushed fully inside her. It wasn't a hard, sudden thrust, rather a smooth, tight glide that had her fighting to hold on to consciousness as his erection stretched her pussy to its limits.

When he was seated in her to the hilt, he drew her to him, lifting to meet her lips in a kiss so profound she could only whisper his name in return.

"Now, my love," he whispered as he lay back. "Ride me now, Ariel. However you need it, I am here."

And he was there. A thick, heavy weight lodged so deep and hard inside her cunt, that she wondered if he had pierced her soul as well. An inferno of sensation was pounding inside her body, beating at her womb, clenching her pussy. She felt flayed by the tempestuous sensations rocking through her.

She didn't need gentleness this night, she didn't want slow strokes or lazy thrusts. She needed him fast and hard, tearing into her body, ripping away the horrors of the past with the love he gave her. And she took from him what she knew they both needed.

Her hips rose and fell, feeling his cock retreat, then stretching her sensitive muscles again as she rode him furiously. His head tossed on the mattress, his cries joining hers as they both fought their release. It must last to the final brutal second, she thought hazily. Until she could endure no more, until he lost all control with her.

She braced her hands on his powerful chest, feeling the flex of muscles, the hard beat of his heart. Her hips moved powerfully, her thighs gripping his, her cunt stroking, caressing, sliding up and down the thick stalk of his cock with hard, slick strokes.

They were both crying out now. Perspiration coated their flesh, heated moans, harsh cries filling the air.

"Now!" His hands tightened on her hips then, his hips suddenly moving beneath her with a force she couldn't grasp. Her eyes widened at the power behind it, her breath catching in her throat, a strangled scream escaping her as her world exploded around her. A rainbow hue of stars blazed before her eyes as she felt her body explode, felt his cock swell, then the hard blast of his semen shooting deep inside her pussy.

Her head shook, she shuddered, rocking with the shock of her orgasm as it powered through her. Sensation atop more sensation. Flames erupted in her cunt, spread to her womb, then caught in an inferno within her very veins as her orgasm overtook her.

Shanar was there to catch her. To hold her trembling body, to soothe the hard, racking shudders that shook her. He even wiped the tears from her cheeks and held her as she sobbed.

"I love you," she cried against his chest, holding tight to him, suddenly terrified to let him go. "I love you so desperately, I would die without you now."

"Never." He rocked her, rolling over until he could tuck her against his side, enclose her within his arms in a way that warmed her despite the chill of fear suddenly washing over her. "You will never be without me, Ariel. I will be with you always, if only in your heart."

"Forever my heart. Forever my soul," she sobbed. "Forever, Shanar, no matter what."

# Chapter Eleven

ॐ

Devlin watched his wife, her silence, as she stood before the open window of their bedroom and stared out into the darkness of the night. Her shoulders were held stiffly erect, as though the burden she carried on them would shift and break her should she move them in the wrong manner.

The silence that wrapped around her frightened some inner part of him, he admitted. He had finally found the woman of his dreams. Could he survive should Jonar be able to snatch her from him?

Trouble was brewing, he knew it, and he knew that she was aware of it. The bitch Antea seemed to be just around every corner, her deceitful eyes watching, waiting for the slightest excuse to bring pain to her sister.

Now, there was also some unseen threat attempting the life of Arriane. Devlin feared this threat would encompass his wife and her other sisters as well.

"Chantel, it is time we discuss this," he told her as he poured himself a cup of wine. "I would know what the hell is going on here."

There was no mistaking the demand in his voice, and Devlin nearly flinched himself at his harsh tone. But the time had come for answers and he would have them now so he could prepare a defense for the women he now protected.

He watched as his wife's head lowered, and she took a deep breath. He felt as though she were preparing herself for a trial.

Devlin sighed roughly, running his hands through his hair as he fought the frustration rising inside him.

"I do not know how to answer you," she whispered on a sigh, turning finally to meet his gaze. "There are things that even I, who carries the majority of the Mother's powers, cannot know or control. I do not know who is threatening us. I do not know any longer what shall come next."

And she was well used to being able to anticipate any problem, Devlin thought, reading the frustration and the fear in her eyes.

"Chantel, let me send Antea away," he pleaded with her once again. "I cannot help but feel that she lies at the bottom of this."

"Antea has no knowledge of Arriane or her past." She shook her head, her face tightening in determination. "I promised her protection, and there is no place safer for her than here at this castle."

Stubbornness was not always a good quality in a wife, Devlin reflected as he saw the steely core of that quality within her gaze now. She refused to back down on her stand to protect Antea and Devlin could not help but believe the protection of the woman would bring them anything but grief.

"Why do I sense you know more about this than you are saying, Chantel?" he asked her, his eyes narrowing. "Would you hide from me the answers that I need?"

Shock glazed her eyes and paled her face.

"I would never lie to you, nor hide from you answers you would need to bring this to a conclusion, Devlin." She shook her head, her gaze never leaving his. "I have my suspicions and my fears. But they have no place in a discussion until I know more. I will not accuse anyone unjustly, nor use my fears to accuse them."

Perhaps that was all it was, Devlin thought, sensing the truth that surrounded her like a shield. But there was something there in what she said that bothered him. If only he could figure out what it was.

He sighed roughly as he looked around their bedroom, seeing the scattering of his own belongings that mingled with hers. He had found a comfort here that he had never believed he would find elsewhere. The thought of having it taken away from him or threatened in any manner, was more than he could bear.

"What about the cult members?" he asked her. "The ones Galen protects. Tell me about them."

She sighed roughly, moving to the bed and sitting on its side wearily.

"They are no longer part of the Damned." She shook her head. "They would not have done this. They came to Galen when Arriane was first born and stayed with the cult to protect her and keep him informed of a time when he could take her. It was they who told him of Shalene's slow teachings to her, to program her to give her life to the snakes."

"And how can you be certain one of them hasn't decided he misses his old friends?" Devlin asked her.

Chantel's eyes hardened at the thought.

"Should that happen, there will not be a man, woman or child that will escape my father's wrath." The tone of her voice suggested that she would be at her father's side to aid him in his quest for vengeance.

"I need to know the names of the families who were in the cult, Chantel," he told her softly. "I want to at least be assured for myself that I know who and what I am dealing with."

Chantel nodded.

"I have a better idea," she suggested. "Tomorrow, you and I will ride to the village and talk to them ourselves. Then you can ascertain whether or not they are a threat."

Devlin nodded abruptly. That of course would be a preferred action, just one he had yet to find a way to suggest to his already saddened wife.

"I want to put a guard on Antea," he suggested as well, his voice hardening in preparation of her refusal. "I can't discount her obvious jealousy of you, Chantel. I want her watched."

Chantel sighed roughly, closing her eyes as a look of weariness flashed over her face.

"Very well." She finally nodded her approval. "But I do not want her to know that she is under suspicion. You must promise to try to prevent that from happening, Devlin."

Her gaze rose to him, the soft green depths imploring as she watched him. Why, he wondered, did she care so much for a sister who so obviously hated her?

"I promise I will do everything I can to keep that knowledge from her, Chantel." He touched her cheek gently. "But I must be assured of your safety. You understand this, do you not?"

His heart clenched as he saw the shadows in her eyes. Was this something she was hiding or merely her own worry and fears? Devlin allowed himself to believe it was the latter. Surely his wife would care enough about her own safety to give him all he needed to protect her?

\* \* \* \* \*

Chantel sat silently before the Mother, the shadows of the cavern beneath the castle pressing around her, nearly smothering her in the threat she felt from them.

"What is happening?" she asked the thinly illuminated figure that stood before her, the gentle face of the Mother staring back at her in sadness. "So quickly events are being taken from my control. How can I do this if I cannot control it?"

*My child, I never said you would be in control*, the Mother whispered, her voice wrapping around her like a veil of silk. *It has begun, just as you wished. It is no longer in your control, to either stop or move forward.*

Chantel's breath halted in her throat, a cry of pain squeezed back until she felt her heart would burst from the agony.

"How can I protect them then?" She fought to stem the fear growing within her.

172

*You cannot, Chantel. There is no longer any protection afforded them. The destiny set into motion has stripped the need for it from them.*

"No." Chantel shook her head, her arms clasping across her chest as she fought the unbearable agony of her choice. "It was not to be this way."

*It is the way it shall be,* the Mother assured her, her voice still wise and infinitely gentle. *It will proceed as I told you, but I can no longer stop the forces that work against my daughters. The time for that has now past. A decision you chose, my child.*

A tear slipped from Chantel's cheek as she acknowledged the truth of the Mother's statement. She had set this course in motion, and now had none to blame but herself for the torments that would rise to haunt her sisters.

"I am frightened." Chantel whispered the words, fighting to be strong, growing angry with herself that she had weakened this far.

*Of course you are frightened, my daughter.* The Mother's voice was filled now with love and a torment all her own. *The choice you made was a difficult one, and yet the course you chose was the wisest. You must pay the cost now for the life you shall later lead.*

"Suddenly I am so frightened it will never be," Chantel confessed, staring up at the figure in abject apology. "My doubts and my fears curl inside my heart and strike with a blow as painful as the vipers would have for Arriane last night."

The lightened form moved closer, the warm mists of the Mother's spirit reaching out to caress the child she had chosen to wield her greatest power.

*Have I ever lied to you, Chantel?* she asked her gently, her voice softly chiding.

"Never, Mother." Chantel shook her head, knowing above all things, the spirit of Mother Earth had been nothing but honest.

*Then would I lie and say that your life shall be greater for your sacrifice now, only to allow it to be snatched from your grasp later?*

*The future shall be in your hands after this service you give unto the earth, Chantel. Whether you accept the destiny then, or turn your back on it, is up to you. But I tell you now, when the time comes, I shall come to you once again, and I shall bring you all you need to vanquish the demons of the past and fulfill the destiny I promised you.*

Chantel swallowed tightly, fighting the tears that still spilled slowly from her eyes, fighting the fears that wormed their way into her soul no matter how hard she fought them.

"I am sorry. I should never doubt you," she whispered tearfully.

*You would not be human did you not doubt the future that could arise from the events soon to come. You would not be the daughter I have waited and watched for all these centuries did you not question your fate at least once or twice,* the Mother assured her.

"Their pain, it pricks at my conscience. The thought of what they shall soon face, and I will be unable to lead them through it, it tears at my heart," Chantel admitted.

*No amount of guidance can prepare them. No words can alter this course, nor set their minds at ease, my child,* the Mother told her softly. *All you can do is that which you know you must. The rest is left up to fate and the cruel injustices of man. You waste your energy in attempting to save what cannot be saved at this time.*

Chantel felt her soul bleed as the Mother whispered these words. She had not anticipated this, to be faced with her sisters' pain, their torments in this way. She had fought to preserve their futures and to assure them of more than a bleak existence of growing old while their lovers stayed young and fit.

It was a choice she alone had made so many years ago. A choice to save the children who would have died, to bring to them a choice they could have never had otherwise. She wondered if they would forgive her for it if they knew the truth.

*You torment yourself with questions that do not apply, Daughter.* The Mother wavered before her, her voice stern as she looked down at Chantel. *These questions you ask yourself do no more than chip away at an already aching heart. You have preserved their futures,*

*as well as your own. In the end, they shall all be thankful for the*
*choices you have made.*

The shimmering image slowly faded from view as her parting words echoed around Chantel. She could do nothing now but lower her head, her tears whispering achingly over her cheeks and dropping heedlessly to the hands that were wrapped around the faint glow of the crystal she held.

She could feel their pain, their fears. For Ariel, Chantel could feel the sharp bite of her humiliation as she told Shanar of her past. For Arriane, Chantel could feel the rage, the horror that was barely contained beneath the shield protecting her emotions. And Caitlin, God help her, Chantel thought, Caitlin had no knowledge to prepare herself for this. At least Ariel and Arriane were forewarned in small ways. Caitlin existed but within a dream, a dream her fair Prince would one day rue to the very depths of his spirit. What pain. What betrayal. And it had fallen from the hand of one they trusted above all others.

The pain her sisters faced now, and would face in the future, lay upon her shoulders and within her own heart. She wondered if she had made the same choices so many years ago had she known the pain those sisters would face.

"Chantel?" Her father's voice had her turning swiftly, staring into the darkness of the passageway that led back to the castle.

When he walked into view, she suppressed her tears and could only smile sadly at the concern in his face.

"You should be resting," he told her as he entered the cavern. "It's been an eventful day for you."

"There will be time to rest later," she reassured him. "There is much that I need to do now."

Galen sighed wearily, moving further into the room, the candles along the wall flaring to life as he passed by them.

In his eyes, Chantel saw the knowledge and the sadness that knowledge brought him.

"You heard," she whispered. It wasn't a question. She knew by the look on his face that he now knew.

Galen's sigh whispered through the room.

"I do not like this choice you've made." He sat down beside her, his arm moving to her shoulders to pull her close to his side. "But I will do all I can to aid you in achieving what you seek."

Chantel could hear the tears in his voice, feel the aching sorrow that moved through his body.

"One day, perhaps we shall look back on these days with fondness. The beginning of our journeys?" Chantel could not see that day coming, but she wanted only to see her father happy once again.

"Perhaps, child." She could tell by his voice that he doubted that day would ever come.

"You know what I would ask of you, Father?" she whispered painfully, feeling her heart break at the knowledge of what must come.

"I know. I think I've known since she walked through those doors and I saw the grief that crossed your face." Chantel could hear his tears, and her heart shattered.

"It is for the best, for now." She wondered how much longer it would take for her to convince herself of this. "Promise me, when it comes to pass, that you will wipe my memory from his mind. He will not fight, he will not go on with such pain inside his soul."

Galen's head lowered and she watched, as a single tear passed over his cheek.

"I promise, daughter. I will do what I must."

# Chapter Twelve

∞

Antea lay over her lover, her heartbeat slowly returning to its normal rhythm, her breathing becoming less harsh as she relaxed against his big, muscular body.

He wasn't Devlin, but he was strong and warm, and his sexual experience greater than that of her own. She had not expected to find such pleasure in his arms, a big man who she thought knew only warring. Who would have known that he could also be the gentle lover of hours past?

She felt his hands, still tangled in her hair as he softly caressed the long strands that flowed around them.

His lips touched her forehead gently, as he seemed to nestle her closer against his body, relaxing with her, in no hurry to rush from the hidden room after attaining his climax.

It was a rare opportunity for Antea, to relax and enjoy the warmth of a man's body after the sexual appetite had been appeased. It was something she had greatly needed to enjoy many times, but her lovers had never been wont to linger long.

This warrior, he called himself Aaron, was everything she had craved in a man since her first lesson in the sexual arts.

"Your body feels good against mine," he whispered against her hair as his hands moved to the contours of her back.

She wanted to arch like a cat as she felt the rough, calloused hands moving slowly over her skin. His fingers touched her, pressing gently where it felt best, smoothing lightly over skin more sensitive.

She kissed his broad chest, with its light scattering of hair, and closed her eyes in contentment.

"What was the commotion earlier, upstairs?" His voice was drowsy, as though on the edge of sleep as those gentle hands moved slowly up her back. Her cunt pulsed in renewed desire, a lazy, wanton sensation that had her rubbing herself against him to prolong the feeling.

"Mm, someone was wont to play tricks on the witch Arriane." She felt at ease with this man, held safely within his arms.

Her hand smoothed over his abdomen, her fingers playing softly as she felt the muscles there clench in pleasure.

"I could understand why they would want to," he grunted as he turned with her in his arms, tucking her in close to his body as his warmth wrapped around her.

Antea giggled at his tone of voice. It appeared there was another who held no great love for the sisters of Chantel. Fortunately he did not hold it against her, she thought.

"They nearly succeeded." She smiled, remembering the glazed horror she had glimpsed on Arriane's face as Joshua led her down the hall. "The snakes would have been effective had she done as I hear she was once programmed to do."

"Programmed? How?" He stroked her hips, the sparse contours of her buttocks.

"Ahh, you have not yet heard who she is?" Antea rose up, her gaze going to his, catching the confusion in his face as he watched her.

"She is Lady Chantel's sister." Oh, she loved that tone of disgust she heard in his voice. Finally a man who was not besotted with her sister.

"She is much more than that, though they are careful to keep her identity hidden," she informed him as she lay back against him.

"So who else could she be?" There was the suggestion in his voice that she could be no one important.

Antea smiled against his chest, pleased to be able to give her lover a piece of information that evidently Galen thought he could keep hidden forever.

"The bitch is Jonar's granddaughter. The one it is said he believes the gods stole from him at the death of his daughter. Galen has raised her since the night the gods took her from Jonar's fortress. They say her mother controlled her mind to the extent that she should have walked eagerly into the nest of vipers awaiting her."

Antea felt the surprised jerk of his body and ran her hand caressingly down the flat plane of his stomach.

"How did you learn this?" he asked her softly.

Antea shrugged. "It is common knowledge, though never spoken about where Galen or his daughters can hear the news. It is said that the members of the Damned who aided Galen now live within the village. What Galen is unaware of is that they still practice their faith to an extent. It would not surprise me were they not somehow behind the attack on her."

"But no one can enter the upper floors, except with Galen's permission," Aaron reminded her.

Antea shrugged. She was not so certain of that anymore.

"I heard something outside my own window when darkness first fell," she admitted to him. "I think the intruder perhaps came in from a way other than within the castle."

She felt the soft expulsion of air, a surprised breath as his grip tightened on her.

"They did not try to come in on you?" he asked her, concern marking his tone.

"No." Antea shook her head. "But I have said nothing about this for a reason. I know you can access the battlements from outside the castle. Could you not access any room within the castle from there as well?"

Aaron was quiet for long moments.

"It could be done," he answered her carefully.

She rose back up to stare into his face, pleasure radiating through her body.

"Then perhaps you could come to my room? Sleep with me within my bed?" She was aware she was frankly pleading, but cared little how it would appear.

Aaron was gentler, more caring with her than any lover she had ever known. His virility was amazing, as was his stamina.

"That could work," he seemed to speak cautiously. Likely he wanted to be certain Galen could not learn of him doing it, Antea thought. "I will have to check it out. Perhaps tomorrow night, I could meet you there."

Antea felt a glow of contentment suffuse her body. She had never awakened with a lover at her side or been held close and warm through the night. How strange such an experience would be.

"We must leave here soon." His voice was regretful as his hands began roaming her body more demandingly, turning her as he rose over her, his smile flashing in the darkness. "Can you take me again so soon?"

Antea's legs opened for the strong thighs that pushed between them, her breathing became ragged as her blood once again began to race quickly through her body. Oh yes, she thought as his lips took hers in a kiss that sealed her affection for him. She could definitely take him again this night.

\* \* \* \* \*

Dawn had barely arrived when Aaron slipped silently into the small hut that sat just outside the forest. The door was closed softly, his gaze going to the single figure that slept on the rickety cot there.

He paced over to the bed and gave the fragile wooden frame a vicious kick, sending the man sleeping there to the floor.

"Vipers take you," he cursed as the soldier came to his feet, his large body preparing for battle until he saw the man who stood before him. "Why the hell did you awake me so?" he snapped instead as he hitched his dirty breeches about his hips and stalked to a basin of water.

"You were seen," Aaron bit out, hooking a chair from beneath the small table and straddling it as he watched the man. "Don't let it happen again."

"Seen?" Manden turned back in surprise, the cloth he would have used to wash his face now hanging slack in his fingers. "How was I seen?"

"Because you made too much damned noise," Aaron bit out. "One of the inhabitants of the second floor heard you scaling the wall. Why the hell were you down that low?"

Manden shrugged. "It was dark. I misjudged my direction. It will not happen again."

"Of course it won't." Aaron wanted to slap the man. "You won't get another chance to get caught. Arriane has been moved permanently to her husband's room. He no longer wishes to get rid of her."

Manden was silent now, then snorted in disgust.

"Rumor was he hated her," he remarked.

"Rumors are becoming surprisingly unreliable. I believe the last rumor was that none but Galen and his daughters knew of Arriane's heritage. It seems everyone knows now."

Manden moved slowly to the chair left beneath the table. He pulled it out then sat down thoughtfully.

"Marissa won't like that," he growled. "She wanted the woman dead before she arrives at the castle."

"Then you can make your excuses." Aaron shrugged, caring little what the whore Widow Denning wanted. He had his own job to complete, but had hoped that the death of Arriane would aid it.

"So what do we do now?" Manden scratched his chin in confusion as he watched Aaron.

Aaron wondered how he had gotten stuck with such an oaf. Manden followed orders, usually to the letter until now, but he had little initiative.

"I'm working on it." He leaned back in his chair with a lazy smile. "The Lady Antea seems more than willing to spill her secrets when well-satisfied and cuddling in comfort within my arms. I should have another plan soon."

Aaron watched as Manden's eyes widened in surprise at this news.

"I thought she gave little notice to the men of the castle. Last I heard it had something to do with the stables." He chuckled. For months, Antea's secret nickname had been the Castle Mare, she was caught fucking so often within the stables.

"I found her a bed to enjoy," Aaron informed him with a broad smile. "Amazing what a little comfort will do to warm a woman to a man."

"That little whore would warm to a dog if his cock was big enough," Manden growled in disgust. "Too bad you couldn't get beneath the Lady Chantel's skirts, as you first planned to. It would have made this venture move more quickly."

Aaron felt a flash of anger at his defeat there. Antea was a poor comparison to the Lady Chantel, but she would be much easier to use. That was more important than the lust he held for her sister.

"Be prepared." Aaron stood as he glanced out the window and saw the light slowly rising outside it. "I must go now. I will let you know what our further plans are."

"And I guess I will inform the Lady Denning that she must now face the witch, Arriane." Manden sighed, obviously not looking forward to facing the volatile widow. "She should arrive at the castle soon."

"Only to be escorted to a house in the village." Aaron laughed, remembering the talk he had heard that evening within the castle. "Arriane has put her foot down and the Mystic seems unwilling to knock her on her ass for it. Marissa will not be permitted to take up residence there after all."

"And I guess you expect me to inform her of this?" Manden was angry now, not relishing the prospect of the woman's fury.

"Why tell her?" Aaron laughed. "Let her find out on her own from her lover. It will serve her right for being so certain of his desires for her."

"This is going to get ugly, Aaron." Manden shook his head as he rose to his feet as well. "Very ugly, before it's finished."

"And we will be sitting fat and rich in some seaside port laughing at the lot of them," Aaron assured him, thankful that he had those plans worked out at least. "The Damned shall rise again, Manden, we will see to it."

Aaron left the hut, a sense of contentment filling him now. All he had to do was complete the assignment he had been given and he would receive enough gold to build a dozen shrines to the Viper Queen he worshipped. That would assure him of her favor and the riches he knew she would provide him afterward.

* * * * *

Several days later Chantel stood beside Arriane as the loaded coach pulled into the gates of the castle. The seal on its side proclaimed the royal lineage encased within it, the guards riding with it proclaimed the money and power of its owner.

As the team of horses that drew the dust-coated coach pulled to a stop, their driver jumped to the ground and moved quickly to open the door.

Chantel heard Arriane's gasp as the woman exited. She stood tall, aristocratic, her dark brown eyes looking over the immaculate courtyard with smug satisfaction.

When she spied Chantel and Arriane standing at the doors of the great hall, Chantel watched as malicious spite joined the satisfaction in the sneer at her mouth.

Marissa Denning was a beautiful woman, there was no doubt about this. She was stately, long-limbed and slender, her long brown hair laying about her face and shoulders in long curls, her dark brown eyes wide, her skin clear and unmarked despite her age. Chantel knew the woman to be nearing her thirty-fifth year, but her looks marked her as at least a decade younger.

Insultingly, the widow's eyes traveled over Arriane's small frame for a second, then she reached into the coach and lifted the small child from the interior. As the boy's feet touched the ground, Chantel clenched her teeth at the pain she could feel resonating from her sister.

"She shall not be here long, Arriane," Chantel assured her quietly, watching as the woman smoothed the devil's black hair back from the child's face and looked around the courtyard searching, Chantel assumed, for Joshua.

"But the child will be here." Arriane's voice shook. "I cannot deny him his child."

Chantel watched the child sadly, seeing the golden brown eyes as they stared at the ground, the tense little body as he waited with his mother.

He couldn't be more than five years, Chantel thought, and he carried sadness with him that tugged at her heart. Poor little boy, she thought, he would soon be a mark for Jonar as well. It amazed her that the dark lord had not tried to kill the child yet. Or perhaps he had, and that was the reason Joshua fought to keep him near.

Too bad, Chantel thought, that the mother came with him. It would be much easier on both Arriane and the child if he were separated from his mother. There was no way that child would ever find happiness while the Widow Denning used him to control his father.

"There is Joshua," Arriane whispered and the edge of pain in her voice caused Chantel to clench her fists in anger.

That man had no care for his wife at all, she thought, as he strode up to the widow, kissed her cheek gently then lifted the child in his arms.

That was a sight to behold. The little boy wrapped his arms around his father's neck with a delighted laugh and childish giggles as Joshua tickled him gently beneath his arms.

Such tenderness, Chantel thought, as the warrior's face seemed to come alive with light and love. He cherished the boy and the Widow Denning was very well aware of this.

"She will not let the child live within the castle." Chantel knew this as surely as she knew the sun would set that night. "She will keep him with her in the village."

"Then there will be no way of being certain he is not bedding her," Arriane finished bitterly. "I have lost him, Chantel."

"You cannot lose him, Arriane," she assured her sister. "His heart is yours, I promise you this."

The bitter little laugh that erupted from her sister's throat had Chantel turning a surprised gaze on her. What met her gaze was less than reassuring. Eyes so blue they seemed to reflect even the color of the sky.

"Who would want him after he shares his body with that bitch again?" Arriane whispered in pain, turning from the sight of the couple and their child. "It does not matter anyway what he does. I should have known better than to care."

The rage that radiated from Arriane was painful to see. The proud lift of her head as she reentered the castle, the tight clench of her fists and her hurried pace as she rushed up the stairs.

Chantel breathed deeply in despair, feeling the hunger and the agony that radiated from her sister.

She narrowed her eyes as she turned back to the scene outside the great hall. The tableau had turned. The Widow Denning was gazing at Joshua in fury, her face flushing as Joshua talked to her quietly.

The child was still held securely in his arms and when the woman moved to take the boy from his father, Joshua denied her sharply.

"Surely you do not expect me to survive in that little town without him?" The furious anger of the other woman's voice drifted through the castle walls. "Since when do you take orders from a woman, Joshua?"

Chantel did not catch his answer as she hid her smile of triumph. The threat Arriane had made had worked. The widow would be sent quickly to the village, but much to Chantel's surprise, it appeared the boy would be staying.

Several pieces of luggage were retrieved from the carriage and an older woman, obviously the nanny, was handed carefully from the darkened interior.

Within moments the Widow Denning was back in the carriage and the force of men was leading it from the courtyard once again. Chantel maintained her stance at the doors, though, watching as Joshua shook his head before turning away from the sight of the receding vehicle.

"Let's hope your sister is pleased," he growled at her as he mounted the steps. "Dealing with a furious Marissa will not be pleasant."

Chantel smiled gently at the child that gazed at her from the shelter of his father's arms.

"What is his name?" she asked Joshua as he entered the doorway.

"His name is Micah." Pride laced Joshua's voice as the boy lay against his chest. "I will get him and his nurse settled if you wouldn't mind arranging for an early dinner." Evidently the man knew how to be cordial when the situation called for it.

"Of course I shall." Chantel followed him into the castle slowly. "When I'm finished, perhaps you would be kind enough then to tell me why you claim a child that shares none of your blood, Joshua. That greatly interests me."

Chantel moved away from him then, enjoying the betraying flinch of his body as he stopped and stared after her. Oh, the boy looked enough like him, Chantel thought. He could even fool Arriane if he wanted to, but Chantel knew better. The child was definitely born of a Guardian parent, but whose blood was much more pure than that of Joshua's. The resonance of power within him was the same and yet different.

What amazed Chantel was that Joshua had allowed the Widow Denning to think she had fooled him so effectively.

* * * * *

Joshua silently cursed Chantel as he went about getting Micah and his nurse Kathleen settled into their room. Micah was overjoyed to be reunited with the man he considered his father, and free of the strict, caustic woman he called his mother. Joshua had no illusions where Marissa was concerned. She was a bitch straight from hell and used the child against him as often as possible.

It didn't matter to Joshua, though, that Micah was not of his blood. The child looked enough like him that he was able to afford him the protection he needed and still repay a debt he owed to the warrior who had sired him.

Of course, Marissa was unaware that Joshua knew the truth and until she became an unbearable irritation, Joshua would not tear the child from her totally.

The fact that Chantel had taken one look at the child and known the truth infuriated him. He wanted no one to know and had gone to extreme measures to ensure that no one suspected that the child was not his.

That meant that if Chantel knew, then Arriane would know as well. Damn, he cursed, each time he fought to throw a shield against her vulnerability and her weakness for him, something happened to break it down.

"Poppa, will Momma stay away?" Micah looked up at him from the bed Joshua placed him on, his big golden brown eyes serious and intent.

"I do not know, Micah," Joshua answered him. "She asked that she be allowed to see you each day."

Micah's lower lips protruded in a soft pout.

"She says if I do not behave and be quiet all the time, then she will not let me be with you anymore, Poppa," he whined, moving cautiously back to the shelter of his father's arms. "Do you not want me unless I am silent?"

"Micah, you know this is not true." Joshua moved the little boy back so he could watch him closely. "Your chatter brightens my day. Have I not told you this many times?"

"Momma says she will take me away, Poppa. Far, far away where I will never see you again."

Fury filled Joshua as big tears built in the child's eyes and his misery seemed to echo in his quiet voice.

"I promise you, Micah. Momma can never take you where I cannot find you." Joshua fought to contain his anger as the bedroom door opened.

He turned, expecting to see Micah's nurse, but saw the curious face of his wife instead. Her eyes were big and a velvety blue as she gazed at the child who hid his head shyly in Joshua's chest when he saw her.

Joshua frowned at her, wondering if she would speak of the fact that he was not Micah's father. Chantel had been careful to keep her voice pitched for his ears only, protecting the boy. Joshua hoped Arriane would be as kind.

He was further surprised when his little wife smiled shyly at Micah, but came no further into the room. She merely opened the door wider and made way for the stout Irish nurse and the young maid who carried a tray laden with food.

"Chantel has sent food and a few toys as well." She moved further into the room when several large boys began packing in a huge carving of a horse, built onto bent slats that would provide a rocking motion.

The horse was outfitted in miniature warrior's saddle, a polished leather bridle, and bright black eyes.

Micah's eyes rounded in excitement, his head turning to watch as the young boys set it on the floor, as well as a small chest of miniature soldiers.

"They were my toys, when my Poppa first brought me to live here," she told Micah softly. "They shall be yours as long as you are here with us."

Arriane obviously expected no answer. With a last gentle smile, she turned and left the room, motioning the boys and the maid to follow her.

As she left the room, Micah could contain his excitement no longer as he squealed in joy and wiggled against Joshua to be released.

"Our little warrior has finally found a steed worthy of him, Sire." Kathleen laughed as Micah climbed quickly upon the grinning rocker. "Please extend my thanks to your wife. It was a lovely gift she has given the child."

Joshua frowned at the nurse's voice.

"I sent Micah a steed similar last winter," he informed her slowly. "Why did Marissa not bring it with him?"

Kathleen frowned. "I saw no such gift, Sire," she said softly, twisting her hands now in agitation.

"Does Micah have any toys, Kathleen?" He fought to hide his anger from the now nervous nurse.

"Madam Denning believes toys are the devil's mischief makers," she whispered, keeping her voice low so Micah would not hear. "The child has no toys, Sir Joshua."

Joshua breathed in deeply, gritting his teeth in fury, determined that perhaps it was time to remove the boy from his mother's cruelty now that he had a home in which to raise him.

He turned and left the room. First he would deal with his wife, who seemed much too complacent about the child now. Then he would deal with Marissa.

# Chapter Thirteen

**ɛɔ**

Devlin found Chantel that next night, stretched out on their bed, her breathing softened in sleep. He stood at the end of the bed, feeling something in his heart lighten further at the sight of her.

Her white-blonde hair fanned around her head and shoulders like a halo. She wore only a gown of the palest blue, one hand lying in relaxation against the flat of her stomach.

He swallowed tightly, feeling the fire in his gut that she always seemed to ignite. This woman, his wife, he thought, he would never tire of watching her, of touching her.

He felt the still unfamiliar smile that crossed his lips as his shaft began to harden, to throb at the sight of her.

The past few days had been merciless on them, causing them to fall to the bed to sleep rather than in passion, when it came time to find their beds.

Peace had finally settled once again upon the castle. The preparations he had in place to protect the women had been difficult to set up, but had finally been arranged. He now had the rest of the day, the rest of the night, to concentrate solely on his wife.

His clothing was dispatched quickly as he watched her. They were left on the floor where he dropped them as he moved slowly, quietly to the bed where she slumbered.

Carefully, so as not to awaken her just yet, Devlin moved beside her on the bed. He stretched out along her body, reluctant as yet to touch her, knowing that when he did his own unruly passions would swiftly overtake him.

He could not keep his hands from her for long though. He picked up a long white strand of hair, inhaling the fresh scent of the soap she used on it and a fragrance that was just distinctively Chantel.

Then his hand moved to the bodice of her gown, which dipped low, baring the tops of her full, perfect breasts. He stroked the backs of his fingers over the tops of those smooth mounds slowly.

Her skin was so warm and radiant, he thought. Each time he touched her it was like being close to a carefully banked fire.

At her throat, he watched as the blood pumping through her veins seemed to throb. She moaned faintly, her body seeming to lift toward him in a passion she felt even in her sleep.

Breathing harshly in the silence of the room, Devlin lowered his head until his lips could caress the smooth perfection of her skin there.

Ah, control, he thought as he felt the fever rising inside his body to take her now. He wanted to lift her gown and plunge his cock quickly inside her. He was never more complete than he was while making love to his wife.

Her strangled moan had him lifting his head, his gaze rising to stare into her slumberous, passion-filled eyes.

"Tell me you are now fully awake and willing," he growled. "I swear, wife, it feels as though it has been ages since I've touched your body."

"Ages at least." She lifted to him, her words a dark silken moan lost in the warmth of his mouth as his lips covered hers.

His hands clenched in the silk of her garment, as his arm gathered her closer to his body. Slowly, in increments, he lifted the material.

The smooth perfection of her legs, the rising fullness of her rounded buttocks, the indention of her shapely hips were carefully mapped as the silk was lifted free of her skin.

Finally, she lay before him, dressed only in the rays of moonlight that fell through the windows, her dark eyes watching him with slumberous sensuality as he leaned over her.

His lips covered hers once again, his tongue sneaking past her lips for a taste, then pulling back, teasing her with the heady brew of their passion.

Her broken moan washed over him, the heat of her passion wrapped around him like a blanket of the softest threads.

Her hands, so small and graceful, rose to grip his shoulders, her fingers pressing against him, the slight roundness of her nails scoring his skin.

Devlin gathered her gently in his arms, pressing his body against her, resisting the growl of pleasure that rose from his gut as he felt his erection press against the softness of her silken thighs.

Slowly, he cautioned himself. He would take her slowly, exquisitely, show her all the parts of loving that he had yet to teach her. He would show her all this, if only he could hold onto his control long enough, he thought in torment.

Her hands now gripped his shoulders imperatively as his tongue slid over the silk perfection of her full lower lip, then his teeth nipped at it gently.

Her moan was a sigh of desperation as he moved to her neck, touching her, caressing the tender skin with his lips and tongue.

"Devlin." Her cry shattered the stillness of the room when his lips went to her breast, his tongue laving the nipple gently.

Her legs twined with him, her body arching against him as she fought to get closer, to align her body more perfectly for the thrust of his cock.

"Not yet, love," he breathed roughly against her breast, his hand smoothing down her flat stomach to the nest of curls that lay between her thighs. "Let me love you first."

"I cannot bear the torment," she whispered, panting for breath, her thighs opening for his hand.

"Surely, for but a few moments more?" Devlin wanted to cry out himself when he felt the heat of her inner body sear his fingers.

A few moments more was all he would have, he thought, as his lips covered hers and his fingers moved gently against her passionate core. Just a little longer, just another taste of her soft heat.

His head moved lower as he felt his control slipping by degrees. He was desperate for the taste of her, the sound of her cries as her body shattered beneath his caress, the feel of her hands clenching fiercely in his hair.

His tongue touched her, and he knew he was lost. His hands gripped her thighs, spreading them further as he tasted her deeply, relishing the broken cries that erupted from her small body.

"Devlin, please." Ah yes, her hands gripped his hair as she cried out his name.

His tongue raked across the sensitive skin. He tasted her, laved her, and groaned her name against the damp flesh before he rose above her, his blood heating at the arousal on her face, the love in her eyes as she stared up at him.

Her arms went around his shoulders, her legs lifting to cradle his hips as he thrust heavily into the welcome heat of the moist depths of her body.

He fought the cry welling in his throat, the trembling in his limbs as he stroked inside her. He relished her broken pleas for completion, the thrashing of her head against the bed, her nails biting into his skin.

His pace increased, his hips thrusting them both closer to oblivion, then suddenly it was upon them. With a throttled shout of ecstasy he felt her silken sheath clench, tremble, the molten heat of her release more than he could bear.

As his climax rushed over him, he threw his head back, his teeth clenching, his body tightening until he could no longer control the surging tide of completion.

Devlin collapsed against his wife, breathing harshly, clasping her close as sanity slowly returned.

"How could I live without you now?" he whispered against her ear, knowing there would be no life without the joy he found in her arms.

The words, whispered in the throes of his passion, chilled Chantel's heart. Her eyes closed tightly, her arms refusing to lift free of the desperate grip she had on his shoulders.

She could feel his devotion, like nothing she had ever known in her life, wrapping around her, seeking to comfort her.

She realized as she held his quaking body in her arms that she prayed for a quick resolution, an end to the bitterness she knew would soon come. The sooner it ended, she told herself, the sooner she could return to him, and bring relief to the heart she knew would be black with grief.

"Remember always my love for you," she whispered against his dampened skin. "Always, my love, let your heart remember."

She felt the warmth of the crystal at her breast flare suddenly to life. Felt his groan as its opposite side flared against Devlin as well. Then she lost her breath, her eyes widening in alarm, in shattered pleasure at the doorway she seemed to have opened.

She felt him flow into her, felt a part of her own soul flow into him, and the agony and the ecstasy of that union was as near perfection as the climax that had torn through her earlier.

*Let your heart always remember.* The words trembled across her body as her eyes closed in weary contentment.

He was her warrior. She may be forced to leave him for a while, but she knew her return would ease the pain of that parting. His heart would await her, just as she knew hers would always long for him.

The vow she had secured from her father would ease his pain, she assured herself. The power the crystal had just given him would ensure that he would never forget their love, and that too would be a comfort for him. It would be small comfort, but perhaps enough to ensure his will to live, she prayed.

# Chapter Fourteen
*Jonar's Fortress*

🙰

Jonar studied the two men before him silently. He was aware of their fear, sometimes he even enjoyed it. Right now he was aware that it was complicating an extremely delicate situation, a situation that could be disastrous if they did not handle it correctly.

"Let me understand this," he stated coolly as the men trembled before him. "There are two candidates, each residing within Galen's castle and you cannot take the one I seek?"

"Sire, we cannot tell them apart." The older man trembled in his worn, dirty clothes. The stench of fear was nearly as overpowering as the stench of his unwashed body. "They are identical in looks and in bearing. Which one should we take is not the question."

The question was the wizard's wrath if his daughter was killed. Jonar feared no man, but he greatly respected the power Galen commanded.

Jonar leaned back against the padded back of his chair and regarded the two men quietly. This could be a problem, he admitted. Galen could make his life very uncomfortable if he put his mind to it.

"Have you tried to determine between the two?" he asked them. "I hear Lady Chantel is wed. Surely she does not share a room with the other one?"

"We cannot reach the second level of the castle." The other man, a knight in Galen's employ admitted. This man did not tremble nearly as badly as the other. He was the one Jonar had thought would succeed in this quest. "Galen's magic allows only a trusted few past the first level. There are no men allowed past it at all except himself and his sons-in-law."

Frustration bit at Jonar. Surely there was some way to be certain.

"Sire, we have tried everything. Mistress Antea is aware of your determination to find her though. Lady Chantel is just as determined to protect her half-sister. They foil us at every opportunity," the other man whined.

Jonar's fist clenched. He admired Lady Chantel's loyalty, even as it infuriated him.

There had to be a way past this, he frowned as he pondered the problem. Even a wizard as great as Galen must have some weakness that would allow them past the first floor of the castle.

"There could be a way," a voice spoke from the shadows of the room, causing the men before Jonar to jump in fright.

"And that would be?" Jonar glanced over as the shadows shifted and Oberon moved slowly into the room.

Oberon's presence caused the weaker man to shudder and the other to glance at him nervously. Jonar knew that the Seeker's mercilessness was well known, as was his joy in inflicting pain.

"To bring them both here. Lady Chantel's loyalty is admirable, but how strong would it be when faced with her own death?"

Jonar looked to the two men who stared at Oberon with abject horror.

"Well, you should know her well enough by now," Jonar told them coldly. "Would she declare herself if her own life were in danger?"

"I-I…believe she would." The knight nodded fearfully and Jonar worried that the man's own fear would cause him to say anything that would appease the man he believed to be a demon.

Jonar sighed roughly.

"Leave me." He motioned them from the room. "I will call for you when I have decided what shall be done about the sisters."

The men wasted no time but rushed from the room, nearly stumbling over their own feet in their haste to escape.

"You need to do something about relations with others, Oberon," Jonar told him with a mocking smile as the door slammed behind the men. "My most fierce warriors now tremble at your sight."

"These humans are worthless as warriors and inept as men." Bitterness coursed through the Seeker's voice as he sat heavily in the chair that faced Jonar's desk.

Oberon was extraordinarily handsome, but his reputation for cruelty had others shrinking in fear. He was a monster, Jonar reflected. With his dark face, smooth handsome features and cold, pale gray eyes, he looked every bit as inhuman as he was.

"Galen is not a man I would like to make an enemy of, my friend," Jonar told him as he watched him closely. "If we take his daughter, we will make an enemy of him."

"He is only human." Oberon shrugged. "Little more than a pest that may buzz at us occasionally. Finding Antea is more important than worrying about his trifling anger."

Jonar leaned forward now in his chair, his eyes narrowing on the younger man as he considered the dangers of taking both women.

"And if Antea fools us somehow and we kill the wizard's daughter?" he asked him softly. "Do you believe he will be little more than a pest then? The power he wields is greater than you know, Oberon."

"The woman is wed to the Shadow Warrior. Are you certain it is not the Guardians' chosen champion that you fear?" Oberon charged him with just a hint of malice.

Jonar shrugged, leaning back in his chair slowly.

"That concerns me," he admitted. "The Shadow and his men hold powers nearly equal to our own. Now they merely battle us. Take one of their own and the war will become gravely personal."

Oberon leaned his blond head back against the chair he sat in and gazed up at the ceiling. Jonar wasn't fooled by his relaxed manner. The warrior was debating, calculating and estimating their odds should they end up in a personal war against the Shadow and his men.

This was one of the reasons Jonar depended on him so heavily. Oberon had a way of looking at each man's strengths and weaknesses and determining the most effective way to defeat him. He had been invaluable in the past years to the battle Jonar waged.

"It is rumored that the Shadow is so enchanted with his new bride, that were anything to happen to her, he would not remain sane," Oberon reflected. "Should a mistake be made…"

"A mistake is not acceptable." Jonar's fist nearly splintered the wood of the heavy table as his fury backed the strength of the blow. "I don't give a rat's ass about the Shadow's bride, alive or dead, but Antea must die before she reaches her twenty-first year."

She had to die before she reached the age of inheritance. Just as Shalene had died.

"Then the answer would be to kill them both," Oberon suggested archly. "There would be no reason to worry whether or not you had made a mistake."

Jonar sighed. There were times that Oberon could be a brilliant strategist, other times he seemed exceedingly lacking in imagination.

"We must make all effort to secure the safety of Galen's daughter," he decided, giving Oberon a firm look as he spoke his decision. "I want Lady Chantel returned to her family as soon as possible."

"Then we take them both?" Oberon leaned forward, an edge of excitement in his voice.

Jonar had feared just this. He had been careful to steer well clear of Galen, as well as the Shadow Warriors as often as possible. This had given Oberon a greater excitement at the thought of pitting himself against either or both of them.

"I will take charge of this then." Oberon rubbed his hands together in enjoyment. "I have a man in place already, one who as yet has not secured the confidence we need in taking the correct one, but one who can aid us in slipping into the castle."

The Seeker's obvious relish at the prospect of taking both women worried Jonar, especially in light of his more deviant practices with the human women of the Fortress.

"Oberon." Jonar's voice was warning as he once again leaned forward. "Take care, my friend. I would be greatly displeased were I to learn you had harmed either of those women before they are brought before me. Do you understand this?"

Oberon frowned, much like a child when denied a favorite treat. Jonar remembered much that same expression crossing his granddaughter's face when he had had possession of her.

He swept that thought away quickly. Better to not remember, to not think about the child who had been snatched so ruthlessly from him.

"I understand you well, Jonar," he finally sighed as he rose to his feet. "The women shall not have a scratch on them or one harsh memory of their kidnapping before they are brought to you."

Jonar nodded sharply, his expression controlled as the Seeker left the room quickly to make his plans.

Jonar stared worriedly at the closed door, wondering if he shouldn't wait, give it more time. Perhaps in time, Antea or Chantel would slip up and the knight he had bribed would be able to kidnap the right woman.

Time was quickly running out, though, he admitted. Antea was nearing her twentieth year quickly. Soon, there would be no time left and the Guardians would possibly bestow her inheritance on her. Jonar refused to allow that to happen, even if it meant killing both women to ensure it didn't.

The child of Konar would suffer the same fate he had decreed that Jonar's child should suffer. She would know the same pain, her screams would echo throughout the halls of this castle, just as Shalene's had done when her murderers had found her.

Jonar only wished that the bitch had a child as well. He would take that child, as the Guardians had taken his, and would raise it in the manner he imagined his own grandchild was being raised. Suffering, lost and without the tender care he would have given her.

Bitterness, hot and black, seared through his chest as his heart clenched with the pain, even after all these long years.

Shalene had been his one light, his one soft edge within this world he had first been exiled to. Exiled, then reviled as the Guardians returned to finish the judgment made against him. They had not known the effects this land would have on him and the Seekers they had confined here. They had not known how powerless their own laws would make them in their fight to destroy him.

They had nearly succeeded once, but he had learned, became stronger, and found the secrets of living in this land.

He had also learned other secrets. The secrets Konar had thought he would never know. He would find them all, the brats the Guardians had sired in the hopes of once again taking back what the Seekers had stolen in their homeland. Jonar would find them and he would destroy them, as surely as he would destroy the one they called Antea now.

# Chapter Fifteen

§

Chantel awoke from sleep, her breath bursting from her lungs, her cry echoing in the room as she fought the arms that suddenly closed around her. Terror snaked through her body, pain radiating from the very center of her being as the nightmare that had gripped her suddenly seemed just as real as it had in her dream.

"Chantel." Devlin's voice was frantic as she fought him, shocking her from the fear, the mind-numbing agony of the realization that what belonged to her warrior was being forcibly taken by another.

"Oh God!" Her heart lurched as his voice penetrated the haze that had wrapped around her.

Her arms gripped him closer, whimpering cries issuing from her throat as her body ached from the remembered brutality of the dream.

She had to have been experiencing another of her sister's nightmares, she thought frantically. Why else would such visions of horrifying pain seep into her dreams?

She had done this before, she assured herself. When Ariel had first come to them, during those long months of her recovery, before she had been gifted with her crystal, the horror of her pain at Jonar's hands had tormented Chantel nightly.

That was all it was. Just a nightmare caused by the pain Ariel still felt at the memory. It was nothing more.

"Chantel, what is happening to you?" Devlin moved away from her, quickly lighting a candle on the bedside table before returning to her and pulling her back into his embrace. "This is the third dream in as many nights. What is going on?"

She could only shake her head, still gasping for breath, still seeking the safety of his arms and his touch.

"Chantel, talk to me." She could hear the concern in his voice as his arms tightened around her. "Tell me what is frightening you so."

Her tears soaked his chest, she could feel the dampness in the soft mat her head pressed into. Just as she could hear the rapid pace of his heart, the fear that filled him, yet she could not stop her tears. The unimagined pain, the humiliation of the events that washed over her in the dream was too unbearable to speak of. If this was what Ariel had truly endured, how had she managed to live through it?

"For God's sake, Chantel, tell me what is doing this to you." He pushed her back, his hands gripping her arms as her head lowered and silent sobs shook her body.

She could not tell him the dreams. She could not tell him the terrors that suddenly haunted her sleep. Pray God this was not a glimpse into her own death, she screamed silently. *Dear Mother, please protect me from such an end.*

"Chantel, speak to me," Devlin's voice rose as she could only sob, her breath catching in her throat, her tears dripping slowly onto the linen sheets of the bed.

"A nightmare," she gasped, shaking her head. "'Tis only a nightmare. They shall end soon. It is the fear, that is all. The snakes..." She grasped at any reason she could find to still the violence she could feel emanating from him.

Did the dreams not stop soon, then she feared he would guess the true nature of the danger they were all in.

"God, Chantel, you are terrifying me with these dreams of yours." He pulled her back into his arms, rocking her gently as she continued to cry against his chest. "Tell me how I can help you stop them. Tell me what to do."

She shook her head against his chest. There was naught he could do and this she knew. She had gifted a precious bit of her power to Arriane and in doing so had left herself vulnerable to the demons that would slip into her sleep on silent wings.

"I shall be fine," she whispered tearfully, her hands locked around his neck, her body pressed tightly to his as she absorbed the safety and security that he afforded her now.

No harm would come to her, she told herself bleakly, not as long as his arms were around her and his heart beat steadily against her ear. She was safe here, at this moment.

"You are not fine." His hand caressed her back, beneath the fall of her hair. "Whatever torments your sleep is making you weary. Do you think I do not see this?"

"They will go away soon." She fought to stop her tears as she spoke.

The terror lancing through her still made her body tremble, her breath shudder through her body. She must find control, she thought desperately. If she did not, then Devlin would surely begin to seek the answers to questions she did not wish him to ask.

"I am no fool, madam. Nor so ensnared by my love for you that I do not realize you are hiding something from me." If his tone was anything to go by, then Chantel feared it was too late to keep the suspicions from him.

He released her slowly, looking down at her for long moments before he left their bed and stalked to the table across the room.

There, he lifted a clean goblet and poured it full of the potent wine he had taken to bringing to their room for her to sip after the dreams awoke her, sweating and screaming from her sleep.

"Drink this slowly," he ordered her as he wrapped her fingers around the goblet. "Too quickly and tomorrow your head will feel twice its size."

Still naked, he sat down on the bed beside her, watching her broodingly as she sipped the wine, and slowly calmed beneath its intoxicating effects.

Long minutes later the shuddering sobs had stopped and the tears no longer fell from her eyes. The potency of the wine eased the trembling in her body and brought a measure of peace to her mind. No longer did the vision of Jonar straining above her haunt her restless mind.

"Are you ready to talk now?" he asked her, his tone hard. "And I warn you now, should I see that damned crystal flare and feel my need for answers begin to evaporate then I shall rip it from your neck."

Startled, she looked into his face. It seemed carved from stone, the harsh angles that were usually softened in love were now bleak with purpose.

He had known. The thought rippled through her mind with a feeling of unease. He had known that she was blocking his suspicions before they had even completely formed within his own mind.

"As I said, I am not a fool," he told her harshly, reading her startled look. "There are many things about the gifts I possess myself, wife, that your earth magic cannot touch. Parts of me that no magic could ever filter through. So best you begin explaining to me now."

Chantel's hand trembled as she lifted the glass to her lips and swallowed deeply from the potent wine. To hell with tomorrow's headache, she thought. She needed the false courage to face her husband this night.

Devlin's look was uncompromising. There was no longer a plea in his gaze, it now held only determination to get to the bottom of the nightmares tormenting her.

"I'm waiting, Chantel. And don't bother trying to lie to me. You should know I would be aware of it the moment you do so."

She looked up at him, startled.

"I have never lied to you, Devlin," she whispered brokenly. "I would never lie to you."

It hurt her that he would think she would. She would not lie, but she knew there were things she could not tell him as well. She glanced at the remainder of the wine. Perhaps enough of it would drown out the nightmares and the fears that were haunting her.

"Then tell me what the dreams are about," he ordered her, taking the goblet from her as she went to drink from it again. "And you've had enough. You are drinking it much too swiftly."

"Stop ordering me about." Anger flashed through her, unreasonable and frightening as she jumped from the bed and jerked her robe over her arms. "You would think I was a child the way you are treating me."

As she belted it tightly at her waist, she turned her back on her husband and paced to the window. There, she did as she noticed she was doing each night, staring into the darkness outside as though there were some unseen threat.

"Perhaps it is because you are acting like a child, Chantel," he suggested angrily. "I am your husband, I have a right to know what torments you."

"You have no right to order me about." She felt like clawing at her own hair as the visions of her dreams rose before her once again. "I do not need that from you."

"Someone needs to order you about." Devlin moved behind her, his hands clasping her shoulders as he turned her to face him. "For God's sake, Chantel, you are running yourself into the ground. What the hell is wrong with you? Do you think I will stand idly by while you destroy yourself this way?"

She stared up into his hard face, the ache in her heart a physical thing as she realized how deeply this was hurting him as well.

How could she stop it? she wondered. It was too late to back away from the destiny unfolding, too late to go back and save her sister from the rape Jonar had inflicted upon her.

"I don't know how to stop it," she whispered, knowing it for the truth. "The nightmares..." She fought the need to gag as the visions that had raged through her sleep were remembered now while she was awake. "They must be Ariel's fears. I knew she was going to tell Shanar, but I did not anticipate how it would affect her."

She glanced up at his face, watching the startled knowledge that leapt into his eyes.

"The rape," Devlin bit out in fury. "You are experiencing her terror. Her rape at Jonar's hands, are you not? God. Dammit it, Chantel, is there no way you can break this link with your sisters for even a few hours? Long enough to sleep?"

She met his furious gaze and realized that her nightmares were hurting him as deeply as they hurt her.

"I have tried," she cried out, her hands clenching the bunched muscles in his arms as she stared up at him pleadingly. "I do not know how, Devlin. Help me, for I cannot bear this terror much longer. I swear I cannot fathom how Ariel survived such pain."

A startled gasp left her lips as he jerked her in his arms and they tightened around her. She knew he was fighting the fact that what was happening to her was out of his control. God help them both, she thought, it was out of everyone's control now.

"Tell me what to do, Chantel," his voice was a ragged whisper at her ear. "Tell me and I will surely do it."

"I do not know," she whispered against his chest. "Just hold me, Devlin. As long as your arms are around me, I know I am safe from all harm. Just hold me."

And hold her he did. He picked her up, carrying her back to the bed and pulling her close to his body as he lay down beside her. His body was hard and warm, his grip about her secure and reassuring.

"Let me love you," he groaned as her lips whispered over his chest, his fingers pulling at the belt of her robe and loosening it quickly. "Let me fill you with nothing but our love for each other."

"Yes," she groaned against his lips, her arms tightening about him as he rolled her to her back, then moved over her quickly. "Love me. Take away the darkness, Devlin."

Her own hands were not idle. One speared into the silky thickness of his hair as the other ran slowly down his arm.

"You are my life, Chantel. Promise me it will always be so," he seemed to beg as his lips trailed to her throat and his arms tightened around her back with near bruising intensity. "Promise me you will never leave me."

"I shall always be with you, Devlin," she swore as the diabolical warmth of his mouth trailed to her breasts, sipping, nipping at their pointed crests.

Chantel arched her back, fighting to get closer, to meld her very skin with his so they could never be parted in any way. She felt his groan vibrate against her stomach, felt the heat and steel-hard length of his shaft as it nestled against her leg.

His mouth tormented her breasts, his hands roaming over her body, first with gentleness then with a need born of the white-hot passion that flared between them.

Chantel cried out in pleasure, not in torment, as he rose over her, his thighs parting hers swiftly, his engorged cock spearing into the very center of her body.

She seemed to lose her breath as he lodged in her to the hilt. Their breathing was harsh in the silence of the room, their moans a broken symphony of pleasure and ecstatic torment as he began to move slowly inside her.

"You are torturing me," she accused him raggedly as he stroked slowly.

Pulling back until only the very tip of his erection rested inside her, then pushing back by slow degrees, Devlin taunted her with the ecstasy just out of reach.

"Do not tease me," she demanded as his hands held her hips still, his big body controlling her frantic movements. "'Tis most unfair."

"Then perhaps you should learn to ride," he growled a second before he lifted her, rolling onto his back without breaking his possession of her body.

Chantel stared down at him in amazement as she found herself suddenly astride his hips, his cock pulsing hot and hard inside her body.

"You do not know how to ride, perhaps?" he asked her huskily as he flexed his hips, caressing the inner recesses of her body.

Her cry shattered the candlelit darkness around them as she did just that. Her hips rising and falling languidly, her thighs gripping him, her cunt caressing him until they reached oblivion, their cries mingling as their bodies shuddered in unison.

* * * * *

From outside their bedroom window, standing silently on the small ledge that ran around the base of the second floor of the castle, Aaron stood and watched in growing arousal as Chantel rose above her husband, moving against him slowly.

His eyes narrowed as he watched the graceful movements of her body. The full, perfect, pink-tipped breasts that Devlin's large hands covered in passion. The slender, perfectly formed legs that straddled the dark thighs of her lover.

She moved against him, her cries shattering the night and echoing past the paned window as she began to ride him harder. Her hips moving, pumping his glistening cock ever harder inside the softness of her body.

Hunger rose inside Aaron with the swiftness of a storm moving in from the seas. It hardened his own flesh against the taut confines of his pants, dampened his palms, and caused his heart to race faster in his need to possess the lovely Chantel.

He had hoped he could rid himself of this crazed passion with the whore Antea. For the most part, he succeeded. She looked well enough like her, but no way, Aaron thought, could she move against a man with the grace Chantel used in taking her lover into her body.

He watched in jealousy as Devlin's hands gripped her hips then moved fluidly to the gentle curve of Chantel's buttocks. There, the dark fingers clenched against the pale skin as his hips began to piston fiercely, driving his shaft deeper into her, his own cries now echoing with hers as their climaxes rushed over them.

Aaron shook his head then moved cautiously along the edge to escape any threat of discovery as he made his way to Antea's room. His cock was raging with the need to bury itself in the slender body of the woman still entwined with her husband's body.

Antea was a poor substitute, but she would do well in the fantasy he envisioned of Chantel.

He grimaced as he remembered the sight of her riding Devlin's hard body. If only, he thought, he could convince Antea to climb above his body and ride him so well.

\* \* \* \* \*

The next afternoon Chantel sat alone in the gardens, staring into the dark clouds rising above the mountains in the distance. In them she saw the riders coming, the end to the perfection she had found within her life.

Swirling in shades of black and gray, the clouds were topping the far mountain, and she knew that soon they would begin their ride across the sky. With them would come the dark forces set on destroying all that could have been built.

She lowered her head, staring at her hands clasped sedately in her lap. It was all she could do at such times to keep herself from collapsing on the ground in misery.

Chantel was thankful that this day Devlin was away from the castle, with her father at the outlying farms. There was no way she could hide from him the fear that the sight of those clouds brought to her. Besides, it gave her the chance to finish the last of her plans to protect the man she loved.

A sense of betraying her husband sliced viciously across her heart. Had he known what she was about, the destiny she was about to curse him with, he would be enraged. Chantel had a feeling there would be no controlling the beast that such information would loose.

She sat within the gardens, the smell of summer's blooms drifting around her, bees buzzing above the nectar they sought, the wind whispering gently through the trees as she awaited the man who would drive the final stake into the heart of her beloved.

"Lady, I should kill you for this." Joshua's voice was low, dark and violent as he moved toward her with all the grace and deadly intent of a wolf on the hunt. "Should I find a way to return payment to you for this deed, then surely I will."

He stood before her now, tall, threatening, as his golden eyes stared down at her from a face so darkly savage it caused her heart to clench within her breast.

"Your name is not Joshua," she whispered. "You were born Joshau, a prince among a people who no longer even exist."

Shocked surprise flared in his eyes as he faced her. His body tightened, shadows of denial, of a lingering rage darkened his eyes.

Chantel lowered her head once again and took a deep, weary breath.

"My father's magic will not work entirely against one such as you, Joshau," she told him quietly. "I must have your assurance that you will not interfere."

Chantel heard the disgusted growl that emanated from his throat.

"You will kill him." Fury filled his voice, and the desperation she heard behind it broke her heart.

Devlin was their rock, she realized. The other three had no concept how to fight Jonar without the one who saw beneath shadows and had learned how to merge within them.

"Nay, not kill him." She shook her head. "'Twill break his heart, but he shall not know the reason why, until that break can be repaired. I would have your assurance that you will support him during this time."

"I would first know exactly what it is that will happen, without the confusion your power fills my brain with. Tell me now," he demanded harshly.

Slowly, revealing only that part that would involve her, Chantel opened a doorway past her power that Joshua's mystical abilities could reach through and probe.

She watched him for long moments. Watched the slow paling of his skin, watched the pain, the despair that filled his eyes.

He sank slowly to the stone seat across from her, staring at her in blind shock.

"God have mercy, do not allow this to happen, Chantel," he whispered despairingly. "Devlin deserves much more than this fate you are consigning him to."

"It is because of my love for him, my desire to see him live the life always meant for him, that I do this, Joshau," she cried out, tears now filling her eyes and wetting her cheeks slowly. "But I must know you will not stand in Father's way. I must know you will not kill as my husband would have you do should he know the truth."

Joshua shook his head.

"My father's power will do it where the other three are concerned, but I know well it cannot touch you. So I must ask you to stay your hand and to let this see through. I swear to you on all I hold sacred and holy, that the time shall come when the bitterness and the pain shall fade, and because of this destiny I set in motion, Devlin shall defeat Jonar. He will see him destroyed, no longer able to kill or to maim. I swear to you, Joshau, all will be right in the end."

"And you?" Joshua lowered his head now, Chantel knew, to hide the tears that would have come into his own eyes. "Do you know what you shall face, Lady? Do you have any idea the unimagined pain that could be dealt to you?"

"My power protects me. Jonar cannot touch me. But I must know that you would not reveal the true purpose of the trip to my husband. I must ask that when the time comes, no matter the cause, no matter the fury you hold yourself, that you will not stand in my father's way."

Joshua raised his head and gazed out at the storm clouds rising over the distant mountains.

"Does Arriane know what is to come? Will he take her as well?"

"He will never take her, I swear it," Chantel promised him. "But if you do not do as I have asked, then he will learn of her existence and take her from us forever. This way, he shall never know who she is, until it is too late to take her from you."

The deception she practiced on this man nearly strangled her. She told no lies, but that was no comfort for not telling the truth either. This deception would haunt her, she knew, as nothing else in her life ever would.

Joshua took a breath and shook his head as though fighting to clear the knowledge she had given him from it.

"If I allow this, then he will not be able to touch her?" he asked her.

"I swear it," she promised him yet again.

Chantel knew that he would regret this day for the rest of his life, but she also knew that by the time he learned the full scope of their fate, he would be silenced by Devlin's need.

Slowly, he nodded. "Very well. I shall aid you in this."

Chantel hid her sigh of relief.

"The messenger shall arrive tomorrow. You will ride out the next afternoon. He must not be allowed to return before the messenger comes for him. Agreed?"

Joshua's jaw worked in fury as the muscles there bunched from the pressure of his teeth grinding against each other.

"Agreed," he snapped, rising to his feet. "But know this, Lady, should the Shadow or my wife be harmed by this venture, then I will not hesitate to tell Devlin the full and unvarnished truth of this game you play."

He rose to his feet and stalked away. Chantel looked down at her hands now as they trembled in her lap. He would know when the messenger came that she had hidden the full truth from him. By then, there would be naught he could do.

Destiny and fate now worked hand in hand. The events were out of her control. She could not heal the pain that would come from them. She would do as she had always known she must and in that she knew that she would pay the ultimate price.

\* \* \* \* \*

Oberon entered the hut silently, his eyes narrowed as he faced the two men who answered only to him.

"Has the king been apprised of the attack?" he softly asked the knight who stood by the fireplace.

Aaron was the best at what he did that Oberon had found, a master tactician, a man as hard and as loyal to the Viper goddess as Oberon himself was.

Aaron nodded. "The message was sent and received. He should come for the warriors by morning."

Oberon smiled in pleasure.

"Everything is now in place to take the women?" he asked Aaron.

Aaron nodded once again, frowning.

"Be careful of the magic of that place when you enter the walls." He shook his head. "You come out with knowledge, only to have it slowly slip your grasp at the oddest times. Galen has done everything to protect the women that his sorcerer's magic can conjure. We must be careful."

Oberon nodded. "You will take care of the forces outside, I shall enter and take the women with my own men. His magic has little effect on the Seekers. It will be accomplished quickly and we will ride for the Fortress the moment we are free."

"I will have my men be certain that both women are in the great hall at that time," Aaron promised him. "Do we ride with you to the Fortress, or do we stay here to further complicate their search?"

"Whichever you choose." Oberon shrugged. "If you ride with us, we can set a plan in motion that makes it appear you rescued the Lady Chantel. Perhaps she will pay you accordingly," he sneered.

Aaron nodded in approval of the plan.

"My men will be in place tomorrow," Oberon informed him. "Make certain this works, Aaron, and you shall be paid accordingly by Jonar. I am certain you can find use for the gold he has promised you."

Oberon left the hut quickly, the satisfaction in this meeting lingering within its walls as he disappeared into the forests behind it.

Aaron moved to the table and poured a large measure of the wine sitting there. He downed it quickly, wishing there was some way to wash away the regret that sat like a heavy stone in his gut.

It was not every day that a man aided in the death of his lover and Aaron found that it did not sit right with him. What good would it do him to save the Lady Chantel? She would have no reward for him, her body would never lie under him in passion, twisting and moaning in heat as he pushed his cock into her.

His hunger for her was a disease eating into him, but he knew the truth of her. She would take one look at him and know he had betrayed her and her sister.

No, other plans must be made there, Aaron thought. Saving Lady Chantel would gain him nothing, but saving Antea would gain him much.

His eyes narrowed as he stared thoughtfully at the wine atop the table. Many things could go wrong, many ways plans could be altered, but first he would have to assure himself that Antea would do as he wanted her to do.

He could not risk telling her his plans. Her love for her sister, twisted as it was by her jealousy, could be a stumbling block. But a suggestion here and there could very well achieve what he needed.

He smiled for the first time since receiving Oberon's summons. It could work, he thought, if he worked quickly, and worked surely.

He set his half-finished goblet on the table then stalked from the hut. There was much work to be done to ensure his plans were realized. It would be a simple matter, he assured himself as he mounted his horse. Lady Chantel's life would not benefit him. But Antea's could very well be worth more than the gold Jonar had promised him if he could pull his own deception off.

# Chapter Sixteen

🔊

They were gone. Chantel stared at the cloud of dust that marked the passing of the huge warhorses Devlin and his men rode. Any source of protection she had was now moving further and further into the distance.

Behind her, Antea stood nervously. Chantel could smell her fear, her lies. From the few feet that separated them she could feel the deception her sister thought she was practicing with every pore of her body.

"Where are your other sisters?" Antea asked her, her voice a bit high, trembling slightly in the demand.

"They sleep," Chantel answered her. There was no sense in revealing that they slept only because of the potion Chantel herself had slipped into their wine.

The others were already suspicious and Chantel knew they would have stood before her and the men now riding toward the castle.

Chantel touched the crystal at her breast as she sensed Antea slipping the small vial of sleeping potion into a hidden pocket of her gown. Chantel had left the bottle purposefully on the table where her sister would have no trouble finding it.

"It grows dark soon." Antea moved to the open doors of the great hall. "There's a storm coming. It looks like a bad one."

"Yes, it will be a very bad storm," Chantel told her, fighting to hide the bleak sorrow in her soul. "But I am certain you shall survive it."

Chantel took a seat before the small fire that had been built. It was full summer, but she felt chilled, so cold that even the heat of the flames could not penetrate the ice forming over her soul.

Silence filled the great hall. Slowly, darkness began to fall, and from the courtyard the sounds of life slowly diminished. Those who were still left to guard the outside wall would be sleeping soon. Antea's lover, Aaron, had seen to that, Chantel knew. She was not the only one who would use a sleeping potion to render unconscious those who would stand in the way of destiny.

"Chantel?" Antea moved beside her, her voice hesitant.

"Yes, Antea?" Chantel continued to stare into the flames, to gather her courage and fight the raw fear brewing in her stomach.

"I love you, sister," Antea whispered, her voice suddenly sounding small and unsure.

"I know you do, Antea." Chantel could not raise her gaze to stare into the darkness of her sister's gaze.

The plans had already been made, she knew. Aaron had placed the seeds of betrayal and now they began to grow within the fertile jealousy of her sister's heart.

Regret shimmered in the air between them, but Chantel knew it would make no difference. In the end destiny would have its way.

She leaned her head against the high back of the chair and closed her eyes as she thought of Devlin. He had ridden from the castle, clearly unwilling to do so, but gaining confidence from Joshua's assurances that Chantel's power would be enough to protect the castle.

Galen had ridden off as well, though Chantel had no idea where. Her father had been unable to face this night, unable to assure her that he would not kill Antea before the betrayal took place.

The sound of horses riding furiously over the drawbridge had her opening her eyes. Fighting the terror, she turned a falsely inquisitive look on Antea.

"Have they returned so soon, do you think?" she asked Antea as she rose to her feet and headed for the large double doors still open to the late evening air. "Come, let us greet them."

Chantel moved slowly, her knees weak, her heart thundering in rapid fear as the sick feeling of regret filled her. *God protect my husband and all that I hold dear*, she whispered silently, knowing that only part of that prayer would be answered.

As she neared the doors, a dozen knights and soldiers rushed into the room, led by one whose beauty was only overshadowed by the evil that clung to him like a cloak of raw terror.

Chantel stopped quickly, suddenly overcome by the ramifications of this mood.

*There's still time*, her mind whispered frantically. *Your power can shield both you and Antea. It can protect you until Devlin's return, it can push the enemy away.*

*Forgive me, Devlin*, she cried out silently, her fists clenching against the need to call upon the power. *Forgive me, my love.*

* * * * *

"Forgive me, Devlin." The voice was at his side, causing Devlin to rein the black horse abruptly from its course and stare around in a flash of unreasoned fear.

It was Chantel's voice, Chantel's terror that seemed to reach out to him.

"We're nearly there, Devlin." Joshua reined in beside him, his voice dark, quiet. "Why are we stopping?"

"Do you feel anything odd, Joshua?" Devlin frowned as he stared around the forests, suddenly quiet, its inhabitants watchful.

Joshua was silent for long moments, his eyes narrowed and staring, almost angrily, into the forests around them.

"I feel nothing but the scent of victory," he finally answered. "Do we ride now or camp for the night?"

"A storm is coming," Devlin told him in distraction as he stared back the way they had come. "The caves would be better as a campsite."

"Then we ride before it storms?" Joshua asked, his voice careful in its sarcasm.

"Yes, before it storms." Devlin shook his head, fighting the unreasonable sense of worry that had plagued him since leaving the castle.

He urged the horse back into its ground-eating gallop and fought to ignore the cry in his mind that urged him to return instead. All would be well, he thought. Should Chantel need him, she would send the wolves or the eagles of the air to convey her message.

It had been her promise. Should she need him, she would send for him. He was turning into a besotted fool, he chastised himself, mooning after her, worrying for her every moment they were apart.

He would return to her in a few days and love her until she was unable to walk from his bed. Their reunion would be well worth the few days he would not be at her side.

* * * * *

Joshua rode behind Devlin, fury rising inside him, concern growing with each mile the horses covered. Something was wrong, he admitted to himself, and he had a feeling it was much more than Chantel had allowed him to see the other day.

He had not felt easy since their conversation. For some reason, the feeling that she hid more than she had revealed had grown steadily over the hours since their departure.

And too, Joshua had heard the whispered prayer that had caused Devlin to halt his horse so quickly. Forgive me, she had whispered. Why would she plead his forgiveness so forlornly if all was going to be well?

Perhaps he had misjudged her, he thought. Could she have deceived him while still yet holding to the truth? His hands tightened on the reins. Of course she could have, he thought furiously. She was the Mistress of that damned power she possessed, she could likely do any damned thing she pleased. Even fool a warrior so filled with his own confidence that he could resist those powers.

What had he done, Joshua asked himself as he rode behind his commander and his friend. Had he aided Devlin's future or had he suddenly become a pawn in destroying it?

\* \* \* \* \*

Chantel knew the moment Antea spilled the sleeping draught into the crude cup that held the wine Jonar had left for them.

She closed her eyes against the pain, accepting the small mug and drinking from it quickly, deeply before she could change the course destiny had demanded.

She set the cup on the floor then settled her head against the rough pillow of the bed as she stared across the room at the rough, dark wall that wavered just slightly before her gaze.

Chantel stared in dazed fascination at the damp stone walls of the room she and Antea were being held in. She had drunk the wine her sister had handed her, had tasted the evil of the potion that had been slipped into it, and had awaited the sleep that would come.

Now, as she watched the stones blur, she thought she saw the Mother's saddened face watching her from within it. Were those tears on her face? Chantel wondered, as a drop of water seemed to slide slowly from one brick to another.

The form of the Mother seemed to coalesce from the darkness, the soft illumination of her spirit weaker and less clear than it was at her father's castle.

Chantel raised her head just enough to glance at Antea and wonder if she too could sense the Mother's visit. Perhaps not, she assured herself as her sister showed no surprise, no fear.

Antea sat on the crude bed at her feet, staring at the wall as well. Chantel wondered if the woman saw her own fate on the filth displayed before her. Betrayal shall be met with betrayal, her father had sworn to her before leaving the castle that morn. *How harsh then will my own punishment be*, Chantel wondered dismally.

*Gentle, child*, the Mother's voice seemed to whisper over her. *How great shall be your reward for this sacrifice. Know you, that when you return, all that was once yours shall be returned tenfold.*

Returned from what? This was but one of the questions that Chantel had always been careful not to ask. Do not ask questions of the Mother that you do not want answers to, her father had once warned her. When Chantel had learned the destiny unfolding around her, she had heeded his words to the letter.

"I'm frightened," Chantel whispered back, fighting the drowsiness taking her over. "There is naught now that you can do to ease the coming pain. Naught you can accomplish in this place of evil."

Chantel knew well the evil Jonar and Oberon could practice. Had they not nearly killed Ariel with the pain alone?

*Precious child, for every moment of pain you shall know, for every cry that whispers from your lips, so shall Antea pay. For every mark placed on your skin, for every touch of evil, the earth shall exact its revenge on the one whose greedy and jealous heart should betray you. I make this vow to you.*

She could ask no more than that, Chantel knew. And for that, she was more than grateful. But she could not allow Antea to pay. What fairness was there in that? she asked herself. Antea had been destined to betray her, and fate had but given her the tools to do so.

"She was but a pawn to the whims of fate and destiny. I will not have her punished." It was not loyalty that urged this refusal of Antea's punishment, but only fairness. "Were it not her, it would have been another."

Chantel wondered if the betrayal would have been easier to bear if it were another. A stranger, someone who had no tie, no bond of blood with her.

*Nay, Chantel,* the Mother whispered. *Let not your tender heart steer fate and destiny from her punishment.*

Chantel could hear the flare of anger in the Mother's voice, and though she well understood the reason for the anger, she could still not condone it.

"It is my right. It is my request as I give my life for the earth, that the earth exact no vengeance for her part."

Silence greeted her plea for long moments.

*Very well, the earth shall not.* Chantel nearly smiled.

No, the earth would not, for her father would see to it that Antea paid in full.

"I must sleep now, Mother." Her eyes began to slowly close as darkness filled her vision. "Remember your vow. Protect him for me, for I can no longer see to it myself."

*He is protected, Chantel. Until his eyes are opened, and he can see the glory of all that is now being taken, he shall be protected for you.*

Darkness closed over her, as the sleeping potion could be fought no longer. For but a while, sweet peace filled her as the Mother brought to her one last perfect vision of the warrior and the love they shared so sweetly.

\* \* \* \* \*

Antea knew the moment Chantel slipped into sleep. A tear fell unchecked down her cheek and her hands clenched as she fought what she knew she must do.

There was no help for it. Chantel was smart and she would have a greater chance of convincing Jonar to stay his hand. Antea knew that her life depended on getting out of the Fortress and making her way to where Aaron had promised to meet her.

She rose silently from the cot, moving carefully, though she knew there was no danger of waking her sleeping sister. Before she could talk herself from her course, she lifted the crystal from Chantel's neck and slipped it carefully over her own head. Then she left the room.

Antea moved silently through the darkened halls of the unsecured dungeons, heading quickly to the only barred door within the underground structure. The door that would lead to the one who could set her free.

At her breast lay the warmth of the crystal, vibrating against her skin, bringing to her images, feelings, guilt. Guilt?

That feeling was so unknown to her. How long had it been since she had known it? How had she recognized the feeling so easily, for she realized she had not made its acquaintance until this night.

She had never known the soul-deep cringe of what she could possibly — nay, definitely — be doing to another.

The young woman who slumbered so deeply within her cell would die before the morning's light, she knew. With her betrayal, with her theft of the stone, she had assured her that destiny.

Antea regretted the necessity of her death, but Aaron had been frighteningly clear in explaining the death Jonar had in store for Antea. Were it only the rape, Antea could have borne it. It was not as if it would have been the first rape she would have suffered through. But the weapon they had chosen to kill her with, the thought of it sent a shiver of pure terror up her spine.

Antea approached the large wooden door slowly, glancing behind her often. She expected, almost wished the other girl would come running to reclaim her life. But the hall was empty, silent.

She stopped at the barrier, her slender fist rapping against the wood.

"What do ye want?" An eye-level panel slid open as dazed, dark eyes regarded her in suspicion.

"Jonar bid us to let him know, should we have the answers he seeks," she said softly. "Tell him that Chantel of Charlea has the answer."

The guard watched her for long moments, his eyes narrowing at the commanding tone in her voice.

"Wait there," he ordered her shortly. "I will tell me master yur ready to talk."

The small portal was closed quickly and Antea waited as her heart thudded with her nerves. Why could they not hurry? The longer she had to wait, the less it seemed her courage grew. She should have felt confident, recharged with the power she could feel against her breast.

The crystal was filled with ancient power and secret gifts. Surely as a sister of Chantel's, Antea thought, she could harness that power as well.

Perhaps she could repay Chantel in that way. She could use the power that had once been Chantel's to do the work that meant so much to her. Protecting the castle and her sisters. Of course, she thought, surely then they would not hate her so deeply. The power was needed, it was the reason Chantel was protected so fiercely by them.

They needed her power to complete their own and to assure that the warriors they were wed to would not stray from them. Had Chantel not touched the crystal and used its power each time she spoke to Joshua concerning Arriane's happiness?

Had Chantel not used that very same power to aid Arriane in overcoming her husband's hatred of her? If it could do that, then surely it could overcome their hatred of Antea when they learned that she had betrayed Chantel.

As the thought drifted through her mind, the door was opened and the soldier motioned her through with a jerky movement.

"He'll see you now. But beware, he ain't got no time for games. So ye best be playing none."

Antea had heard of Jonar for years. The powerful dark lord who ruled the deserts and sought to defeat this land as well. She stood before him, gaining strength in the warmth that curled throughout her body.

"My man tells me you wish to declare yourself." He frowned down at her, his brilliant blue eyes lit by the fire of evil, his darkly tanned face devoid of expression.

He was nothing as she had expected when she had first met him. Tall and handsome, despite the dark power he radiated. Black hair, blue eyes, muscular and finely built—she felt a thrill of arousal when she was in his presence and the look in his eyes showed he knew.

"I declare myself as Chantel, daughter of Galen." She raised her head proudly, taking the name and sealing the other girl's fate.

"And how do I know you are truly Chantel?" His thin lips twisted in a parody of a smile. "It is easy to declare yourself, now you must prove to me that you are not the one I seek."

She lifted the crystal from the bodice of her gown and allowed it to fall against her silk-covered breast.

"Check with the guards who betrayed my father," she told him softly. "The daughters of Galen all possess such stones. These stones were gifts of love, as well as identity. All know that his daughters wear them, they are a sign of his protection."

Jonar's eyes narrowed. The crystals, magically inset with other precious stones were beautiful, as well as proof that she was who she claimed to be. It was as he had suspected, but he could not make such a mistake as to kill a daughter of the sorcerer.

"So you are the eldest." He sighed briefly and she thought perhaps regretfully. "You shall be returned to your cell and the daughter of the traitor Guardians shall be brought to me."

"Why do you wish the daughter of the Guardians?" she asked him quickly, curious, needing to know why he sought her death. And it was her death he sought, she knew.

He watched her carefully, making her wonder if her question had caused him to somehow doubt her declaration.

"Revenge, my dear." He finally smiled tightly. "A child for a child. A life for a life. Is that not how you humans see it? They took from me my daughter and from them I shall take theirs as well."

A life for a life. That sentence caused a chill of alarm to shiver over her body. She prayed Galen would not see it the same. Somehow, she had to find a way to escape before he arrived.

She had to reach Aaron, who would know the next steps to take in securing her future within Galen's home.

"Release me now," she whispered, fighting to hide her desperation. "I gave you what you sought, now release me as you promised."

"Now?" His brows arched questioningly. "Would you leave alone? You may wait in your cell for your father's arrival while I deal with the daughter of the Guardians."

"I will meet them in the village we passed coming here." She had to leave quickly, she thought, she couldn't let Devlin or Galen catch her alone.

He shrugged. "I have what I want, it makes no difference now."

He motioned to the guard who waited at the door. "Release this one. Bring to me the other who is in the cell, so I and Oberon may deal with her."

Relief washed over Antea. If luck held with her, then she would be on her way with Aaron before Galen and his companions arrived to rescue her sister.

* * * * *

Desperation filled Devlin as horse's hooves pounded along the old dirt road that led to the Fortress of the Damned. His heart echoed the fierce thunder vibrating overhead, his blood pounding through his body at a speed that rivaled his steed.

Behind him rode his warriors, at the end of the line Galen followed, his magic reaching out over the men and sheltering them from the fury of the storm overhead.

Devlin could feel the warmth of his cheeks as his tears mixed with the rain that ran in slow rivulets down his face. He prayed to make it there in time, prayed that despite his growing fears, the message Oberon had left at the castle had been true.

He had given his Seeker's oath that the Lady Chantel would not be harmed, unless she refused to acknowledge herself. Surely to God she would not stand and stay silent, accepting a death meant for Antea, Devlin thought.

That thought had him spurring his horse to a great speed, as they grew ever closer to the stone fortress Jonar had taken from the snake worshippers decades past.

God protect her, he prayed as he felt the hope in his heart dwindling beneath the fear in his gut.

He had seen the deaths that came to the women who were marked as the Guardian children. Jonar was wont to let the women live until at least their sixteenth year. It would have been better for them were they to die at birth.

The brutality of the rapes Devlin had seen left him shaking in terror that Jonar and Oberon would dare to touch his wife in such a way. There was no way anyone could mistake the warmth and sincerity of his wife or the cold calculation that filled every bone in Antea's body.

It was not a death he would wish even upon the hated Antea. For after the rapes had ended, Jonar used a magic that no sorcerer or warrior could combat. A small metal rod whose light radiated to the center of the body, destroying the insides, searing them to such a degree that there could be no repair and no healing unless the gifts of the Guardians had been received. And even then, the pain was unbearable, driving many warriors to insanity while in the grip of it.

He would reach her in time, Devlin swore, fighting to ignore the soft, insistent voice that echoed in his heart that said he was already too late.

# Chapter Seventeen

☙

Chantel was dragged roughly from sleep, stumbling in clumsy disorientation as the guards hauled her out of the room and down the long corridor toward the dungeon's entrance.

The drugged fog that had held her in peaceful slumber was slowly dissipating beneath the fear and the laughing jeers of the soldiers. What was it they had said when they jerked her from her bed? What dark evil could they have meant about Oberon and Jonar sharing their pleasure?

Too quickly it seemed, Chantel stood before the dark lord, feeling bereft, naked without the crystal, which had been stripped from her. She could feel the missing part of her, the link to her sisters, to her father, that she had grown used to in such a short time.

A link she knew was about to be severed forever. The moment she had glimpsed the expression in Jonar's eyes, she had known that her death was at hand.

The destiny Mother Earth had predicted so many years ago was now at hand. There was no longer reason to fear the day coming, nor to worry about the deceptions practiced. There was now only the time for acceptance.

God help her, but she prayed the pain would be brief. The horror she knew would follow her even unto death, but it was now the pain before death that she feared. That and the loneliness that filled her, due to the loss of the crystal.

Chantel could no longer feel the power of the crystal or the strength that had once been inside her. She felt weakened, frightened, though she was determined that this monster would never see that fear.

"So, you are the daughter of Konar." He watched her with eyes a brilliant blue and lacking in any warmth or mercy.

Chantel could feel her heart thunder now in fear as he watched her. She fought to breathe, to remind herself that it was for the greater good. One day, the Shadow would be victorious because of the sacrifice she now made. But may Mother Earth and God have mercy on her, for she feared had she the choice now, she would turn away from what was to come.

Beside him, Oberon sat on a low-built, crude stone altar. The leer on his face was nearly more than she could bear.

Chantel's skin crawled as she watched his hand move slowly between his own thighs, watching her as he massaged the erection that had grown beneath his pants. The sight of it sent icy chills of horror racing over her skin.

Chantel prayed her heart would burst from the fear before the stench of his evil could touch her.

"I am Chantel. Daughter of Galen," she repeated, standing tall, proud, as she knew her father would expect her to despite the trembling in her body. Proclaiming herself now would do no good, she knew. She had signed her own death when she accepted Antea into the castle.

Chantel hoped she did not beg when the end came. Begging would do her no good and she felt these creatures would relish her pleas. She had a feeling that when the time came, she would be more than willing to beg though.

"Then show me the necklace which proclaims you as the daughter of the sorcerer," he suggested quietly. "The talisman he gifted to his daughters."

"It has been stolen from me," she whispered, meeting his eyes and glimpsing a strange fury within them as she blinked back her tears. "The other woman that you held stole that which was mine. The fourth in a circle of four gifted to the daughters of Galen, chosen by Mother Earth to wield her power."

"Cease!" His voice echoed with anger as her calmly spoken words began to fill him with doubt. "Only a child of Konar's could speak with such strength as she faced me. Only the daughter of my bastard brother would know the words to say. The child of Galen is released, as I swore she would be. Now you, Antea, shall die, just as I swore to Konar you would."

"Konar's daughter is not I," she whispered fighting the breathless fear that threatened to take her voice. "But even she is innocent in this vendetta you wage against the Guardians."

"As was my daughter innocent." He spoke harshly, his voice filled with an anger she knew must have grown over the years. "You cannot dissuade me, Antea. I swore to Konar the fate you will now receive."

"What are you going to do?" She could not resist the fear in her voice or her struggles against the men who held her. "Oh God, please no…"

She fought, raged, inside her soul screamed as they tore her clothing from her, as the pain of their possession began. She begged the Mother for courage and knew a veil of distance. She pleaded for strength and felt the pain ease. She did not plead to be taken from her destiny, from the price fate extracted for its aid when her life would begin yet again.

She stared into the darkness of her own mind and thought instead of a time when she would triumph. When she would stand before these two and would know triumph. When she would watch their blood flow and know the land she so loved, the man she breathed for, would know peace.

They took what was not theirs to take, cursing the Guardians, believing they defiled the enemy, that they had struck a blow against the greatest of those false gods. Such games warped minds played. Such horrors they beget…

And when it was over, she knew the worst was yet to come. She stared from the stone altar they had forced her to, her body now damaged, her spirit weak, and she felt the full fury of her choice rain upon her. The hatred, hatred such as she had never known in her life, branding her soul. Marking these two forever as enemies of the very land they thought to conquer so easily.

Until her return, the earth would extract vengeance, one slow drop at a time.

"You fought better than most." Jonar's demeanor was cheerful, triumphant. "Konar will see now that he will strike me upon this land without losing the children he holds in such regard. Vengeance is done."

If only such were true.

She did not argue his declaration, merely watched as he tightened his breeches then before turning away. When he returned, in his hand he held a small wand. She had heard of this weapon. One that would wound and maim from within and yet never touch the skin. Aiming it at her stomach, he pressed the side and a ray of light lit the area at her navel.

Her body heaved as she felt the flesh tear inside her abdomen. Screams were but a harsh cry as the breath left her body in a pain so resounding it nearly broke her mind as she rolled brokenly to the floor, convulsing with the agony.

The agonizing pain lasted only briefly. But she knew that whatever this damage had done would soon take her life. As the heat in her subsided, she looked up at him, knowing that in her life she had never known hatred as fierce as what she now knew.

"Jonar?" She could barely put sound to her voice as he leaned near, mild curiosity on his face.

"Yes, my dear?" he inquired, satisfaction filling his eyes as he regarded her dying body.

"I am Chantel. Daughter to Galen. Sister to Arriane. She will know, Jonar, that you have taken that which she loves. She will know and by her hand shall your blood flow. Yours and the demon who follows you."

She watched as Jonar's eyes widened in sudden shock, his face paling. He opened his mouth to speak, but was halted by the door to the altar room swinging open.

"The Shadow Warriors, sire!" the guard screamed out desperately. "They have breached the Fortress and now come this way. God's blood, but the Shadow is cutting through each man who gets in his way."

His eyes came back to hers.

"Chantel," he whispered, grief, resignation and regret filling his eyes.

"You will burn in hell for this day," she swore. "And the Shadow will be the one to light the fire."

"Come now, Jonar, we will deal with this later," Oberon yelled from the door. "Come now, while we can still escape."

Jonar shook his head, then turned and rushed out the door, leaving Chantel alone in her grief and her pain. She closed her eyes, knowing Devlin would soon be there, wishing with all she knew that she had known the torment he would have to face.

She felt the tears that fell down her cheeks, the sobs that racked her, her cries as the pain seeped slowly throughout her body.

*It hurts, oh God, Devlin, it hurts so badly*, she cried silently.

Then suddenly, she was no longer alone. Chantel opened her eyes as her sisters ran through the door, each dressed in men's clothes, their crystals beacons at their breasts. They had come for her, hoping to save her.

Chantel heard Ariel's terrified cries as they found her on the floor. Heard her tearful pleas that Mother Earth surely would not have allowed this.

Then she felt herself being lifted, heard the anguished cries of her sisters as they wrapped a blanket carefully about her and held her in their arms.

As their cries echoed in the room, she felt the warmth of their crystals as they were laid about her neck. The pain began slowly to ease, but Chantel knew that nothing could stem the tide of death that was slowly cresting over her.

"I will kill them myself, Chantel," Ariel the warrior woman swore, knowing it was by Antea's betrayal that such had happened. "They shall not escape unharmed."

Chantel lifted her hand to the tear-streaked face of her sister and touched her gently. She would have spoken, would have tried to ease the tears had she not heard the tormented cry of the warrior as he burst upon the scene.

She glimpsed Devlin's ravaged, terror-shocked face as her sisters eased back. The fire of fury in his black eyes, the disbelief that left him shaking as he eased her in his arms.

"Chantel." He touched her face, her neck, then looked in horror at the spot she knew marked her stomach. Then tears ran slowly from his eyes as his gaze came back to hers. "I tried. I tried to reach you. Oh God, baby, I tried."

From her navel, her lifeblood slowly oozed from her body. She had felt the warmth when it began. Jonar's weapon was amazingly efficient. The wound so vicious that even magic could not heal it.

"Do something!" Devlin raged, his eyes lifting to the sorcerer who fell to his knees beside her.

Chantel turned her eyes to her father, as her grip tightened on her warrior's hand.

"Remember your vow," she whispered raggedly, feeling the sluggishness, which seemed to make it hard to speak. "You must do as you swore now."

"She will pay," Galen promised her softly, his eyes wet with his own tears. "They shall all pay for this, Chantel."

"No." She shook her head slowly, feeling the drowsiness drifting over her. "Use her, she has the power to do so. She can help. Remember, Father, she is a sister as well."

"Chantel." Devlin's voice whispered over her senses as though from a distance. "Hang on. Don't you leave me. Please God, Chantel, do not leave me."

His tears, the ragged agony reflected in his voice was a wound deeper and more painful than the one Jonar had given her.

"I love you, my warrior." She smiled up at him as she felt the life slowly begin to drain away from her body. "I shall always be close."

She heard his screams of denial as darkness closed gently over her, and for an instant, hatred flared in her for the sister whose betrayal had caused it.

"Joshua!" Devlin screamed, turning to the pale, disbelieving expression of the Mystic. "Contact the Guardians now. I will pay any price for her life. Any price. Tell them now, damn you. Contact them now. Ah God, any price, Joshua."

Desperation clawed at his heart, his very soul as he felt the life leave his wife's body.

"Now, Joshua." He was aware of the sobs tearing from his chest, the grief washing over him in waves so fierce he felt he would never survive the tumult.

"It is too late, Shadow." He felt Galen's hand at his shoulder. "She is not of the Guardians. They can do nothing now."

"Goddamn you, no!" he screamed as he bent over Chantel's body, the agony radiating from his very being too intense for him to stay upright. "No, bring her back to me, Galen. Please God, bring her back to me."

The sobs were torn from his chest. He who had never cried in his life did so now in great racking waves as he held his wife close to his heart.

She had said she would always be safe as long as he held her there, next to his heart. God help him, but she was no longer safe and he knew he could never survive the pain of her loss.

"Antea must be found." He heard Galen behind him, speaking now to the others. "It was by her hand. She has stolen Chantel's crystal, taken her identity. She must be found."

Devlin's body shook, his head rising to stare into the lifeless face he cherished above all others in his life. She was gone. God help him, but she was gone and the whore she called sister was the cause.

"We take care of my wife first," he ordered the men who stood around him. Men whose arms were wrapped around the sobbing, but still healthy bodies of their wives. "We take care of my wife, then I shall find the demon whore and I shall return her to hell."

It was a vow he made to himself. There, as he rocked his precious wife, feeling the life and the laughter freeze inside him. He would find Antea himself and he would hurt her, he vowed. He would destroy her with pain before he used his sword to cut her lying, deceptive heart from her breast.

\* \* \* \* \*

The crystal throbbed at her breast. Antea rode silently behind Aaron as they sped away from the Fortress of the Damned. She was aware of the tears on her cheeks, the ache in her breast. Guilt built upon her until it was like a raging storm far greater than the one that clashed around them.

She had traded Chantel's life for her own. Had she waited only a while longer, Galen and Devlin's forces would have arrived. She had seen them as Aaron had led her through the woods instead of the main road. The sound of their horses thundering along the road had shaken her with terror.

She had wanted to return to the castle. There would be no return now, she admitted to herself. What she had done would likely result in her death anyway. Galen would never allow her to live now.

A shiver shook her body at that thought, then a cold chill chased down her spine. She could hide from men, but she had no illusions that she could hide from the sorcerer's magic.

Aaron carried the gold that had been his payment for allowing Jonar entrance to the castle. Galen's magic protected the castle as long as certain measures were taken. The drawbridge must be up if he was away. The doors to the great hall must be closed. In that way, they would have been protected.

Antea knew she could have prevented Chantel's death in any number of ways. She lowered her head against the driving rain as regret and guilt filled her heart. She would regret this day as long as she lived, she knew, and if Galen had his way, she would not live much longer.

* * * * *

Devlin wrapped the blanket tenderly around his wife's broken body. He had tried to clean the blood from her, but there had been too much of it.

He still knelt on the rough stone altar, his trembling fingers whispering over her beloved face. His breath still heaved with the sobs that were, only now, diminishing. But his soul was freezing, his heart hardening within his chest. He could not go on, he admitted to himself. He would live long enough to find Antea and kill her before he would swiftly follow Chantel to whatever afterlife she had found. And follow her he would, he swore.

"Devlin, let us go after Antea." Joshua now stood separate from his wife, his cold voice echoing through the room despite its softness. "The longer we wait…"

"No." Devlin shook his head as he tucked the ends of the blanket securely about Chantel's cold, still body. "She will not escape us, nor will the one who aided her. I will take care of my wife, then I will find her myself."

Devlin picked Chantel up in his arms, staring down at her as the world faded away. Dear God, he thought, how could he be expected to go on after this?

"We will take her to the caves I had prepared for my own death," Galen told him, his voice husky with his unshed tears, rage trembling along every syllable he spoke. "She would be at rest there, near the castle."

Devlin nodded, knowing the ride would be a hard one to get there in time. Galen was right though, Chantel would rest easier knowing that she was in a place much loved by her father and her sisters. It was the one last thing he could do for her.

"Let us ride then." He moved through the room, the stench of evil and of death nearly overpowering as her blood soaked along the bottom of the stone of the altar stained by evil and Chantel's blood.

Joshua moved aside as Devlin passed, his hands clenching at the futility on the other man's face and the deception Chantel had practiced on him. She had known this would happen, he realized. What reason had she had to court her own death in this horrifying manner? What had made this sacrifice seem an alternative to her life with Devlin?

He watched as Arriane roused herself and followed behind Devlin slowly. She was apart, and he could see the distance she had placed around herself and the others.

Ariel was wrapped in Shanar's arms, her sobs having long eased. Caitlin likewise was held close to Derek's side. They all moved slowly ahead of Arriane, unaware of how she followed alone, unprotected.

He had tried to hold her close, but she had fought his embrace. For the first time since he had known her she had been unwilling to be near him, to allow him to hold her. She seemed to have surrounded herself instead with the grief of her own loss, drawing deeper within her sadness.

Joshua wondered if Chantel had known when she made her fateful decision to allow Jonar's men to kidnap her and Antea what would happen. He could imagine no woman willingly taking steps to endure such death.

It made no sense to him, Joshua thought, but hell, nothing else had made sense to him since first stepping into that cursed castle. Why should this?

\* \* \* \* \*

## Galen's Castle

They wrapped her in linen and laid her on a cool stone bed. Arriane brought the pillow that had once graced Chantel's bed and placed it gently beneath her head.

Caitlin and Ariel were wrapped in their husband's arms, clinging to the safety and the love they had found there. Arriane clung to no one.

Her father sat in mourning, his head lowered as the priest whispered holy words over Chantel's body. The words were meaningless to the priest. It was as though Arriane could hear his thoughts. *Heathens!* His mind had whispered the word as he entered the dim confines of the cool crypt.

Joshua stood beside Devlin, his expression closed, his amber eyes burning within the darkened skin of his face. He had made certain he had the least contact with his wife that could be managed. He would ride out with Devlin and the others after the crypt was closed. They would ride out in search of the whore that Galen had already secured.

Her father thought she didn't know. He thought she was unaware of the prisoners slowly amassing in the cavern beneath the castle. One of those prisoners was Antea, another the lover who had aided her in her deception. They were bound by chains of magic, held secure for whatever judgment Galen would place against them.

The others were the members of the cult, followers of the Damned, those who still worshipped the snake goddess and had aided Oberon in securing the castle and taking Antea and Chantel.

Arriane glanced at his face. He was pale, his blue eyes dim and nearly uncomprehending as the priest finished his eulogy. Soon, he would send Devlin and his men seeking the woman he now hid from them.

Arriane would have shaken her head had she the energy. Devlin would know and if he did not, then Joshua surely would. They would return before Galen passed whatever judgment he made against the woman.

Finally, the last words were said and the priest bowed and hurriedly left the chamber. Devlin still stood silently. It had been his demand that the priest say the words, his fears that Chantel could not pass were she not blessed first.

Arriane would be the last to assure him that his actions were in vain. She could feel the air hum with her sister's presence and wondered why the others were not aware of it as well.

"Antea was sighted near the ports with her lover two days ago." His voice suddenly broke the silence of the crypt. "I will go after her."

"It will take us several hours to prepare for the journey, Devlin," Shanar spoke as his hands caressed his wife's back gently.

"No." Devlin shook his head as he continued to stare at his wife's still face. "I ride alone. Kanna will be arriving here at any time. Please explain to her what has happened and send her home. Tell her she will find all she needs to secure my lands there hidden within my desk. She will know what to do then."

His voice was carefully controlled, without a hint of warmth, his hand gripping the hilt of the sword that had been strapped to his hips.

"What the hell are you talking about?" Derek spoke up now, and Arriane realized that in the days he had been in the castle they had seen little of him or Caitlin. She knew so little about him. "Secure your lands? You talk as though you will not return."

Devlin touched his wife's cheek and Arriane saw the promise his soul was making. He intended to join her as soon as he sent Antea to hell. In his mind, there was nothing left to live for. How one gifted with eternal life could achieve his death, she was not certain. But she knew that if Devlin left alone, then he would not return.

"You will return to the castle first," Galen told him quietly. "I need her body, much as you hate it. That is unless you wish her to find peace in death?" Crafty bastard, Arriane thought to herself. Her father was carefully maneuvering Devlin, but to what purpose?

Devlin raised his gaze from his wife and Arriane flinched. His eyes were dead. There was no fire, no warmth left there within the dark recesses. His heart still beat, yet he had joined Chantel already.

"Then I shall return her to you." He shrugged and for a moment hatred flared then died as surely as a flame could be extinguished.

"I will ride with you," Joshua spoke from beside him and Arriane noticed that he too had prepared for battle.

She caught his gaze and held the amber accusation for long moments before he turned his eyes from her. *Ah*, she thought, *once again he has found yet another way to blame me for the ills befalling the warriors.*

"Then ride swiftly, my young warrior." Galen nodded and Arriane wondered why the others were not protesting what they must surely see. Devlin intended to kill himself the moment life left Antea. He had no intention of fighting any longer, of serving the Guardians who had not answered his call for help.

"We shall all ride with you, Devlin." Shanar's embrace tightened around his wife as she flinched at his announcement. "I seek revenge on Ariel's behalf, just as Derek does on Caitlin's. We ride together."

It was apparent that it made little difference to Devlin who rode with him.

"My sword will be the one to shed her blood." His order was made in a voice soft with deadly purpose. "Do you all understand this?"

They looked to each other in concern, then nodded slowly.

243

"Very well, then prepare to ride." With one last trembling caress to the cold, still lips of his wife's face, Devlin turned and left the room quickly.

Moments later, the others had followed and Arriane was left alone with her father.

"She's here, beneath the castle," Arriane told him softly. "When will he know?"

Galen raised his eyes, then moved slowly to his daughter.

"You have stood alone in your grief," he whispered, his arms opening to embrace her. "Forgive me for allowing that."

Arriane flinched, stepping back from him. She could not bear the touch, the love she felt from him.

"Arriane?" He looked at her, shock and pain filling his eyes.

"Do not touch me, Father." She shook her head, fighting the tears she had not shed, even with her sister's death.

"Ah, child, this is no fault of yours." He ignored the command, pulling her against the warmth of his body, his strong arms enfolding her in the love she had always known he held for her. "This is no sin of yours, child."

"Jonar's blood forever taints me." The pain of that knowledge was nearly enough to bring her to her knees. "Even Joshua cannot look at me now."

"Joshua is a fool, I have always said so." His hands rubbed her back as he tried to soothe her. "Your sister loved you, Arriane. Never forget that. What she did, she did to secure so much more than you shall ever know. I swear to you now, her death was not in vain."

"They have destroyed us all." Arriane fought the tears, the gut-wrenching pain that filled her. "As we prepared her body, we cleaned the evil of what they had done to her away, Father, but there is no way to cleanse the knowledge of it."

Her grandfather's evil magic had taken all hope for the future. With his evil, his taint of demonic hatred, he had killed her, just as he had once killed Ariel's mother. Ariel had broken down into complete hysteria when she had seen the wound on Chantel's abdomen.

She had fallen beside her sister's body on the bed they had laid her in and sobbed as though she herself were enduring the pain. Her arms had gone around her sister, pleas pouring from her throat as she begged her to awaken, to come back, to take the nightmares away.

It was then that Arriane had known. She had known to the soles of her feet that Jonar had been the one who had raped Ariel all those years ago. And Arriane carried his blood, was infected with his evil. She was no longer a sister, but was reviled instead.

Arriane remembered the day Ariel had come to the castle. Her big violet eyes had appeared bruised, her body moving as though it had no will of her own.

Chantel had cried for her. Wrapping her in her arms, rocking her as a mother would a child, she had grieved as the other girl could not.

"Jonar and Oberon will pay for what they have done, just as the whore Antea shall pay," Galen sighed. "But not for a while yet, precious daughter. There is much that Chantel died for and little that I can do against those who caused her death. For a while yet, we must endure the pain of it."

Suspicion flared, anger rising like a mindless beast within her heart as she jerked from her father's arms.

"My God, you are going to let her live," she accused him harshly, her body beginning to tremble in fury and in fear. "She will betray us all, Father."

Sadness and grief filled the air between them.

"She shall betray us all, but only in that final betrayal shall Chantel's plans and the vision of your destinies hold forth. She died for your happiness, Arriane, and her own. Unfortunately, that happiness shall be a long time coming."

# Chapter Eighteen

&

It was as though time had stopped within the castle. Grief, despair, unimagined pain. There was no easing the burden that the loss of Chantel had brought.

Galen sat within the huge, throne-like chair in front of the fire of the Great Hall. Here within the castle he had built to protect his family, he had failed to protect his eldest, his most cherished daughter.

His blue eyes were dim now with the memories that rushed over his heart. The infant, the child, and finally the young woman. Her last words to him had been a prediction of this day. He had trusted in the power of Mother Earth. Trusted in the instincts his daughter had possessed to protect herself, even while sacrificing her life to the future she had been promised.

Galen had never imagined, had never conceived the horror of the death his daughter had endured. Had never imagined that Jonar would be so cruel as to use such tainted magic against a defenseless woman. He would have stopped her had he known, he thought. He would have never allowed the warriors access to his daughters, would have stripped the crystals from their necks before he would have allowed this dark horror to come to one of his children.

But now there was no escaping it. His daughter lay entombed in the crypt Galen had built for himself, and spurred by a fear he could not name, he had commissioned the erection of three other crypt beds within it.

Before any of his other children joined his eldest, he would see to the duty Chantel had made him swear he would carry out. What had possessed him, he now wondered, to agree to such a thing? Surely there was no magic in this world or any other that would still the hatred in Devlin long enough to allow this bitch to live.

Seated in a darkened corner, still bound with the chains of magic he had placed upon her hours before, the traitor sat. The likeness of his own daughter, her face, her hair, the color of her eyes a duplicate of Chantel's. The heart inside her breast was as black and as cold as any evil he had ever known though.

"You betrayed her." He finally spoke into the darkness of the corner. "I would know why."

He saw the sudden shift in the shadows at the sound of his voice.

"Let her alone, the fault is mine," the male secured beside her spoke up in fury.

Strange, that this knight had betrayed him as well, Galen thought. A man he had once trusted, a heart that had held no evil when he first came into the castle.

"And you shall pay for your part in this as well, my friend," Galen promised him quietly. "Your lust for this whore shall be your downfall, Aaron." He then returned to the woman who sobbed within the darkness now. "I ask you again, why did you betray my daughter?"

"I did not want to die." Her voice was hoarse from her tears.

"You lie. You would have known that Jonar would not touch you until he was certain of your identity, just as you would have known that the warriors and I would come to rescue you. So I ask you again, why did you betray my daughter? What possessed you to steal the crystal from her and proclaim yourself a child of Galen?"

"I did not believe you would come in time," she pleaded, weeping as Galen stared at her, his heart stone-hard within his chest.

"Another lie and I will cleave you in two myself," he warned her coldly, harshly.

The steely thread of power, of intent within his voice, echoed throughout the room.

There was silence from the shadows.

"Shall I tell you why you did so?" he asked her finally when she refused to answer.

He knew why. He had torn the crystal from her neck the moment he saw it and had instantly known why she had betrayed his daughter.

"Did you really think the crystal would lead you to the Guardians? Did you really believe that power would give you the knowledge, the ability to reach them and secure for yourself and your lover the destiny you sought?"

"I felt the power," she cried out from the darkness. "It filled me, it made me stronger."

"It was a power not yours to possess. How in mankind and magic you managed to make it respond to you, I cannot fathom." But he did know. The ties of blood had given her the power, and the fault of that was his own.

His own magic had ultimately been his daughter's downfall.

"What am I to do with you now?" he sighed wearily. "Traitor, yet forgiven by one whose heart was too tender to know any better. The vow she has placed on me wearies me, girl. But be warned, there will be more pain in life than death would have ever brought you."

"Please, Galen," she beseeched him, her trembling voice causing his stomach to clench with the need to retch. "Do not punish Aaron for my mistake. Let him go."

The whining, calculating whore thought she could appeal to him, to some sense of honor she thought he had.

The knight was silent now. He knew no amount of pleas would change whatever course Galen had set for them. Nay, Galen thought, not himself, but Chantel had set this course and he knew he would do anything, give anything he possessed to go back and recant the vow he had given her.

"I trusted you, Aaron." Galen could see the bleak misery that came into the knight's eyes. "Why did you betray me?"

"The goddess," Aaron whispered, his voice now filled with loathing. "This is my sin, Galen, not Antea's. It was I who set her on this course. It was I who suggested the betrayal and filled her heart with fear of what Jonar would do. I used her. Punish me, not the woman."

Silence reigned within the great hall. He could feel the knight's need to reach out to the woman who sobbed at his feet, bound by chains of magic and unable to find comfort in each other, yet they reached out to each other anyway. There was emotion there. A caring that sickened him to his very soul. What right had they to care or to have each other, when by their actions, they had destroyed his precious child?

"You shall both be punished," he whispered wearily. "Even now, the members of the Damned swing from the gallows constructed in the courtyard. Death haunts my home for your actions and there shall be no forgiveness in it."

*Used by destiny, led by fate, Galen, Chantel secured your vow for a reason.* The Mother spoke to him once again now. He had not heard her soft, caressing voice since giving Chantel the crystal years before.

"I will kill him at least."

*You need him to secure her agreement. You know what must be done. His mind was clouded, his will weakened for this very reason.*

"He will interfere…"

*Just as he is supposed to interfere. Do not step from the course, my son. We are so very near and yet so very far away. Chantel is now dependent on your willingness to continue in her name. Her destiny and the destiny of your daughters now rest in your hands alone. They rest in your willingness to do as fate has decreed. She must live. She must take Chantel's place, or the warrior who holds the key to the future will not survive. He will hate Antea. His soul will deny even the smallest transgression against the one he loved, but until this is finished, the image of her must remain. It must, Galen, or all she has died for will be lost to her. She shall drift, always alone, a scream, a cry, a broken wound that will cripple her very spirit shall result instead. The image of her must remain. A small consolation to his soul. She is not his heart, and well he knows it. But the soul must be given a measure of ease or your magic will never hold and he will find a way to end his own life. Do as you swore to her.*

The Mother's demand lacked the cool, gentle qualities it always had before. It now contained anger, pain. The earth grieved as he grieved himself.

He needed to kill, Galen admitted to himself. The bodies hanging now from the gallows were not enough. He needed to expend the fury rising inside him as well.

"Kill them now." Devlin's voice spoke from the doorway as he entered the room slowly, advancing on Galen and the couple who now gazed into the face of death. "If you do not have the stomach to kill her, then I am more than ready."

Galen watched as the warrior flexed his fists, his black eyes trained on the corner, his steps propelling him toward them slowly, methodically.

He halted at Galen's chair, staring down at him with eyes black with grief and fury. There was a coldness there that would turn him, that would drive the tenderness from his heart and create the warrior the Guardians had always dreamed of having.

Galen detested giving them, in any way, what they wished, but he knew there was now no hope left to turn the tide. Fate and Destiny, they could touch their children with tenderness or surround them with misery as was their will. Misery would now shroud this young man for years to come.

Galen sighed, staring wearily into the fire once again.

"And how would Chantel feel about your actions?" he asked him. "You heard her last words as well as I. Can you so easily disregard them?"

"I made her no vow," he raged, the agony filling all he was, resonating to touch all who stood near. The man was gone, only the demon the Guardians had fought to create remained... "She is gone because of the harlot and her lover that you now protect. I would have no qualms killing them."

The rage filling the warrior could be felt about the room. The grief and pain rode him hard, the need to destroy the one responsible for that grief was more than he could bear.

Galen himself had vowed to spare her and for a time had considered breaking that vow. Each time he did so, he could hear his daughter's words echo about his soul.

*Use her, Father. She is a sister as well. Should she find a way to secure even the smallest bit of the earth's power, then the end shall come at a far later date. If she cannot, then at least he lives. He must live, Father, or I shall drift as only a ghostly wail, unwilling, unable to find rebirth without the heart I seek.*

Galen knew what Chantel and the Mother had been asking of him. She had known the crystal had responded to the other girl. Known that without her, then the events that must proceed could not. It was the only way even a bit of her power could be harnessed to see the way to the future.

Antea was Chantel's half-sister. The child lost to her mother nine months before her liaison with a sorcerer, which resulted in Chantel's birth.

Galen's incantation on the original crystal, to cleave only to the blood of Chantel, that her sisters only know its power, had been his daughter's destruction. He had not known, could not have guessed, that the child Muriel thought she had lost, had lived.

Now he was faced with a decision he would have given his life not to have to make.

"Do you not kill her, I will," Devlin swore to him, his voice grating harshly as he stared into the corner where the girl cowered. "One day, some way, I will find her and I will kill her, Galen."

Galen was silent. Another decision. Another vow made. He had sworn he would wipe her memory from the warrior should she perish. How could she have known the torment, the fury and bloodlust that would have gripped her warrior?

All that saved Antea now was the magic about her. A magic Galen knew Devlin would find a way to break through. He nearly sighed his regret.

It was the darkest day of his life, he reflected. He would gladly give up his life, his magic, would it bring Chantel back. But he knew that only his magic now would preserve the destiny Chantel had died for.

"Ah, Devlin, valiant knight, if only I could give you your heart's desire," he whispered wearily. "If I could, I would give you this viper who stole our heart, gladly. But my vow to Chantel stays my hand."

"I will find her," Devlin snarled as he leaned forward, his lips curling back from his teeth, his eyes narrowing ferally. "I will find her, Galen, and I will make her scream as she dies, as surely as I heard Chantel's screams within my soul. She will not live."

Pity and anguish stilled Galen's tongue. His only response was to lift his hand and place it at the temple of the warrior who bent close to him.

"Be at ease, young knight," he whispered. "Return to your bed and when you awaken, your heart, your soul shall be at ease. The rest will come in time."

Devlin's expression cleared, the flame of fury fading within his eyes, his body relaxing, though only slightly. He rose, looked down at the magician one last time and then walked slowly from the room.

"What did you do to him?" Aaron's voice came from the darkness, the suspicion and the fear causing Galen to grin mirthlessly.

He turned back to the couple, a mocking smile playing about his lips, fury still reflected in his eyes.

"I just secured a husband for your harlot," he bit out. "I am sure you will admire my plan. Devlin cannot seek death as he wishes, so his vision of Chantel, his dreams and his memories must have a replacement. Your whore shall replace her in his bed. You may live, but the conditions are mine. And should you fail, the crystal you deceived her sister to possess shall become your worst nightmares. Heed my words, Aaron, you live only because your life will gain her cooperation. Cross me and your death shall be her punishment."

Galen looked into the shadows, his heart lying heavily within his chest, unshed tears choking him.

"When the warrior awakens on the morrow, he will no longer remember the one who was taken from him. For another image shall confront him. Chantel's image, her voice, and the dreams they weaved together have all been shrouded in mists and darkness. He will not remember the bride of his heart, for another shall face him. You, Antea. You shall ease the soul of what it has lost. You shall play wife to the warrior and complete the circle of the crystals. You shall, for if you fail, you shall find the crystal a cold, barren place which shall harbor your traitorous soul."

# Chapter Nineteen
*Six months later*

ഔ

Devlin awoke as the sun was spreading its gentle rays through the window across his face. He blinked slowly, his eyes opening, staring in blind confusion at the ceiling over his head.

Had he drunk too much again? he wondered. It wasn't inconceivable that he would do such a thing. Perhaps once again fought with the bitch he had married? He turned his head and saw her body on the bed beside him. Even now, after all these months, he felt a sense of disorientation when he awoke to find her sleeping beside him.

She used no pillow, though he admitted this was his fault. For some reason the sight of a pillow beneath her head was more than he could bear.

He frowned, chasing an elusive memory, a feeling of overwhelming grief. It was like this each time he fell asleep in their bed. He awoke with an overpowering sadness, a grief he could not name.

At her breast lay the cold crystal he had married to own. Mirthlessly he admitted that such a description described her heart as well. A cold, barren desert that he had no desire to ever touch.

He had not taken his wife once in his memory. Several nights after he had begun to heal from whatever sickness had consumed him, he had rolled over, his cock demanding attention. He had attempted to take her, hearing her cries of pleasure as he touched her and feeling a betrayal his heart could not name.

He had become so physically ill after catching the scent of her passion in the air that he had vomited off and on for hours.

He had finally moved from the room entirely, though he had been forced to take the woman with him. He had locked the other room after ordering it cleaned, staring at the door, wondering why it hurt so deeply. He still could not explain the pain of that memory or his soul-deep knowledge that he had come close to betraying not just his heart, but a part of his soul.

It was several days later that he had walked into his room and found his wife sharing his bed with one of the castle knights. Even now, Devlin wondered why he had felt no surprise when he had seen the dark-haired man rutting between his wife's thighs. It had meant so little to him that he had merely backed out of the room and given them time to finish before returning for what he had sought.

Rubbing a hand wearily across his face, Devlin rose from the bed and began to dress quickly. He hated sharing a bed with the woman. It had been his thought for weeks now to move to a room farther down the hall.

As was his habit, his mind was quickly made. After adjusting the wide belt at his hips, he began moving his few belongings that were laid out into the large chest at the end of the bed.

His wife and her lover could have this bed all they pleased then. There would no longer be any need for her to sneak her knight in while he was training soldiers or seeing to the running of the castle.

"What are you doing?" Her voice was only mildly curious as she rose from the bed, pulling the blankets about her body as she did so.

"Moving to another room," he answered her as he shut the lid on the chest, then collected his sword.

"Why? Dammit, Devlin, I don't feel like moving again. Why should we? You have not touched me in this bed."

He paused to glance at her. The frown on her face, the irritation in her eyes. For some reason he kept expecting to see something more when he looked at her. Something warm and kind and absent of artifice or deception.

"I did not say you were moving, I said I was." He shook his head at his fanciful imaginings. "You can have your lover anytime you choose now. I've tired of the attempt to keep up appearances."

He watched her face pale as he informed her of his knowledge of the warrior.

"You know?" she whispered, sinking slowly to the chair beside the bed. "What are you going to do?"

"The same thing I did months ago when I walked in here to find him humping between your thighs." He shrugged. "Absolutely nothing."

What was this unreasonable hatred he had for this woman? he wondered. He could look at her and some days he wanted nothing more than to bury his dagger at her breast.

Her mouth opened, then closed as she fought for a reply.

"Don't distress yourself, Antea." He opened the door, lifting the chest and carrying it with him. "No reprisals. Hell, it's not like I can bear to touch you myself."

He walked away from her, weariness clenching his gut, his head throbbing with emotions he could not put a name to. Devlin felt sometimes as though he were going insane. Even the men he fought with attested to the fact that there was something gravely wrong within this castle where he was concerned.

He opened the door to the other bedroom, set his chest inside then turned the key that was nestled within the lock. This he slipped into the small leather pouch attached to his belt. He felt no comfort in being able to lock his belongings up.

"Devlin." Joshua stood now in the doorway, watching him carefully. "Is there a problem?"

"No problem." Devlin turned to him as he began to make his way down to the steps that led to the great hall. "Why?"

"Well, you did just move from your wife's room," he pointed out. "That usually involves a problem."

Devlin shrugged.

"Already she sends for her lover," Joshua grunted. "She is making a fool of you."

This surprised Devlin. He turned back to Joshua with a frown.

"A woman does not make a fool of a man when it matters not to him who she fucks," he assured the Mystic. "Perhaps I will find a lover myself."

Though some knowledge inside him said he would not.

"That does not mean she should be given leave to do the same." Devlin could hear the fury in Joshua's voice. "She should be more circumspect."

Devlin halted at the end of the steps, turning to watch Joshua with mild irritation.

"I agree she doesn't deserve such freedom," he grunted. "But I haven't the energy nor the desire to watch her movements or her lovers, and neither do you have the time."

"So we assign someone," Joshua bit out.

"If you must, then assign Aaron. He seems to be doing quite well at the job," Devlin laughed sarcastically. "Let it go, Joshua. Kanna will be here later and she will take over the running of the castle and the duties as its mistress. I no longer care what Antea does…"

"She is your wife," Joshua broke in.

Fury, hot and deep, flared in Devlin's chest. He imagined he heard a keening cry rip through the castle that echoed the one he could feel in his soul.

"That woman is no wife of mine," he snarled, barely controlling the violence raging through his system. "Call her such again and I will call you out for it."

He turned and stomped from the castle, aware as he did so that several glasses shattered and the huge mirror above the fireplace cracked from its top corner to the opposing bottom corner.

His powers were becoming stronger, his use of them more constant with these bitter rages that seemed to fill him, he knew. He had once known the secret of controlling the black moods. It now seemed as though they controlled him.

Galen watched Joshua from where he stood within the hallway, a frown marking his brow.

"My magic is not so easy to break through, Mystic. You will merely cause your friend more pain."

"I mentioned her name thrice," Joshua whispered in confusion. "It was as though he never heard it."

"Because he did not," Galen assured him, moving slowly into the great hall as Joshua followed him. "The magic surrounds his soul, Joshua, even my death would not break the bonds that hold the memories at bay. You do no more than cause him to hurt and to feel confusion at the reason why."

"Will you allow that whore the freedom he gives her?" Joshua demanded as he followed him. "You can stop it."

"I could," Galen, agreed taking his favorite seat in front of the low fire burning within the fireplace. "I have given Devlin this castle, these lands, and all that he would have received were he my son. I will not interfere. To do so is to attempt to change the course Fate and Destiny have laid out for your commander."

Galen was aware of Joshua's helpless rage in the face of this announcement. Of the men who fought with Devlin, only Joshua had been unaffected by the spell that had woven around the castle. None remembered her now. None save himself, Joshua and Arriane.

"Then perhaps I am free do so as well," Joshua sneered.

Galen shrugged, though his heart broke for his daughter.

"Perhaps it would be best should you reinstall the Widow Denning in the village," Galen reflected. "You sear my daughter's heart with each word from your lips. It would but give her a bit of peace should you do so."

Galen had attempted to hold his daughter just the night before. To ease the horrible shadows in her eyes that came with Joshua's continual refusal to be a husband to her. His refusal to allow her to care for the child he had installed in the castle was scarring her in ways he feared she would never recover from.

She had taken to spending more and more time within the underground chamber of the castle. She could feel Chantel more clearly there, she said. It brought her comfort where nothing else could.

"This castle is cursed," Joshua whispered. "Even Shanar and Derek sense the darkness about it. They are ready to leave, you know this, do you not?" Joshua asked him sarcastically, knowing such a move would break the man's heart.

"I am aware of this. Fate has decreed it, Destiny sets it in motion." Galen could already feel the emptiness of the castle, the tragedies soon to come.

"Tell me, Galen," Joshua moved to sit in the chair beside him. "For God's sake, do not do to me as your daughter did, it is slowly destroying me."

"As you are destroying my other daughter?" Galen asked him softly.

Joshua was silent for long moments, his gaze meeting Galen's and seeing in it the anger at Arriane's pain.

"I will make you a deal," Joshua told him softly. "Tell me. Tell me what is to come and I will show her nothing but kindness. I will speak to her with warmth at all times. I will swear this to you."

"You do not want that curse, my friend." Galen closed his eyes as he fought the need to give his daughter a brief chance at happiness.

"It is my choice," Joshua argued. "Your magic blocks every attempt I make to reason with my friends, whether in the castle or miles away. I cannot change what is to come, at least allow me to know."

Galen opened his eyes and stared into the flames rising within the grate. In them, he saw so much and at times prayed he was blind to it as well.

"There is a time coming, the blackest days the warriors could ever know. You shall all share Devlin's sorrow, his grief and his pain, though you will not have the comfort of magic to hide the reason why." He ignored Joshua's paling face, the shock in his eyes.

"All of them?" he seemed to gasp.

"Even Arriane." Galen swallowed tightly. "Nothing can change it, nothing can stand in its way."

"Why? Goddamn you, sorcerer. Why can we not change it?" Joshua cursed, revealing his own softer feelings for the wife he professed to despise.

"A day shall also come with it that shall herald a dawning of happiness, of peace with the destruction of Jonar. These women shall be yours once again, in laughter and in love. They shall not be gone forever."

"You are lying." Joshua jumped to his feet, staring down in fury at the man who looked up at him. "Both events are not possible."

"Both are entirely possible," Galen told him quietly. "But you, Mystic, you may lose even that. Your rage and black hatred shall one day turn the gentle heart your bride has offered you time and again. I do not lie, you know this to be a fact. Know as a fact as well. Arriane shall pierce that stone you call a heart, and when she does, you may not survive the encounter. Now, I expect to see a smile on my daughter's face soon. She deserves it more than most."

Joshua watched as the bastard sorcerer left the room and knew that somehow, some way, he was not lying. He may perhaps be wrong about Arriane piercing his heart, but he knew he did not lie, nor was he wrong about the other.

He shook his head, running his hands over his face as he fought to accept this information. It made sense. If Chantel knew they would die anyway, she would have sacrificed herself to any pain, no matter how great, to be assured of being with Devlin later.

The question in Joshua's mind was how much later and how would it happen? She was dead. He checked the crypt often and knew her body was still there.

How many times, he wondered to himself, had he sat within the darkness of that stone chamber and spoken to her? Cursing her for what she had done to Devlin, questioning the legacy she had left them.

Joshua did not believe in the dead rising, other than Christ, and he did not believe in rebirth. How then, he wondered, was a sorcerer and Mother Earth going to pull this one off?

\* \* \* \* \*

He found Arriane in their room. Closing the door behind him, Joshua stared at her, seeing once again how pale she had become, how lost she appeared.

She sat on the window seat, staring out at the valley below, her head lying against the rough stone sill. Hair as black as the darkest night flowed around her, the heavy weight appearing too much for her fragile neck to bear.

The dark gray and midnight blue of her gown gave him a glimpse of the storm he knew was brewing in her soul now. Each night he slipped into her dreams, holding her close, trying to ease the pain that struck at her. The guilt and suffering were nearly too much for him to bear. How, he wondered, did she carry such burdens alone?

And she had carried them alone. Other than when she slept and he slipped into her mind to ease the horror of her dreams, she carried all her fears and all her pain alone.

Guilt flayed Joshua's soul. Rarely had his actions caused him to wonder at his own brutal nature, but now, at this moment, he wondered at those he had taken against his own wife. The woman who, in his dreams, had eased him after countless battles, had soothed his soul, had touched him in passion and in enraptured love.

"Arriane?" He spoke her name softly as he walked toward her.

She became aware of him with a hard shudder of her body. Her head turned, her brilliant blue eyes glistening with unshed tears.

"I'm sorry." She rose to her feet as though the movement took more energy than she had to spare. "I did not know you were here. I will return when you are finished."

As she moved to walk past him, Joshua caught her arm in a firm, though gentle grip. She stopped. Silent and still she stood beside him, her head lowered, her body vibrating with her suppressed anguish.

"You need to rest," he told her softly, uncertain what to say or to do to ease her pain.

"I will rest later." There was just cold finality to her voice and he wondered if she knew the destiny awaiting her. Surely she was protected from such knowledge, such brutal clarity of future events.

Joshua shook his head. Of course she was. Did she know the events to come, then he would have glimpsed them in her dreams.

"I cannot play your games now, Joshua," she whispered as she tugged her arm against his grip.

"Arriane, forgive me." He kept his voice just as soft as her own, allowing his regret, his shame to be revealed. "I am no fit husband for you, but I would be one now, if you would allow it."

A shudder worked over her body, as though terror were striking at her very soul.

"No." Her voice was filled with fear. "Please, Joshua, do not use my emotions against me now. I cannot bear more pain."

Joshua grimaced. What had he done to his little wife? In his attempt to save his own damned soul, had he broken hers?

"Arriane." He turned her more fully to him and when she would not raise her gaze to his, his hand cupped her chin, forcing her to gaze up at him.

A shattered scream of denial echoed through his head, his heart. Never in his life had he seen such ragged emotions, such terror in a single person's gaze. Her eyes were dark with it, her soul laid bare to him, crimson with her inner wounds.

"I am doomed," she whispered bleakly as he watched her with shaken intensity. "The very blood that runs in my veins has cursed me and all those that I love. Beware, my husband, that you are not caught in that trap. For as God is my witness, I love you more than all others."

He shook his head, barely able to grasp the painful honesty in her voice and in her eyes.

"The fault is not yours…"

"She is my sister and she haunts me." Ragged pain shredded her voice. "I can feel her all around me and my guilt only grows. She would wrap me in comfort, but there is no comfort for one such as myself."

"No, Arriane," he protested the searing guilt she would take upon her slender shoulders. "You cannot take the blame for this. You cannot allow yourself—"

"He is my grandfather." Hatred and shame filled her voice. "He destroyed my mother and led her on the course of her destruction. He has raped two of my sisters and he has killed one. His blood is evil and I am tainted."

"Stop it." He shook her gently, terrified by the willing acceptance to take the blame for Jonar's actions. "What have you done, Arriane, to make you believe such things? I have tempted you to murder every second of our time together and still you have faced me with only truth and devotion. What in your bereaved mind makes you believe that Chantel's death was any fault of yours?"

"Because I live." Her desperate wail echoed around him then. It was a broken, pleading sound that tore at his heart. "I live to watch everything and everyone I love broken and discarded by that bastard. And you, Joshua, most beloved by me, will be next. I have seen your blood and your hatred, and God help me, I cannot bear the pain."

The excess of her desperation nearly drove her to her knees. Joshua caught her as she sobbed out against him, holding her fragile body in his arms as shock coursed through his system. There were no tears, only that haunting, never-ending pain.

He lifted her into his arms, bearing her to their bed as she shuddered in his arms. Unable to shed her tears, her pain was so great, she would only turn her head from him, fighting his embrace and any comfort he would give her.

"You will not do this," he bit out, gripping her chin and making her look at him as he stared down at her in a blinding haze of fear and pain. She would destroy herself if she continued on this course. "Will you undo the sacrifice Chantel made for you, Arriane, by grieving in such a way forever? Will you take away the great love she held for you, by refusing any happiness that would come your way?"

"What happiness?" She jerked her chin from his grasp, bucking against his body in an attempt to be free. "What happiness is there now for me to look forward to? I am wife to a man who hates me and granddaughter to one whose perverted desires would destroy me further. Tell me, Joshua, what hope is left?"

"There is this." He could not bear such agony any longer. He could not bear to see her in such overriding pain, such desperate need, and not react.

His lips slanted over hers, catching her surprised gasp as his tongue pushed forcefully into her mouth. The taste of spiced wine and gentle woman instantly overwhelmed his senses. As though his kiss had opened some untapped well inside her, she came alive within his arms.

Her lips opened to him with a needy groan, her tongue reaching out to meet his as her arms wrapped about his neck, her fingers gripping at his hair to hold him to her. She was a flame burning only for him. An untapped well of such passion that he knew she would destroy him.

"Do not leave me," she cried out as he tore his lips from hers to search out the silken, fragrant skin of her neck. "Please, Joshua, do not leave me aching again."

"Never," he growled, so desperate for her now that he prayed for the control not to damage her.

He dispensed of their clothing quickly. Some was ripped beyond repair as he tossed the shreds to the floor.

She whispered his name with such need, such emotion that his cock became a raging beast, hardening between his thighs with a swiftness that he knew should not surprise him.

Joshua stared down at her, fighting for control as his gaze touched her full, swollen breasts, then moved to the naked, plump lips of her cunt. They glistened with her juices, drawing him with a scent so sweet and delicate it would haunt him unto death.

"I do not want to harm you," he whispered, his hand going between her thighs, his fingers sliding through the honey of her arousal as they slid easily down the narrow slit that separated it. "You are so tiny, Arriane, and I am not a small man."

She shivered. His gaze went quickly to her face to see if it was fear that caused such a reaction. He clenched his teeth at what he saw there. Naked, unabashed arousal glittered in her eyes and filled her expression. Her lips were swollen from his kisses, her cheeks flushed with her lusts.

Her hair spread out around her in wanton disarray as she stared up at him in a fever of need, her lips reddened, parting, tempting him to taste them again.

"You will only hurt me if you leave me again." Her hand reached out to him, her fingers running over the heavy length of his engorged cock. "How many times I have dreamed of you taking me, Joshua. I beg of you, do not turn from me again."

Remorse flayed him. She had needed him. Needed more from him than just the easing of her dreams. She had needed to be held, to be comforted, and he had not provided even that simple comfort to her.

"Forgive me, Arriane." He lifted her hand from his cock, kissed her silken palm then laid it on her abdomen. "You must not touch me. Not this time, promise me this."

She frowned, her eyes so solemn they broke his heart.

"But I enjoy touching you," she whispered. "The feel of you brings me much pleasure."

"My touch will bring you even more," he promised her, attempting to smile, but fearing it appeared more a grimace than a smile. "My control is tenuous at best. If you touch me, I may lose what little I have and I am terrified of harming you."

His hand skimmed over the wet silk of her pussy again. His fingers parted her, his gaze unable to stay away from the pink and cream perfection of her most tempting flesh.

"You will not harm me." She was breathing hard now, rough, her hips shifting against his touch as the translucent juices coated her further.

"You are so small." His fingers slid down as her hips lifted to him, his finger testing the entrance to her heated vagina. She was soft and fiery and his cock was screaming for a relief that could only be found within her snug pussy.

Joshua knew he would not be able to wait much longer. He leaned to her, his lips covering hers again, his tongue sweeping into her mouth as her hands moved to the quilt, her fists bunching the fabric there. She whimpered, her tongue tangling with his, her hard nipples rasping over his chest as she lifted herself closer to him.

Joshua felt the blood thundering through his veins, throbbing in his cock. His flesh was ultrasensitive, his entire being sensitized from the outpouring of passion between them. Never had another woman's kiss been so sweet, so tempting. Never had he known such heat and longing.

Tearing his lips from hers, he kissed her desperately from her neck to the swollen mounds of her breasts. Covering a nipple, he drew on her repeatedly, ravenous for the taste of her flesh that seemed infused with her female lusts.

"Joshua, I cannot bear it." Arriane was panting now, the sound of her desire-thick voice shredding his control.

"You will burn me alive." His lips trailed to her abdomen as he caught the scent of her passions, earthy and alive with the promise of a rapturous heat.

He could not resist the allure of it any longer. His mouth watered, his cock straining at the leash of his control but first, first he needed to taste the liquid pleasure that poured from her body.

Arriane was nearly mindless with the pleasure consuming her. She tossed her head against the mattress of the bed, her fists clenching in the blankets and still he did not stop. His lips ventured further, further down her body…

"Oh God. Joshua…" She wailed his name as his tongue stroked through her slit, setting fire to her cunt.

Her legs shifted, opening easily as he moved between them, her body desperate for more of the sensations that shot through her nerve endings like stars exploding in the sky. Her hips lifted, and in her mindless need for more, pressed her pussy into the greedy hunger of his mouth. As though the action loosed some beast of passion inside him, Joshua's hands gripped her hips, his mouth burrowing more firmly against sensitive flesh as his tongue plunged forcefully into her vagina.

Arriane felt shock ricochet over her body. His tongue was moving inside her, stroking her, slurping at the thick juices running from her. The sensations were indescribable, exhilarating, burning her alive with the rising crescendo of heat.

His hands held her to his mouth as he lay between her thighs, lifting her, angling her hips so he could fuck her with the rapid, quick movements of his tongue.

Arriane bucked against him, her feet bracing on his shoulders as tremors racked her body. It wasn't pleasure. Nothing so intense, so blinding could be called pleasure. It was enraptured agony. An exquisite torture that was blinding and numbed the brain. She was but a creature of sensation now, her hands locking in his hair, her hips rotating against the hard thrusts inside her tormented cunt.

Each hard thrust stoked the fires hotter, brighter inside her quaking flesh. She shuddered against him as her womb convulsed with a flood of intense, breath-halting rapture.

She screamed or thought she did. Her thighs locked around his head as she felt her cunt clench, spasm, then explode in an ecstasy she knew must lead to death. She shook in the firestorm that erupted through her body, only barely aware of Joshua tearing free of her, coming over her.

She felt his cock press into her, surging through the pulsing muscles of her cunt. He was crying out her name as her sweat coated their bodies and Arriane could do nothing but ride the wave of yet another exploding starburst of sensation.

His cock was thick and steel-hard, spreading the tightening flesh, tearing into her like a heated stalk of pure fire. And he did not stop, did not halt his own rush to completion then. The engorged flesh thrust into her repeatedly, lengthening her orgasm until she was sobbing, desperate, her body racked by such powerful shudders that she was held suspended in a state of orgasmic bliss.

Then his harsh male shout sounded in her ears, his cock throbbed, swelled further, then flooded her with a heat and fire that tore her very soul loose from its moorings. Then she was adrift in exquisite pleasure. Her body pulsing, her inner core floating free of its human restraints to merge with his. White-hot and intense, a flaming benediction to the release that still thundered through her veins.

"I love you." She could not still the vow that trembled from her lips as consciousness slowly receded. "'Til the end of time, Joshua. I will love you."

* * * * *

"No! No!" Jonar came upright in his bed, his body trembling, rage coursing through him.

The vibrations of his granddaughter's power could be felt all around him, pulsing with her pleasure, her devotion to her lover. He shuddered in agony, in such need that his body rocked with it.

But even through the haze of pain and lust, a thread of satisfaction wove through his mind. His hold on her was still there. The bonds he had set in place so many years ago would still hold. He would rid her of her Guardian lover and all that she held dear. She would come to him then. Then she would know her place was by his side.

"You will pay for this, Arriane," he whispered desperately, staring into the darkness of his room, the sounds of her pleasure, her vows of love to her demon lover rocking him to the core. "I will be certain he reviles you. I will ensure his rage and his hatred toward you are profound. I will not release you, Arriane."

Her soul had touched the warrior, but, he smiled in satisfaction, the warrior's had not touched hers. Had it been so, then he would have never felt the release of her power, would have never known of her pleasure. The warrior did not love. And for that, he would pay with his life.

# Chapter Twenty

**ΕΟ**

Kanna arrived at daylight the next day, escorted by a troop of Guardian warriors, and obviously weary from her long journey.

Kanna, like the warriors, was gifted by the gods, but her battle was not fought on the fields of honor. Rather her battle had been to keep the hearts and the sanity of the Shadow Warriors intact.

She had raised them when they were boys and she was little more than a child herself. She had been barely sixteen when she accepted the proposal the gods had given her. Care for the four hungry misfits, raise them until the time they could be trained at warriors' arts, and her life would want for nothing. She was twenty-three when they had been sent to foster in training with other knights of the king's realm.

There had been years there that they had neither heard from her, nor known about her whereabouts. When she had returned there had been an edge of sadness in her and she had been given the gift of immortality, the same as the warriors received when they turned twenty-one.

Kanna was slight of build, barely five-foot-five in her stocking feet, but she was often a force to be reckoned with. She tolerated fools not at all and when there was work to be done, she rarely had problems finding anyone to do the work.

As she stepped inside the great hall, Devlin saw the look of horror that crossed her face. In the past months, the interior of the castle had steadily gone downhill. As mistress of the castle, Antea did little more than order the servants to see to her own general welfare and they seemed little inclined to do more than they were ordered.

The situation had become intolerable for Devlin. Filth seemed to invade every corner of the castle. The dirty rushes on the floor, the littered remains of food that caked it in places, and the stench of neglect were beginning to wear on them all. All of them but Antea, who kept her dainty little nose in her room, where the servants were berated until it was kept merely passable.

Kanna's eyes rounded, her soft face going slack with surprise as she stared into Devlin's face.

"Devlin?" she questioned him as though she did not know him. "What has happened to you?"

Devlin shook his head, feeling his throat tighten with an emotion that nearly strangled him.

Kanna had forever been the one to soothe his hurts as a child, to hold him when the nightmares of death haunted him. He was a grown man now, and though he no longer remembered the nightmares, he realized he still needed her comfort.

"I don't know, Kanna," he sighed roughly. "The year has been difficult. But welcome to Charlea, what there is left of it."

"Your wife?" Kanna stared around in mild surprise. "She has been ill?"

"She is no wife." He barely contained the rage and disgust in his voice. "Our belongings shall be moved from my own lands and brought here. I am now master of this castle and it will serve as our home."

Devlin watched as Kanna breathed in roughly.

"I cannot leave here, Kanna, it has become home. Even with its many difficulties and trials, I would stay here. I hope that once again you would take on the task of keeping my home for me," he asked her, suddenly wary. Perhaps, he thought, she had no desire to leave the estate in England that she cared for in his absence.

"Your..." She paused, and in her eyes he saw the memory of his protest to the word *wife*. "The lady of this castle may not appreciate that."

"Then she can leave." He shrugged, looking around once again at the filth. "I've assigned one of the castle guards to you. You can trust him. I want this castle back in shape within the next fortnight. Whoever refuses to help, then return them to the village with no wage and hire others. I don't care how you manage it, just get the stink out of here."

She smoothed her hands down the light blue linen dress she wore and looked around once again, her eyes narrowing.

"I have complete rein and it shall not be taken from me?" she asked him, obviously well set to the idea that if the lady of the castle could not manage, then neither would she stand in her way.

"Should Antea try to interfere, let me know and I shall deal with her," he told her. "There is much you need to know, but first I will show you around so you may see the difficulty of your task."

As he showed her around the castle, he confided in her the problems that faced him. Antea and her lover, his own lover's arrival within the castle and how he preferred that Sarah be given the lighter tasks, as she fulfilled his greatest need.

The afternoon was gone before it was settled and Devlin had Antea called from her room. He could tell the knowledge of Kanna's position did not sit well with her, but a warning glance in Aaron's direction stifled her comments.

As long as having her lover around kept her in line, Devlin had no problems with him. But he would have him stripped of his shield and exiled did Antea not do as he ordered.

"Well, at least it's a challenge." Kanna looked around the kitchens, her nose turning up at the filth that lay there. "Get out of here and let me get started. And I will need every bit of that fortnight you promised me.

* * * * *

There were the deepest pits of hell, Devlin thought, that surely were not as dark as his soul felt these days. He wandered out onto the battlements of the castle and stared into the star-studded night, wondering if there was some way to die and yet to still breathe.

A corpse of battle perhaps, he thought. Had he died in that last battle against Jonar and somehow been revived by those cursed Guardians, to roam the earth, not as a warm, living, vital man, but as one of the dead who are forever haunted by some unnamed cry within his soul?

That was the best he could describe it. He stared into the night. His eyes probed the black velvet night with its diamond points scattered in a maze of designs wondrous to the eyes.

Somewhere out there the Guardians awaited. Had they not once told him they were the children of the stars and one with the night? Demons, he reminded himself, were one with the night. He should have never accepted their gifts, nor trusted in their power.

He was doomed. He would walk the earth and fight their battles for years untold, never growing older, forever losing any who would be dear to him as he was forced to watch them age, watch them die and pass forever from his life.

As he concentrated on those stars within the night, it was as though the breeze carried a taunting whiff of some elusive fragrance. He frowned, wondering why roses and the smell of rainwater so tempted him. What secrets were lurking in those hours of battle he had hopelessly forgotten all those months ago?

"Devlin?" Shanar's voice was quiet, subdued, as he stepped slowly from the entrance to the castle and joined him on the narrow walkway of the battlements.

"The night has secrets, Shanar." Devlin frowned, leaning against the wall as he contemplated the land shrouded in those secrets. "Why, I wonder, do they whisper to me?"

He heard Shanar's sigh, soft and filled with resignation. Devlin was aware that all his men were slowly growing fed up with him and the life he was leading. He was drinking too much, fighting too often, and seemed determined to end his life on Jonar's sword. They had fought more battles against the Black Terror of the Guardians in the past six months than they had in their lives.

"So what brings you out here to keep me company, my friend?" Devlin asked, fighting to ignore the caress of the wind and the memory of gentle hands. He still did not know why he missed such a gentle caress, for he had never known such.

"Derek, Joshua and I. We want to take our wives away for a while, Devlin. We've grown weary of the fighting. We need a break."

A break, Devlin knew, barely described the wearied needs of his men.

He sighed roughly. With them gone, he was confined to this castle alone, with no army to back him should he decide to fight.

"How long?" he asked him, wondering at this sentence he was being given.

"A year, Devlin." Shanar's voice was hard now, brooking no refusal. Devlin was very nearly amused at the Viking's sudden defensive position. "We are tired, as are our wives." He paused shaking his head. "I don't know, saddened. We want to take them away from here for a while, find someplace where they can find peace."

Shanar's little wife, more than the others, needed that rest. She awoke nearly nightly in terror, her screams echoing through the castle. She remembered little of the demons that haunted her, but the terror that swept through her was real enough.

"What has happened to us, Shanar?" Devlin frowned as he stared into the sky once again. "Were we not happy here once? Strange, but I feel we once were."

"I do not know what happened, Devlin." Shanar sighed. "Perhaps it was merely wishful thinking on our part. I know each month we are here Ariel's nightmares grow worse and Derek swears his wife Caitlin is wasting away to nothing."

Derek frowned—something bothered him there. Caitlin had never avoided the rest of them. Her pale green eyes were ghostly, her expressions rarely showing emotion or warmth.

What the hell had happened? He swore he could remember laughter in this castle, yet he could not bring to mind a single memory of it.

Finally, he sighed deeply.

"Go." He waved the big warrior away with a careless flick of his wrist. "I'll see you in a year or so, then we shall resume."

"They will leave us one day, Devlin," Shanar whispered. "They will grow old as we stay young and be forever gone. It is only fair that we have this time."

Devlin nodded shortly. Of course it was only fair, he knew well what awaited him. For his part, he cared not how old his wife grew or when she died, as long as she stayed from his sight.

"Go," he repeated. "I'll see you back here when you return."

"Devlin, perhaps you should go as well," Shanar suggested. "You and Antea, it is not natural."

"I will stay here," Devlin told him coldly, unwilling to discuss his wife.

"She is your wife…"

"She is no fucking wife of mine." He turned on Shanar, readily tired of this constant lecture he was receiving from his men. "Antea is nothing to me. Not wife, not friend, not lover. Nothing, Shanar, do you understand this?"

The rages confused him as much as they did his men. He could not tolerate that title going to that woman. He clenched his fists, wanting to scream to the world that the whore was not his wife and deserved not to live, let alone to carry that title. But he could find no reason to do so. It was his fault she had gone to another man, his sickness of her that must have turned her heart cold.

"Of course, Devlin. We will see you in a year's time." Shanar turned and stomped from the battlements, fury lining each inch of his broad body.

Devlin bit off an oath as he raked his fingers through his hair and stared at the ground beneath him. He would jump, but the three-story fall would do little more than break bones that would quickly heal.

A laugh, filled with self-loathing and disgust, erupted from his throat. He didn't blame his men for leaving. Could he bear to do so, then he would leave as well.

Galen watched the exchange, his heart clenching in pain as he felt the tears Devlin could not shed. Magic wrapped around his memories, his heart and his soul. But he dreamed, Galen knew.

Devlin's woman, Sarah, had been led to him through the magic Galen wielded. She told him often of the nights Devlin tossed and turned, crying out a name she did not recognize, tears wetting his cheeks, agony radiating along his body. He still had not taken her as a true lover, but seemed to find comfort in her presence.

Soon, Galen thought, soon the legacy would be complete. The final battle that would destroy the daughters of the earth was quickly growing near. Mother Earth had assured him of it, whispered her sorrow as he cried in lonely agony over the loss. And still her vows echoed in his ears, in his heart. They would come again. They would return and they would be victorious.

"Chantel..." The whispered sigh brought Galen's eyes open in swift surprise.

He watched the warrior closely, his magic delving into the whispered sigh. He watched as the warrior shook his head, the memory drifting through then escaping on the breeze as Devlin stared out in confusion.

He lived, as Chantel had wished. But he was a mere shell of the man he had been. His soul forever sought what it had lost. Galen often caught him looking to Antea, perplexed, seeking to know why he could not send her away, why he hated her with such a fury. The magic hid the memories, preserved the soul. But nothing could ease the pain.

Dear God, what had they done to this man? he thought in agony. What, though, were they about to do to his men as well?

Devlin moved slowly along the battlements, his head down as he returned to the warmth of the castle. Winter was quickly drawing near and the night air was beginning to take a chill to prove it. It would soon be time to rest. It was fruitless, battling Jonar when the cold froze a normal man's bones and made his sword arm sluggish.

"Devlin." Sarah turned to him as he opened his door, her long, dark blonde hair cascading over her shoulders as she brushed it slowly, her hazel eyes watching him with a smile of pleasure. "I was hoping you would be along soon."

"Let me." He took the brush from her hand, pulling its stiff bristles slowly through the golden locks.

"Your touch is so gentle," she whispered as she closed her eyes in enjoyment. "It is one of the things I so love about you."

He frowned as he brushed her hair, falling in long curls past her hips. The silken length was always a pleasure against his skin, especially in the dead of the night, when the moon's glow turned it a glorious white-blonde.

"The others are leaving in the morning," he told her quietly as he pulled a chair behind her stool and continued to stroke her hair with the brush. "They shall be gone a year or more."

"This upsets you." She watched his face in the mirror, but as always, he could not look long into her eyes.

"It should not," he sighed. "Winter is coming on and it does no good to battle Jonar then, anyway. Besides, my rages grow blacker as the days grow shorter. They are growing tired of it."

"And you?" she asked him. "Do you grow tired of your rages as well, Devlin?"

Her voice was soft, understanding, soothing the ragged edges of that inner pain he could not understand.

"I grow tired of them, but I cannot control them." He frowned, watching as the brush went slowly through her hair. "Tell me what to do, Sarah, how to stop the pain."

There was silence in the room now, broken only by the soft drag of the brush through her hair.

"Why do you hurt, Devlin?" she finally asked him tenderly, turning to him, her legs now framed by his as she sat between his thighs.

Devlin looked down at the softness of her shift and the delicacy of her hands. She was a small woman, with gently flared hips, full breasts and shapely thighs. Her presence brought him comfort, but he could not bring himself to return the deep affection he knew she felt for him. Just as he could not bring himself to take her as he knew she needed. There was no passion in him, no lust, no need for anything but a search he could not even define.

"I don't know," he finally answered her, glancing into her eyes for as long as he could. "I don't understand the screams I hear within my nightmares or the sadness I feel within my soul. It was not always like this, Sarah."

"Precious warrior." She stroked his lean cheek gently. "None can know your pain, if you do not know it yourself. I can only hold you when you allow me to and love you as much as I can. Anything more you must provide yourself."

He sighed roughly, hating the tightness of his chest as he heard her gentle voice, the knot of need in his heart that even she could not fulfill.

He leaned to her, his arms going around her as he pulled her into his embrace and held onto her. Her warmth, the feel of her pressed against his body was not nearly enough, but it was all he had.

"Come to bed with me." He stood, drawing her to her feet, then lifting the shift from her body gently. "Keep the nightmares at bay this night."

"This night and any other you will allow, my love," she sighed against his lips as they covered her own.

She ached for him, so tall and brave, so strong and sure, and yet hurting so desperately from that which was taken away from him.

Sarah did not know who or what had been stolen from this warrior, nor did she understand why he did not remember it. But she knew that the pain would break him, bare him to his bones did he not find some ease from it.

As he carried her to the bed and placed her upon it, she made a silent reminder to question Galen more closely concerning it. But as they lay down and he curled his body around her, sadness overshadowed her joy with him. He would not take her this night, just as he did not take her any other night. Devlin had no passion for her, no need for her body. She was his comfort and nothing more.

# Chapter Twenty-One

ജ

"I want her taken." Jonar stood on a windswept hill, his eyes narrowed on the lights shining softly from the castle as he watched it.

"They are too heavily protected." Oberon stood beside him, not nearly as pompous as he had been six months before. "Galen never leaves his castle and death comes quickly to any man or woman who even considers betraying him."

Jonar cursed silently, violently. Since the woman's death, the magic around the castle had become so thick, so heavy, that deceit could not pass its doors, even if it did manage to pass its drawbridge.

"What of the other?" Oberon asked him, well aware by now that they had killed the wrong woman.

"I do not care about that whore daughter of Konar's," he bit out. "I want my granddaughter, Oberon. I want her returned to me and to her home."

Jonar could feel the fierce need growing in him daily to see her, to touch her face, to take her in his arms. He should have known, all these years she had been gone. The Guardians would have given her to her father before stealing her into the stars. It was their way, their law. He should have searched harder for the father all those years ago.

"We will continue to watch and to wait. Perhaps something will develop soon." There was resignation in Oberon's voice as they continued to watch the lights extinguish, room by room, within the castle.

"Do you see the value of heeding my orders, my concerns, Oberon?" Jonar asked him quietly as he stared at the shadowed hulk of stone and mortar. "Had we heeded my concerns, perhaps we would not be where we are now."

Where they were now was not a good place. It was as though the earth had turned on them. The Fortress had collapsed stone by stone within months as the ground beneath it began to shift.

Gardens dried up from lack of rain, the villagers died of plagues, wolves, snakes, and often the fowl of the air beset his own warriors each time they entered a forest. Only the Seekers came from these skirmishes still living.

The bitch had cursed them, just as she had sworn. They were paying for their death of her in spades, over and over again. If it could go wrong, it invariably did.

"Her curse was uncalled for." Oberon pulled his fur-lined mantle closer as he spoke in anger.

"Ahh, of course it was." Jonar nodded, his mockery echoing around him. "We kill a woman in the most painful way possible, rip her insides to pieces and let her bleed to death inside her own body, and her curses are uncalled for. You are a fool, Oberon."

"She was just a human..."

"A human who commanded the great respect and love of some damned spirit of this planet," Jonar raged. "How often do I have to tell you the mystical power of this land? It is not as our own home was, Oberon. It commands powers and life in and of itself. You cannot destroy the ones who hold that power, no matter the provocation. The spirit will not allow it to go unpunished."

Jonar regretted that death. Like nothing he had ever regretted in the centuries he had walked this land, he regretted the death of the sorcerer's daughter. He should have known, he thought, the true Chantel would have never betrayed her sister in such a way. She would have never left her alone, knowing the fate that could be in store for her.

Jonar remembered her screams, her pleas in brutal clarity. He knew the pain the wand could inflict and set its power at the maximum strength. There was no pain on this world or any other that could compare to it.

"We've sat here for weeks, Jonar, barely able to stay hidden. Galen and the warriors will know soon that we watch the castle," Oberon warned him. "What then?"

Jonar sighed wearily. He admitted to himself that he had no idea what would come then. All he knew was that he craved the sight, the scent, the touch of his granddaughter.

He remembered her as she had been so long ago. Barely six, all gangly limbs and big blue eyes with a fall of riotous, silky black curls. Her laughter had shone in her eyes, the warmth of her spirit taking away the chill of exile.

And so easy to train. She had so loved and trusted him that it had been so easy to slip into her mind. The steps he had laid all those years ago would still be in place, he assured himself. He just had to find the right setting, the right moment to breach her defenses, then she would be his once again.

Unless her hatred and her rage overshadowed the ground he had prepared so carefully, he thought, his fists clenching. He knew she had been there, had watched her sister die, had known, just as Chantel had warned him she would, that he had been the cause of her death.

As he stood there, watching the castle, his eyes narrowed against the chill bite of the wind, the sound of approaching feet carried to him.

Jonar turned, watching the darkness as one of his men slid through it and approached him warily.

"You have news?" Jonar asked him, fighting the thrill of anticipation he could feel tightening his gut.

"Aye, Sire." The man grinned, his teeth flashing in the darkness. "The talk is all over the village. All but Devlin prepares to ride out in the morning and head to a more peaceful land for a while with their wives. Joshua and the lady Arriane will be riding for the seaport, they take no guards and no soldiers with them, nor will they have accompanying warriors to aid them in case of trouble. They ride alone."

The anticipation hit him hard, clenching his stomach as anticipation blazed within him. She would be so very near. With only the three men, it would be no problem to take the women, all of them. In time, he knew he could reach Arriane once again.

"Do you know the route they take to the seaport?" he questioned the spy harshly.

"Aye, Sire." Triumph flashed in the man's eyes. "They believe themselves safe, with winter coming on. There was no effort made to hide their destination or the route they would take."

Jonar chuckled in relief. It had paid off, this gamble he had taken. Somehow, according to the gossip in the nearby village, Galen had convinced Devlin to marry the whore Antea, but his men would not be able to stand the woman's presence long and it appeared that neither could her sisters.

"We return to camp. Oberon, gather our warriors together and we will plan our attack as soon as the route is laid out for us. This may be our only chance, let's make certain we get it right."

* * * * *

*The time has come, Galen.* The Mother awoke him from a restless sleep, her illuminated form wavering at the foot of his bed.

"No," he whispered. "I am not ready to lose them all, it is too soon."

*The time is here. Rise from your bed and prepare to see your daughters before they depart from the castle. This shall be your last chance for many, many years, Galen.*

Tears tightened his throat, his chest. He blinked fiercely, attempted to fight the weakness that would have him pleading that this course be changed.

First Chantel and now the others—a father's heart could only bear so much pain.

*Be at ease, Galen, the time shall pass as only a blink of an eye. Soon you shall be reunited with your daughters. Children born once again of your loins. When they are returned to you, their legacies shall hold a much different end. Soon, dear Galen, and you will hold your children and then your grandchildren. Soon...*

The form disappeared, leaving only the ache of sadness, the ache of loss that came with the knowledge of what was to come.

For the first time in years Galen lowered his face to his hands and he sobbed.

\* \* \* \* \*

Devlin stood in the courtyard, watching as supplies and possessions were loaded onto stout wagons and his men prepared to leave with their wives.

The early morning was heavy for some reason, its chill biting sharply through Devlin's clothes. He frowned at that, his eyes narrowing as he watched the people milling around the grounds.

"Duncan," he called out to his squire as he silently berated himself for his paranoia. "Saddle my horse as well. I'll ride with them as far as the mountains."

He watched as the young man ran to do as he ordered, then turned back to the sight of the three loaded wagons and the horses slowly being brought out.

"Don't trust us to ride out on our own, Devlin?" Joshua asked him as he walked slowly from the wagon that held his and Arriane's belongings.

"I've been babysitting you for years, Joshua. I'll enjoy the break," Devlin told him mockingly. "I'm glad to see your little wife knows how to smile after all, though. It's about time you settled into your marriage."

He was curious at the evasive flicker of Joshua's eyes. Curious, but strangely, not concerned enough to bother to question him about it.

Sometimes, the freeze that seemed to encase his emotions, his cares, bothered Devlin. But when he fought to look too deeply into it the thoughts scattered as though driven by an ill wind.

"We're ready, Joshua." Shanar moved up to them, a smile creasing his face for the first time in months. "Let's get moving. If we want to reach the seaport before the week's end, we need to hurry."

"I'll ride with you as far as the mountains." Devlin nodded to the cloud-darkened area he spoke of.

"Antea will be riding with us as well," Joshua informed him. "Arriane had some things she wanted to speak of to her. Do you still wish to ride with us?"

Devlin turned and narrowed his eyes on Antea as she walked slowly to the horse her lover held for her.

"As long as you keep her downwind of me." He shrugged. "That woman's scent sickens me."

Joshua flinched at his words, his amber eyes flaring in a fury that Devlin knew had nothing to with Antea. Devlin sensed things, shadows moving about them all, the echo of some knowledge, a pain they would not reveal. God help him, but he didn't have the energy to pursue it.

Devlin mounted his horse, feeling loneliness, a pit of despair at the sight of his men ready to leave the castle for so very long. They had been together, continually, all these years. Fighting, laughing together. They had been his anchor within this world gone mad and now they were leaving as well.

They rode from the castle courtyard. Three wagons, the warriors and their wives, three guards to escort Antea back to the castle, and Devlin himself rode slowly toward the distant mountains.

His eyes narrowed as he rode beside Shanar, settling his gaze on the darkened clouds that seemed to roll closer.

There was no scent of rain in the air, no reason for that darkness to be approaching so steadily when all around there was blue sky and the gentle rising of the morning sun.

And yet there it was.

"Shanar! Turn back!" Devlin turned to the warrior, yelling out the order as they passed the protection of the forest and entered the valley that led into the mountains. "Get those damned women home."

All hell broke lose. From the very ground the warriors seemed to emerge, their war cries echoing in the valley, their weapons drawn as they surrounded the small party.

Devlin turned his horse in a wide circle, glimpsing the terrified faces of the women as they were moved hastily into a small group, the warriors surrounding them.

Breathing harshly, he stared at the dozen warriors, their sneering faces filled with smug satisfaction.

They weren't here for the warriors, Devlin thought in agony. They were here for the women.

His horse stomped as the opposing warriors stood in a large circle around the Shadow Warriors and their women. They were watching, waiting, Devlin thought. What the hell were they waiting for?

"Shadow." Jonar stepped from the cover of the large boulders at the base of the mountain. "Give me what I want and you may go free. There is only one of you I seek."

The bitch Antea. Devlin heard her cry, saw from the corner of his eye as Aaron's arms went around her, his face twisting with pain. Fuck, just what he needed, the others in danger because of that bitch.

"There is nothing here for you, Jonar," Devlin called out to him. "These women are our own and naught of yours."

There was a silence that filled the clearing. A weight unlike any Devlin had ever known settled on his shoulders. God, where were those cries echoing in his head coming from?

"This is where you are wrong, Shadow," Jonar laughed. "One there is mine and mine alone. I demand my granddaughter and I demand this now."

Arriane felt terror fill her. Her throat closed with it, her stomach clenching in agony. The sudden, remembered sight of Chantel's broken body came to her mind.

"Joshua, swear you will kill me first," she whispered, aching at the thought of leaving this bitter warrior. "Swear it to me."

Joshua was silent for long moments, but she could not bear to look into his face, to see a jeering smile should it be there.

"I swear to you, wife, your body shall never know any man's touch but mine," he whispered.

She glanced into his face now, suppressing a cry when she saw the knowledge in his eyes. At that moment, Arriane knew her own fate, as well as those around her.

"Arriane," Jonar's voice called out to her now. "Come to me, Granddaughter, and I will spare the others. I swear this to you."

Memories, once distant and unclear now, rose to haunt her. The sickening smell of her mother's body after leaving Jonar's room. The knowledge that the love her grandfather had for his daughter was somehow evil and unnatural.

Cries drifted through her soul, pleas and broken sobs in her mother's voice as Oberon and Jonar dragged her roughly from their room.

"Will it spare them, Joshua?" she whispered the question, yet knew the answer.

"Nothing can spare any of you, Arriane." He swallowed tightly, his expression bleak.

"You have no granddaughter here, Jonar," Joshua called back to him. "There is naught for you here but misery, you bastard."

As Joshua's words echoed through the valley, Devlin frowned. As he continued to stare at Jonar, he could feel the rush of pain, the agony, the hatred unlike anything he had ever known.

His hand tightened on his sword as slowly, like a fog dissipating from his mind, memories swirled within him.

Devlin saw her, lying broken, so horribly abused he could feel her soul crying out to him even after death. A warning, a screaming agony, a glimpse of the fate that awaited these women should Jonar take them, screamed through his soul.

Chantel. The word flashed across his mind, though the memories were distant, as though a dream. Chantel, screaming his name, pleading for mercy, begging for the pain to end.

"Chantel." Devlin's cry rang around him as tears filled his eyes, a black rage twisted his gut into bands of agony as her gentle face was reflected now in the grimace of death. "I will kill you, Jonar. Your black heart shall bleed beneath my sword."

\* \* \* \* \*

The battle was bloody, bleak, ringing with the shattered screams of the warriors as one by one, their wives fell helpless beneath the blades being wielded by the dark warriors.

There were too many of them, and despite the pain searing his gut into a mindless rage, Devlin could do nothing to save them. He was surrounded, his men lay near death, despite their gifts, their wives dying or dead beside them.

Antea had been one of the first to fall, just seconds after Aaron had received a deadly blow from the warriors who converged on him.

Shanar and Ariel, both warriors, yet neither strong enough to fight the many men whose swords were like lightning flashing through the fog-enshrouded valley.

Caitlin fell next, and as Derek bent to his bride, he was run through from behind. A killing blow to another man and perhaps even to the warrior the gods had once blessed.

As Devlin was surrounded, only Joshua and Arriane were still standing. As Devlin's sword flashed, a part of his mind intent on reaching them, another part watched in horror as Arriane turned to her husband, her blade sinking into his heart.

Devlin could only stare in amazement, unaware he had dropped his sword in shock as he watched the black-haired beauty, a red glow surrounding her, suddenly plunge that same blade into her own heart as Jonar stood beside her, beseeching her. She fell slowly at his feet, a curse upon her lips.

Then searing pain, a fire spreading through his own body as a sword found its mark deep into his gut.

He could hear Jonar's cries filtering through his own black screams of rage as he fell beneath the blow, his blood soaking the ground beneath him.

Devlin lay helpless, the betrayal of the gods burning an ache in his soul as the fog in his heart was slowly lifted.

"Chantel." His whispered cry was a plea as tears rained down his feet. "I come for you, Chantel."

Then the mists of the gods fell, warm and achingly sweet and he felt his body lifting, moving with an airy motion that signaled his return to them.

"NO! I will not!" He tried to scream, yet knew it was little use. "Let me join her. Let me join her…"

Darkness washed over him as his cries echoed in his mind.

*Let me join her, do not take me from her once again.* The plea was a whispered litany as slowly, gently, the fog returned, the memories receded and the Shadow began to heal.

# Epilogue
*France*
*Present Day*

*She came to him, whether he wished it or not. And though he had always known only hatred, only abiding fury when faced with her in the past, now he knew only gentleness. He needed to kiss the pale pink perfection of her soft lips, needed to touch the full curves of her breasts. He hungered for her, as he had never hungered for anything in his life before this.*

Her nipples, hard little points of tempting fruit beckoned his lips, his stroking tongue. As she knelt before him, he could do no more than lean forward and envelop a tip with his hungry mouth. He was greedy for her, his desires ravenous. She was warm, heating the cold wedge of hatred that surrounded his heart and made him long for her. Made him long for her kiss, her touch.

His hands gripped her small waist, feeling the delicacy of her body and he knew, knew beyond a shadow of a doubt that she was stronger than she appeared. And still his lips sipped at her nipples. He could not get enough. His teeth tugged gently as she cried out, trembling before him, her nails delicate pinpoints of fire against his scalp as she held him to her.

"Remember me," she whispered, desperation and fear reflecting in her voice. "Remember me, Devlin. Save me."

He held tighter to her now, terrified that somehow, something would reach out and snatch her from him. His lips moved from her breasts, over the swollen curves, dropping hard, lustful kisses along her chest and collarbone.

He rose from his bed until he rested on his knees before her, his lips touched her neck, his tongue whispered over the delicate shell of her ear. Her hand, so soft and silken, rather than calloused as he remembered, smoothed over his shoulders, his waist. He sucked in a hard breath as it then traveled to the hard plane of his stomach.

"Touch me," he growled, needing it as he had never needed anything in his life.

The touch of her hand on his cock had him nearly spilling his seed onto the bed. Her grip was warm, tentative, almost shy. Her fingers explored the thick shaft, tracing the bulge of the veins, the flared head that throbbed beneath her touch. Sweet mercy. He fought the eruption he could feel boiling in his scrotum. She set him on fire. He needed more of her, always more of her.

Before he could question himself or his voracious need, his lips covered hers, his hands pulling her tighter against his body as he bore her to the bed beneath him. Her hand gripped his hip then, her moan echoing in the air around them as he made his way between her thighs.

Then the dream shifted. He howled in fury, in desperation as the bed was gone, their naked entwined bodies suddenly separated, no longer blending together in passion and desire. He still held her. She was clasped in his arms, staring up at him in agony, in fear.

Devlin trembled, his hands shaking as they rose to touch the blood that marred her abdomen. Shock and denial filled his soul.

"I love you, Devlin."

"No. No. Do not leave me, Chantel. Chantel…"

\* \* \* \* \*

"Chantel…" He came out of the bed, fury and rage pulsing, pounding through his body even as the knowledge that it was not reality, slid through his soul.

His chest heaved for breath, his hand reaching for his gun before he could shift from nightmare to reality. He shook in the grip of an agony he could not define, memories that drifted away as though they had never been, but left a remnant of loss to sear his soul. His hand reached up to touch his face, his fingers coming back, damp with his own tears. He could feel the moisture in his eyes, the cries in his heart. He trembled, shaking from the vividness of the dream.

He knew the face as Antea, the conniving, vindictive bitch he had once known as wife. He fought his memories as he had before and could not place their wedding, could not place tender emotions for her at any time. Just as he could not place his overriding hatred of her. But he did remember her death and it was not the one of his dreams. And why did the name Chantel still echo in the air around him? He knew her name. Knew her touch, the taste of her kiss, and a joy he could not place at the thought of her.

He threw himself from the bed, then jerked on jeans and a T-shirt with swift, angry movements. He pushed his feet into leather running shoes and strode quickly from his bedroom.

The castle was silent, bathed in darkness with only the rays of the moon that shone through long narrow windows at the end of the hall to light his way. Not that he needed such light. His gifts made it possible to see even in the worst darkness.

He grunted at that thought. Such gifts. They had damned him. But even now, he wasn't certain how. Shaking his head, he headed down the stairs. Coffee, he thought, he would need plenty of it. As usual of late, it would be another sleepless night.

\* \* \* \* \*

*United States
Present Day*

The dream was vivid, more graphic than ever. The crystal suspended by silver, inlaid with precious stones and gleaming in hope, yet always out of reach. Shadows formed, twisted, pain struck at every nerve ending, destroying her, killing her. Chantel fought against the hands that held her, rasping, evil voices that whispered their vile words in her ears as harsh fingers raked her tender flesh. The scent of their evil was overwhelming, their acts too demented and pain-ridden to accept, even to one who knew such evil existed.

They were stripping her very sanity with their touch. Their laughing, jeering voices, their assurances that when death came, she would not be missed. The knowledge that in the acts they forced upon her, they were destroying not just her, but the one she held as most beloved.

Then came the touch to her abdomen. Fire. Agony. She screamed out his name in desperation, a plea, a hopeless cry of need, born of the agony of death.

"Devlin!" The pain was too much to be borne. It ate inside, working slowly, insidiously closer to her heart, seeking to destroy it, to destroy her.

Then he was there, his voice a tormented wail, his hands tender as he drew her to him, his tears hot and wet as they fell to her face. She stared into eyes as black and bleak as her own future and knew her death was at hand.

"Do not leave me, Chantel." His voice was ragged, breaking on the sob that tore from his chest as her blood seeped between them. "Do not leave me, for I cannot survive the darkness without you."

He cried for her, he cried the tears that she could no longer shed, but her heart, her very soul ached for the agony she knew would be inflicted upon him.

"I love you, Devlin," she whispered softly, feeling the dark void of death as it crept over her body. "Forever, my love, I shall love you forever."

Then the darkness became complete. Distantly she heard his wail of denial, felt his hands as they drew her closer and she screamed out silently in return.

\* \* \* \* \*

Chantel awoke to the sounds of her screams echoing in the room, shocking her into sudden awareness. She jumped from her bed, stumbling against the mirrored dresser in dazed, wild terror. She clutched her stomach, the agonizing pain she felt in her dreams still vivid even after waking. Her body shook in hard, deep spasms, her throat emitting whimpers that frightened her nearly as badly as the dream itself. She sounded like a dazed, fear-driven animal to her own ears.

Desperate, strangled cries choked from her throat as she groped for the light switch beside the mirror. Soft light filled the room, revealing only the bedroom where she had fallen asleep. There were no twisting shadows, no evil forms watching her from demented, fury-filled eyes. There was no one there to harm her, no one to rescue her if there were.

She pulled at her plain white gown frantically, her fingers running over her stomach, searching for the gaping wound she received in her nightmares. But all she felt was the warmth of sweat-dampened skin, not the thick, sticky residue of her own blood coating her fingers, draining her life.

"Another dream," she gasped, fighting for breath, fighting the fears and the demons that followed her from her dreams.

Gripping the front of the dresser, she raised her eyes to stare at the vision that greeted her in the mirror. Wide, unusually bright, dark green eyes sparkled from within the glass. They were like brilliant gems washed in dew, glittering from beneath the pale length of her lashes. Those glittering eyes emphasized the stark white features of her face and the terror in her expression. She looked as ghostly and unreal as anything in her nightmares.

Chantel shook her head, trying to calm, to fight down the fears and the jerky whimpers escaping her throat. It was all a dream, she reminded herself desperately. It was just a dream. Nightmares can't harm you, she told herself, still frantic, still searching for demons hiding in the shadows, as her body shook in continued reaction.

She wrapped her arms across her chest, distantly aware of the slight rocking motion of her body. In the back of her mind, she was well aware that she was close to slipping into one of the hysterical episodes that marked her teenage years. But she was alone now. Her mother wouldn't be rushing in to comfort her, or her brother wouldn't be standing in the doorway, confused yet willing to help. The sound of her father's displeasure wouldn't be echoing from his room as she fought the residue of her dreams.

She looked about the small bedroom and the plain wood furnishings. The disheveled bed was there, its forest green and white lace comforter twisted and falling nearly from the bed. The overstuffed chair was sitting in its corner beside it, the antique night table her mother had given her gleaming richly at its side. She was still in the room she had gone to sleep in. The dark stone room of her dreams had disappeared. All that was left of it were faint echoes of remembered screams and the cries of the man who clutched her to his chest.

Chantel was awake but she didn't feel awake. She felt trapped between nightmare and reality, unsure which was which and terrified of being forced to return to the pain and darkness she had just escaped. She wasn't a child any longer, she reminded herself as the fear still pumped harshly through her veins. The nightmares weren't real.

They weren't real. They were induced by stress, fear, an overactive imagination, as her psychologist termed it when she was a teenager. Those weekly sessions with the overbearing, arrogant doctor did no more to help her now than they had at the time. The dreams were not real, she knew that, yet they still haunted her.

Chantel turned and sat on the bed gingerly, covering her face with her hands. They might not be real but they were definitely growing worse, more graphic and disturbingly real than ever before. For the past two weeks, they had become a nightly occurrence. With each nightmare, new and terrifying visions were added.

Until tonight, where she had witnessed the horror and graphic brutality of her own death.

A whimper escaped her once again as she fought back the remembered visions of degradation and pain. Was she seeing the future or her own fears? It wasn't as though her life was calm or orderly on a daily basis, but nothing had led her to believe such a death could be awaiting her.

Chantel looked at her hands, grimacing at how they shook, and knew that sleep would not come again. She glanced at the clock, seeing the small hands that proclaimed it only four in the morning. For something that wasn't real, the harrowing dreams were beginning to interfere with her life and were stealing the rest she needed so desperately.

Shaking her head, she bent to the floor, picking up the long, white flannel robe. Tiredly, she pulled it on, belted it tightly and headed for the kitchen. Sleep was out of the question for now. There was no way she could chance a return of that particular nightmare. She might as well begin the day, as she knew it would proceed, with plenty of caffeine.

Pushing the nightmares away, Chantel concentrated on her just completed mission and her narrow escape from the war-torn country she had been in. She considered asking her father for some time off. She needed rest, before she managed to get herself or someone else killed.

Just the thought of approaching her stern parent with such a request had her grimacing with distaste. She couldn't see Michael Ducaine, head of the elite Terrorist Control Agency, being receptive to such a request. Perhaps after her brother James returned, Chantel thought. He could talk to their father, get the time she needed so desperately. Because she knew if a rest didn't come soon, then she would be no good to herself nor any agent she was assigned to work with. At the rate she was going though, exhaustion would get her before Blackthorne, the organization they were working to bring down, could ever touch her.

The Terrorist Control Agency was a secretly funded and operated organization dedicated exclusively to gathering information and tracking the movements of potentially dangerous terrorist organizations. In the past years, it had focused exclusively on Blackthorne and its leader known only as Jonar, as the smaller, ineffective terrorists groups were swallowed and incorporated into the larger group. From all indications, Blackthorne was emerging as a serious, highly dangerous threat to the tentative balance of power within the world. A power Chantel feared would only become more deadly as time passed.

She tried to still the trembling of her body, the fears rising inside her. Blood and death and a warrior's cries. Breathless sighs, whispered love and a passion that seared her memories. Which was her destiny? Or was it a fate she had already known? One she was given a chance to set right? Fear and anticipation filled her. Terror and exhilaration filled her. Whichever it was, she was ready.

# Why an electronic book?

We live in the Information Age — an exciting time in the history of human civilization, in which technology rules supreme and continues to progress in leaps and bounds every minute of every day. For a multitude of reasons, more and more avid literary fans are opting to purchase e-books instead of paper books. The question from those not yet initiated into the world of electronic reading is simply: *Why?*

1. *Price.* An electronic title at Ellora's Cave Publishing and Cerridwen Press runs anywhere from 40% to 75% less than the cover price of the exact same title in paperback format. Why? Basic mathematics and cost. It is less expensive to publish an e-book (no paper and printing, no warehousing and shipping) than it is to publish a paperback, so the savings are passed along to the consumer.

2. *Space.* Running out of room in your house for your books? That is one worry you will never have with electronic books. For a low one-time cost, you can purchase a handheld device specifically designed for e-reading. Many e-readers have large, convenient screens for viewing. Better yet, hundreds of titles can be stored within your new library — on a single microchip. There are a variety of e-readers from different manufacturers. You can also read e-books on your PC or laptop computer. (Please note that Ellora's

Cave does not endorse any specific brands. You can check our websites at www.ellorascave.com or www.cerridwenpress.com for information we make available to new consumers.)

3. ***Mobility***.  Because your new e-library consists of only a microchip within a small, easily transportable e-reader, your entire cache of books can be taken with you wherever you go.

4. ***Personal Viewing Preferences.***  Are the words you are currently reading too small?  Too large?  Too… ANNOYING? Paperback books cannot be modified according to personal preferences, but e-books can.

5. ***Instant Gratification.***  Is it the middle of the night and all the bookstores near you are closed? Are you tired of waiting days, sometimes weeks, for bookstores to ship the novels you bought? Ellora's Cave Publishing sells instantaneous downloads twenty-four hours a day, seven days a week, every day of the year. Our webstore is never closed. Our e-book delivery system is 100% automated, meaning your order is filled as soon as you pay for it.


   Those are a few of the top reasons why electronic books are replacing paperbacks for many avid readers.

   As always, Ellora's Cave and Cerridwen Press welcome your questions and comments. We invite you to email us at Comments@ellorascave.com or write to us directly at Ellora's Cave Publishing Inc., 1056 Home Avenue, Akron, OH 44310-3502.

# The
# ✝ ELLORA'S CAVE ✝
# Library

Stay up to date with Ellora's Cave Titles in
Print with our Quarterly Catalog.

MAKE EACH DAY MORE *EXCITING* WITH OUR

# ELLORA'S CAVEMEN
## CALENDAR

www.EllorasCave.com

erridwen, the Celtic Goddess of wisdom, was the muse who brought inspiration to story-tellers and those in the creative arts. Cerridwen Press encompasses the best and most innovative stories in all genres of today's fiction. Visit our site and discover the newest titles by talented authors who still get inspired - much like the ancient storytellers did, once upon a time.

Discover for yourself why readers can't get enough of the multiple award-winning publisher

Ellora's Cave.

Whether you prefer e-books or paperbacks,

be sure to visit EC on the web at
www.ellorascave.com

for an erotic reading experience that will leave you breathless.